MIDNIGHT ENCHANTMENT

BOOKS BY MADELINE BAKER

A Whisper in the Wind
Apache Flame
Apache Runaway
Beneath a Midnight Moon
Callie's Cowboy
Chase the Lightning
Chase The Wind
Cheyenne Surrender
Comanche Flame
Dakota Dreams
Dude Ranch Bride
Every Inch a Cowboy
Feather in the Wind
First Love, Wild Love
Forbidden Fires
Hawk's Woman
Kade
Lacey's Way
Lakota Love Song
Lakota Renegade
Love Forevermore
Love in the Wind
Midnight Fire
Prairie Heat
Reckless Desire
Reckless Destiny
Reckless Embrace

MIDNIGHT ENCHANTMENT

AMANDA ASHLEY

Midnight Enchantment

You can reach the author at:
Email: darkwritr@aol.com
Websites: www.amandaashley.net and www.madelinebaker.net

DEDICATION

For Marissa
Because she asked for it

CONTENTS

CHAPTER ONE

Ava Liliana Falconer strolled along Bourbon Street, pausing now and then to peer into one window or another. There were so many interesting places to visit in New Orleans, known far and wide as the Voodoo capital of the world. There were museums and old cemeteries, antebellum mansions and gardens. Not to mention the stores and shops where you could buy all manner of fascinating things, like voodoo dolls and tarot cards, shrunken heads and monkey paws, spell books, charms, and "gris-gris" bags. And books on magic—both light and dark—as well as volumes on the occult, and all manner of mysterious and mystical arts.

Having a vampire for a father and a witch for mother, Lily was no stranger to the supernatural world, and was, in her own right, a rather powerful witch, though her powers were not half as strong as those of her mother, or her great-grandmother, Ava Magdalena. But she was no slouch, either.

The lyrical strains of a guitar drew her toward a nightclub at the far end of the block. She made her way cautiously along the crowded sidewalk. Only months ago, the Knights of the Dark Wood had been hellbent on exterminating the vampire side of her family. Of course, the Knights weren't adverse to killing witches, as well. And although that had changed, thanks to her great-grandmother's magic, New Orleans could still be a dangerous place for a young, unescorted woman.

Lily paused outside the club, all her senses alert, but she didn't detect anything more dangerous inside than the unmistakably earthy scent of pot, something she had never experimented with, although a girlfriend in high school had once dared her to try it. But magic and marijuana didn't go together.

Taking her courage in hand, Lily stepped through the arched doorway. She found a small table near the raised dais where the guitar player sat, felt the notes of his song surround her. He had hair as black as her own, though not as long. When he looked at her, she saw that his eyes were a deep, deep blue, mesmerizing in their intensity. For a moment, it was as if there was no one else in the room, only the two of them caught up in a brief, mystical moment of time.

Rattled by the strange sensation that had passed between them, Lily looked away and the moment was gone.

When she dared to glance his way again, his smile told her he was just as aware of what had passed between them as was she.

Muttering, "This is just too weird," Lily stood and practically bolted out of the club. Outside, she breathed in the cool night air, practically jumped out of her skin when a deep voice behind her said, "Why did you run away?"

Gathering her composure, Lily turned and came face to face with the guitar player. "Excuse me?"

"Why did you run away?"

"I'm sure I don't know what you mean."

His gaze met and held hers. "I'm sure you do."

With a wave of her hand, Lily said, "Stop it!" And smiled when her power arced between them, driving him back a step.

He stared at her, one brow arched in surprise. And then he chuckled. "Witch woman."

"Vampire man."

His deep, masculine laughter sent a shiver of awareness down her spine.

"Well met, milady," he said, admiration in his voice. "How are you called?"

"That's none of your business," Lily said curtly. "Good night, sir." Turning on her heel, she walked briskly down the street.

If she had hoped to elude the maddening creature, she was sorely mistaken. In an instant, he was beside her, matching her stride for stride, his hands tucked in his pants' pockets.

Liliana stopped abruptly. "Why are you following me?"

"Why are you running away again?"

She glared at him. "Because I don't like you. Now leave me alone before I turn you into a newt!"

"A newt?" He threw back his head and laughed.

With an exasperated sigh, Lily began walking again.

And again he fell in beside her. She tried to ignore him, but it was impossible. He was tall and broad-shouldered, with an easy aura of self-confidence that bordered on arrogance.

Not wanting him to follow her home, Lily changed direction and ducked into an occult book store.

Of course, he followed her inside.

Pretending to ignore him, she browsed the shelves, always conscious of the tall, dark stranger behind her. His presence was overwhelming, his scent tantalizing. When she reached the back of the store, she whirled around to face him. "What do you want?"

"Your name."

Lily shook her head. One of the first things she had learned at her great-grandmother's knee was that names had power.

"I will give you mine if you give me yours."

"I don't want it," she said, primly.

His smile was devastating.

Lily's heart began to pound a quick tattoo when he backed her against the wall, his hands flattened on either side of her head, his big body far too close, his breath fanning her cheek. She shivered when she felt his mind brush hers. "Stop that!"

"Why are you afraid of me, Liliana?"

Just as she had feared, he had the power to read her mind. Swallowing hard, she said, "I'm not afraid."

"Yes, you are." He took a deep breath. "I can smell the fear on your skin, hear the rapid beating of your heart." Closing his eyes, he leaned closer. "Smell the blood flowing rich and red in your veins like the finest wine."

Terror rose within her. Frantic, she tried to summon her magic, but fear held her fast in its grip so that all she could do was stare at him, helpless, and more frightened than she had ever been in her life.

"You have nothing to be afraid of," he murmured. "I will not hurt you."

"Why ... why should I believe you?"

"Because I said so." He lowered his hands and took a step back. "I am sorry I frightened you. I did not realize you were so young. So innocent." Taking her hand in his, he kissed her palm. "Please accept my apology."

Liliana closed her eyes and took a deep breath, hoping to still the frantic pounding of heart.

When she opened her eyes again, he was gone.

❧ ❧ ❧

Ava looked up and smiled when Lily entered the living room, but her smile quickly faded when she caught the faint scent of vampire. "Where have you been?" she asked, her voice sharper than she intended. "More importantly, who have you been with?"

"I don't know." Sinking down in the easy chair across from the sofa, Lily clasped her hands in her lap.

"What do you mean, you don't know? I can smell him on you. What on earth were you doing with a Transylvanian vampire?"

"I was walking down Bourbon Street when I heard a guitar. Something about the melody drew me inside. The man playing it looked at me and … the strangest feeling passed between us. It was weird and a little scary and … " She shook her head in wonder. "I've never felt anything like it before. It rattled me and I left. But he followed me."

Ava's eyes widened. "Did he bite you?"

"No! No. Nothing like that. It was like he was looking for someone and thought it might be me. Does that make any sense?"

"Not a bit. What's this guy's name?"

"I don't know."

"Listen to me, young lady," Ava said sternly. "You stay away from the Transylvanian vampires or I'll send you home quicker than you can say abracadabra. Do you understand me?"

Lily nodded.

Ava's gaze moved over her great-granddaughter's face. "Are you sure you're all right?"

"No," Lily murmured. "I'm not sure I'll ever be all right again."

Lily tossed and turned all night long. Every time she closed her eyes, the vampire's image rose in her mind. He wasn't handsome in the usual sense of the word, but he was gorgeous nonetheless, his features strong and masculine and compelling. And his eyes—she had never seen eyes like that. Not just that deep, deep shade of blue but the intensity of his gaze. She'd had the feeling that with one glance, he had discovered everything there was to know about her, every hope of her heart, every secret desire.

It had been most disconcerting. Worst of all, she wanted very much to see him again.

Chapter Two

Late that night, Raedan prowled the residential streets of the city. Houses rose on either side of him, their windows dark, the occupants having gone to bed hours ago. How pathetic their lives were, their days spent in mundane jobs, ruled by the need for nourishment and shelter, the financial means to feed and clothe their young, haunted by the ever-present specter of illness and death.

But they shared one thing—the need for sustenance. Leaving the residential area behind, he wandered the dark underbelly of the city in search of prey, even as his thoughts turned to the young woman, Liliana. She was a witch who came from an old family. He had sensed her power the first time their eyes met. But there had been something more. She also carried the blood of Hungarian vampires, though she, herself, was not a vampire. It was an odd mix. His kind and those of Hungarian ancestry avoided each other whenever possible, but he had sensed their presence in the city when he had returned to the Big Easy a few weeks ago.

Raedan found his prey huddled over a half-empty bottle of cheap booze in the dark doorway of one of the less reputable hotels. He would rather have indulged on the blood of the lovely Liliana, but witch blood tended to be bitter. But no doubt better than this, he thought, as he sank his fangs into the drunken man's throat. Much better. Lifting his head, Raedan turned away. Surely he could find more satisfying prey elsewhere in the city.

Strolling along the dark streets in search of a new victim, his thoughts again turned to the young witch, her body shapely yet slender, her hair the color of ebony, her eyes the dark gray of a dove's wings. Her scent, alluring and slightly exotic, lingered in his nostrils. Liliana.

One way or another, he intended to see her again.

Claret blew out a sigh as she made her way along the sidewalk toward her lair. Life had been boring these past few months, she mused. The old Elder Knight was dead, though she had no cause to mourn his passing. She had no idea what had happened to the warlock, Jasper. With the Elder Knight's death, the curse on the warlock would have been broken and Jasper would have regained his humanity. Her best guess was that he, too, was dead, since she had tried to contact him and found only emptiness.

She turned the corner of Bourbon Street and headed toward one of her favorite hunting grounds. There was a new vampire in town, a very old, very powerful vampire. Thus far, they had not crossed paths, but she had caught his scent on several occasions. What was he doing here? Just passing through? Or did he hope to usurp her position and become the new Master of the City? She could think of no other reason for his presence in her territory.

"Over my dead body," Claret murmured. It was customary for any Transylvanian vampires who entered New Orleans to ask her permission to stay, but it was obvious he had no intention of doing so.

A wave of preternatural power washed over her as she passed the alley behind a seedy hotel. Moving cautiously, she made her way through the darkness, only to come to an abrupt halt when a dark shape turned to face her.

It was the very stranger she had been thinking about. "You!" Claret hissed. "How dare you hunt in my territory without asking my blessing."

"I dare anything I wish, madam."

His hair was long and black, his voice low and dark and dangerous. It sent a ripple of fear down her spine as every instinct she possessed warned her to get out of there before it was too late. Instead, she lifted her chin and squared her shoulders. She had held this territory for more than a hundred years and intended to hold it for a hundred more. "Why are you here?"

"Because I wish to be." He nodded at the inebriated hooker standing motionless in his arms. "If you will excuse me, madam, you are interrupting my dinner."

"Please be discreet," Claret said imperiously. "And clean up any mess you make when you're through."

His amused laughter followed her out of the alley.

Chapter Three

L ily woke feeling out of sorts, which was highly unusual. But then, she hadn't gotten a lick of sleep last night. And it was all that detestable vampire's fault. He'd been arrogant, impertinent. She wasn't used to being treated that way. Back home in Savaria, she was accorded respect. After all, her grandfather, Andras, was the Master of the Hungarian vampires.

Turning on her side, she stared out the window. Transylvanian vampires weren't like her brother or her father, who were both able to be awake during the day, consume human food, and procreate. Transylvanian vampires were like the Undead creatures portrayed in horror movies. They slept in coffins by day and preyed on the innocent by night. Unlike her kinfolk, the other vampires often killed their prey.

She wondered where the stranger passed the daylight hours.

What his name was.

If he would be at that same club tonight.

Lily immediately shook the thought away, only to have it recur while she showered, and again while she prepared breakfast. She was mentally going through her wardrobe, trying to decide what to wear, when her great-grandmother entered the kitchen.

"You're not thinking of doing something stupid, are you?" Ava asked, pulling a chair from the table.

"Of course not," Lily replied acerbically. "Why would you think that?"

"By the look on your face. And the fact that you're burning the eggs."

"Oh!" Grabbing a pot holder, Lily removed the pan from the fire and set it in the sink.

"Maybe I'd better fix breakfast," Ava muttered, and with a wave of her hand and a few magic words, she conjured two plates of sausage, hash browns, scrambled eggs, and toast, and two cups of coffee.

Lily sank into one of the kitchen chairs and picked up her fork.

Brow furrowed, Ava smeared plum jelly on her toast. She wasn't ready to handle another romantic entanglement. It hadn't been that long ago that Lily's twin brother, Dominic, had fallen head over heels in love with Maddy and, in a remarkably short time, had bedded and wedded her in spite of the numerous obstacles they had faced, not the least of which had been the Knights of the Dark Wood, as well as Quill's old nemesis, Claret.

Ava frowned. Perhaps she should get in touch with Quill and Callie and let them know their daughter might be headed down a similar path. "Lily? Liliana!"

Lily looked up. "Did you say something?"

Oh, lordy, Ava thought, it was even worse than she had imagined. "You're not to see that man again," she warned in a voice that brooked no argument.

Lily shrugged. "Stop worrying, Granny," she said glumly. "I don't know anything about him. Not even his name." And in the bright light of day, she wasn't sure she wanted to.

"Keep it that way," Ava said as she buttered another slice of toast, and then, under her breath, muttered, "Maybe we should have stayed in Portland."

"I've been thinking about going back to Savaria," Lily said.

"Oh?"

Lily shrugged. "I miss my folks and my friends." But that wasn't the real reason. She desperately wanted to see a certain Transylvanian vampire again. And she was terribly afraid it would be a dreadful mistake.

Hoping to get him out of her mind, she left the kitchen and picked up the book she'd bought a few days ago. Perhaps a good murder mystery would take her mind off the stranger she shouldn't even be thinking about.

⚜ ⚜ ⚜

Ava looked up when the doorbell rang, frowned when she glanced at the clock over the mantel and saw the time. "I wonder who that could be? It's kind of late for company."

"Only one way to find out," Lily said. "Do you want me to get it?"

"I'll do it." Rising from the sofa, Ava went to the door. "What the devil are you doing here?" she exclaimed when she saw the vampire, Claret, standing on the porch.

"Can I come in?"

"No." Stepping outside, Ava closed the door behind her. "What do you want?"

"There's a vampire in town."

Ava lifted one brow. "More than one, I'll wager."

"This guy is new. I don't mean a fledgling. I mean new in town. And he's scary as hell."

Ava frowned. She didn't know how scary the new vampire was, but if Claret was afraid of him, that was worrisome, indeed. The scent of the vampire's fear was coming off her in waves. "He must be intimidating as hell, to have you shaking in your boots like a fledgling."

"Very funny!" Claret snapped. "Have you heard anything?"

"I'm afraid not. What's his name?"

"I don't know."

"Well, I can't help you then. Good night."

"Wait!" Claret reached out a hand to stop Ava, let out a hiss when the witch's magic repelled her. "Can you give me some kind of talisman against him?"

"Not without knowing who he is." Although Ava had a terrible feeling the vampire in question was the same one Lily had met in the club the night before.

Muttering an oath, Claret vanished from the porch.

"What was that all about?" Lily asked, when Ava returned to the living room.

"Some new vampire in the city has her scared to death," Ava said, picking up the book of spells she had been thumbing through earlier. "I think you'd better stay close to home until we find out what's going on."

"What does Claret have to be afraid of?"

"Apparently, the fact that he's more powerful than she is. And she's likely worried that he's here to take over as Master of the City."

"She has a lot of nerve, coming to us for help."

Ava nodded. "She's got all the nerve in the world and then some." Just months ago, Claret had been both enemy and ally in the battle against the Elder Knight and the Knights of the Dark Wood.

Raedan sealed the wounds in his prey's slender neck, released her from his thrall, and sent her on her way, none the worse for the small amount of blood he'd dined on. There had been a time when he would have drained her dry without a qualm, but that had been centuries ago. He had been a peace-loving man once, with little thought for violence or vengeance. But then the vampires had come and changed everything, including him. For centuries, he had known nothing but blood and bloodshed as he fought in one battle after another. He had been in little danger from mortals. As one of the Undead, his wounds had healed almost instantly. He possessed the strength of twenty men. His hungry blade had claimed hundreds of lives, left bodies to rot on the battlefield in one country after another while he walked away unscathed.

But times had changed. Villages had turned into towns, and towns into cities. Kings and queens had come and gone. The old ways and the old beliefs had been swept away until the world of his youth was gone.

He, too, had changed through the centuries. He had mellowed as he aged, his lust for blood and battle lessening with the passage of time. He had put up his sword, but it had left him with an emptiness inside, a lack of purpose. These days, he rarely killed except in self-defense. Gradually, he had regained the respect for life he had known before being turned, He had learned again to appreciate the world around him—snow-covered mountains, the vastness of the oceans, raging rivers and gentle streams, the stark beauty of the desert, the fragile beauty of a single flower.

He had traveled the earth, seen all there was to see. And yet, the emptiness of his existence remained. Lately, there had been little that amused or excited him or held his interest for more than a fleeting moment. Until he met the witch-woman, Liliana. She was a prize worth fighting for. He wondered if she would show up at the club again. There was no denying the unexpected attraction that had sizzled between them. He knew she had felt it, too. How could she not?

His thoughts turned briefly to the vampire he had met the other night. Feisty little thing. And pretty, too, with a wealth of red hair and a figure that went in and out in all the right places.

But it was the dark-haired female—Liliana—who fired his imagination, who aroused his hunger. And his desire.

Sooner or later, he would find her again.

Lily spent the next day trying to come up with a good excuse for going out that night. But it was no use. Ava was never going to believe any of them. And after Claret's visit, Ava was never going to let her go out alone. In the end, she suggested they go out to dinner.

Ava was in the mood for Creole. Lily wanted Chinese.

They settled on Italian.

"The baby is growing so fast," Lily remarked after they ordered. "The pictures Maddy sent are adorable. I can't believe J.D. is already four months old."

Ava nodded. "He looks just like your brother. No doubt he'll be just as devilishly handsome and charming as Dominic, as well."

"Maddy and Dom are so happy together," Lily remarked with a sigh. "I don't even have a boyfriend."

"You'll find someone," Ava said.

"Before they met, you saw Maddy and Dominic in a vision. Do you see a man in my future?"

Ava started to say no, when an image of Lily in the grasp of a tall, dark-haired man with midnight-blue eyes flashed through her mind. She had never seen the man before but she knew without doubt that it was the vampire Lily had met at the nightclub. And that he would bring her nothing but trouble—a feeling that was re-enforced when Lily talked her into going to a night club on Bourbon Street after dinner.

And the vampire was there, sitting on the dais, strumming a guitar. Clad in black jeans and a long-sleeved, black silk shirt, Ava had to admit he was stunning. Even though he was sitting down, she could tell he was well over six feet tall. Hair as black as Lily's brushed his broad shoulders. Eyes the color of a midnight sky. Foreign, she thought. Even at a distance, she could feel his power. He was one of the old ones. Older than Quill, even older than Quill's father, Andras.

Ava glared at Lily. "You knew he would be here, didn't you?"

"I'd hoped," Lily admitted, her cheeks heating under her great-grandmother's accusing stare.

"One drink and we're out of here," Ava said.

Their drinks had just arrived when the vampire sauntered toward them.

"Hello, Liliana. It is nice to see you again."

His voice moved over her like dark velvet, warm and soft and seductive.

He acknowledged Ava with a glance. "Mind if I sit down?"

"Yes, I do," Ava said, her voice as cold as the grave. "And I advise you not to seek trouble with me."

He nodded curtly, his dark eyes narrowed with barely suppressed anger. "Good evening, Liliana."

Those were the words he spoke aloud. But in her mind, Lily heard him say, *I will see you again.*

"Are you completely out of your mind?" Ava exclaimed when the vampire returned to the dais. "That man is more dangerous than any vampire I've ever met. And that includes your grandfather. If you know what's good for you, you'll stay as far away from him as you can. Do you hear me?"

"I hear you," Lily replied. She watched the vampire out of the corner of her eye, felt a quiver of excitement in the pit of her stomach when he winked at her.

And she heard his words in her mind once more, vowing to see her again.

CHAPTER FOUR

Three days passed. At Ava's insistence, Lily stayed close to home. She spent her days engrossed in Ava's grimoires, learning and practicing intriguing new spells and incantations, doing everything she could to put her great-grandmother's mind at ease.

Evenings, they played Canasta or Scrabble, or conjured a big bowl of hot, buttered popcorn and binge-watched *The Musketeers* on one of the streaming channels.

She went to visit her brother one evening and spent over two hours holding J.D. while watching Dominic and Maddy gaze adoringly at each other and talk about how happy they were, how much they loved being parents. They were planning to take a long-delayed honeymoon to Hawaii as soon as arrangements could be made.

Lily was happy for both of them. And more than a little envious of the happiness they had found together in spite of a warlock named Jasper, a witch named Claret, and a vindictive Elder Knight of the Dark Wood. But all that was in the past now. Ava had used a bit of magic to end the battle between the Hungarian vampires and the Knights and for now, they were at peace.

Late one night, when Ava had fallen asleep on the sofa, Lily went out into the backyard. It was a beautiful evening, the sky clear and studded with stars, the air fragrant with the scents of damp earth and trees and grass. Crickets serenaded the night.

Staring up at the sky, she murmured, "Star light, star bright, grant the wish I wish tonight."

"And what might that wish be?"

Lily whirled around at the sound of his voice, her hand pressed to her heart as she stared up at him. "You! What are you doing here?"

"I wanted to see you, of course."

Close up, he seemed even bigger and broader than she remembered. He was tall, so tall. The top of her head barely reached his shoulder. And he was so ... so big.

Lily glanced at the house. Was Ava inside, watching them? "You shouldn't be here."

"No one tells me where I can or cannot go." His gaze moved over her. "Do you wish me to leave?"

"Would you go if I asked you to?"

A slow smile spread over his face. "No."

A shiver ran down her spine as she suddenly realized that this man—this vampire—was the most dangerous creature she had ever met. "You never told me your name."

"Raedan."

"First or last?"

"It is the only one I use."

"Like Pitbull," she muttered. "Or Madonna."

"Hardly Madonna," he muttered dryly. "You did not tell me what you were wishing for."

"It's none of your business, Mr. Raedan. Good night." She turned on her heel and started toward the house, froze when his hand folded over her shoulder.

"Perhaps I could make your wishes come true."

"I doubt it. Good night, Mr. Raedan," she said again.

"Stay a moment longer." His voice was whisper-soft but she caught a faint note of longing. Of loneliness.

"Why should I?"

"The nights are long and I am new in town."

When she glanced pointedly at his hand on her shoulder, he released her.

"New Orleans is full of people," she said with an airy wave of her hand. "I'm sure you can find someone to accommodate you."

"I would rather spend my time with you."

Suddenly curious about this strange man—this decidedly attractive man—she moved to one of the patio chairs and sat down, her arms folded across her breasts.

He gestured at the chair on the other side of the white wrought-iron table. "May I?"

He had impeccable manners, Lily thought, as she nodded her permission. "So, tell me about yourself. Why are you in New Orleans?"

"I have to be somewhere," he replied with a faint smile. "It has been a while since I visited Louisiana."

"What do you do for a living?"

"You might say I am between jobs at the moment," he said, looking amused.

"I guess you don't work, do you?"

"Not lately." He gazed into the distance. "There was a time when I raised some of the finest horses in the world."

"What happened?" Lily leaned forward, her curiosity growing. "Why did you stop?"

"Things change," he said, his eyes suddenly haunted. "Times change. Tell me about you."

"There's nothing to tell. I'm visiting my great-grandmother."

"How long will you be here?"

"I'm not sure. I was thinking I might go home next month."

"Back to Hungary?"

"How did you know?"

"You have a slight accent. Why are you not married?"

"How do you know I'm not?"

He glanced at her left hand. "No ring."

Lily shrugged. "My marital status is none of your business."

"But you would like to be a wife, wouldn't you?"

Lily stared at him. He saw way too much, she thought. And yet, she felt strangely drawn to him. There was something in his dark eyes, something eternally sad. She wondered if he was mourning the loss of someone he loved, if that was why he was lonely, why his eyes were haunted. "Are you married?"

"Not anymore."

"I'm sorry."

"She has been gone a long time. You remind me of her. Her hair was thick and black, like yours, her eyes gray, like yours, though not so dark." His gaze slid away from her.

And in that moment, Lily's heart went out to him. How many people had he lost through the years? Or was it centuries?

"I would very much like to see you again," he said.

Ava had forbidden it, Lily thought. Good thing Granny was still asleep, or she would be out here demanding that Raedan leave at once. Her parents and Dominic would most certainly object. And with that in mind, she searched for the right words to refuse. But she couldn't find them. Instead, she whispered, "I'd like that."

"Tomorrow night?"

"All right. But I'd better meet you somewhere. My great-grandmother doesn't want me to see you again."

Lily frowned thoughtfully, then said, "I'll meet you at the Prytania at eight."

"Eight o'clock." Rising effortlessly to his feet, he rounded the table and lightly kissed the top of her head. Bowing from the waist, he said, "Thank you, Liliana."

She smiled at the old world gesture as she watched him stride toward the gate, a tall, dark figure who blended into the night and was gone.

"Raedan," she murmured. And felt a wave of excitement flood through her at the thought of seeing him again, quickly followed by doubts as she realized what she'd done.

She didn't want to think of what would happen if her parents, or Ava, found out she had a date with a vampire—and the wrong kind of vampire, at that. And then she grinned. Luckily, she was a witch. A simple incantation would cloak her whereabouts and block the family from knowing what she was doing—and who she was doing it with.

Some hours later, Raedan replayed his conversation with the young witch as he strolled down Esplanade Avenue, home of La Belle Esplanade, the most colorful hotel he had ever seen. He hadn't been able to think of anything but Liliana since seeing her the first time. She was quite lovely, a little whimsical, and far too trusting for her own good. He had sensed her sympathy when he mentioned his last wife, Mary Elizabeth. Though Mary had been gone more than forty years, he still missed her. She had been a sweet, gentle soul. He could have saved her, but she had refused. *I love you, my dark angel,* she had whispered on her death bed, *but I do not want to be what you are.* Of all his wives, he had loved her the most.

Perhaps the lovely Liliana would be his next.

CHAPTER FIVE

Ava regarded her great grand-daughter over the rim of her coffee cup at breakfast the next morning. Something was up, but try as she might, she couldn't determine what the girl was hiding. But she was definitely hiding something. All her walls were up.

"What would you like to do today?" Ava asked, reaching for another slice of toast.

"I'd like to go shopping. I haven't bought anything new in ages."

"Are you planning to take a new wardrobe back to Savaria when you go?"

Lily shrugged. "Maybe. Actually, I've been thinking I might stay here a little longer. J.D. is so cute, I hate to leave him. I can't believe how much he's changed in just the last few weeks. I never realized babies grew so fast. Maybe I'll stay until Dom and Maddy leave for Hawaii."

"J.D. is adorable," Ava agreed. "Is he the only reason you've decided to stay?"

"What other reason could there be?" Lily asked with wide-eyed innocence.

"I don't know," Ava said dryly. "You tell me."

"Granny, are you going shopping with me or not?"

"What do you think?"

❦ ❦ ❦

They headed for Macy's early that afternoon. Lily wandered through the Ladies Department, picking out anything that caught her fancy. Anything that was sexy but not too revealing. Anything that might appeal to a man of the world like Raedan.

In the dressing room, she tried on jeans, sweaters, and skirts, along with several casual dresses. She ended up with two pairs of jeans, black and white, and a navy skirt and three sweaters, one white, one hot pink, and one black. She picked out three dresses as well, a pretty blue-and-white polka-dot with a flared skirt, a black sheath that managed to be sexy and modest at the same time, and a turquoise-blue silk with long sleeves.

Ava pursed her lips when they took the elevator to the lingerie department, where Lily picked out several lacy bras and matching panties.

Shoes came next.

It was late afternoon by the time they left the mall. After dropping Lily's purchases into the trunk of the car, they drove to Ava's favorite restaurant for lunch. It was a lovely day and they chose to sit outside. After ordering, Ava regarded her great-granddaughter thoughtfully.

"Why are you looking at me like that?" Lily asked, somewhat defensively.

"Do I need a reason?"

"I feel like a bug under a microscope."

"I'm just wondering what you're not telling me. And afraid that I already know the answer."

"I don't know what you're talking about. I've got nothing to hide."

"Don't you?"

Lily lowered her gaze, uncomfortable under Ava's scrutiny.

"Talk to me, child."

Lily took a deep breath and let it out in a long, slow sigh. "There's something about him, Granny. I'm not sure what it is, but I want to see him again."

Ava huffed a sigh of her own. "He's dangerous, Liliana. And he's hiding something."

"What do you mean?"

"I'm not sure. But I detect more than vampire when he's around. And whatever it is, it's not good I don't want you to be alone with him.."

"I don't need a babysitter. I'm twenty-five years old and a witch!" Lily exclaimed. "I can take care of myself."

"Can you?"

"I don't want to talk about it," Lily said as the waitress brought their orders. "Okay?"

Ava nodded. "All right," she agreed. *For now.*

That night, after dinner, Lily tried to think of a plausible reason for going out that wouldn't raise Ava's suspicions. She had about run out of ideas when Ava knocked on her bedroom door.

"Lily?"

"Come in."

Ava opened the door, but remained in the doorway. "I just had a call from a friend of mine."

Lily's brows shot up. "I didn't know you had any friends in New Orleans."

"I don't. Joanna lives in Portland. Her husband is ill and the doctors have no idea what's wrong with him. She wants me to come up and see if I can help."

"Of course, you have to go. Is there anything I can do?"

"Just say a prayer, dear. Will you be all right, here, alone?"

"Granny, I'll be fine."

Looking doubtful, Ava said, "Maybe you should come with me. I'm sure Joanna wouldn't mind."

Lily blew out a sigh. "I'm a big girl now. Besides, Dominic and Maddy are just a phone call away and the house is warded against everything that walks, talks, or crawls. How long will you be gone?"

"Hopefully just overnight."

"Stop worrying about me and go help your friend." Lily made a shooing motion with her hands. "Maybe you should hurry?"

"You're right, you're right." Ava conjured an overnight bag that Lily knew was already packed. "Keep the doors locked," she admonished. "And the windows, too."

"Yes, Granny."

"Okay, okay, I'm going."

"Don't forget your broom," Lily said with a grin.

"Ha-ha." With a whispered word and a wave of her hand, Ava was gone.

Stomach churning with excitement, Lily changed her clothes, brushed out her hair, and applied her lipstick. With luck, she wouldn't be late.

Raedan stood outside the movie theater, wondering if Liliana was merely late or had changed her mind. He guessed the latter, no doubt due to her great-grandmother's suspicions. The woman was right to be concerned, but he meant the girl no harm. All he wanted was the company of a beautiful young woman to remind him that there was still good in the world.

He caught her scent wafting from the parking lot even before he saw her hurrying toward him, a vision in a blue-and-white polka-dot dress and white heels. A pink flower adorned her hair. She smiled uncertainly when she saw him.

"Sorry I'm late," she said, cheeks flushed.

"No need to apologize." He gestured toward the box office. "Shall we?"

Lily studied Raedan while he paid for their tickets. He was the most strikingly attractive man she had ever seen, and that was saying a lot, because all the men in her family were insanely handsome.

Inside, he gestured at the concession stand. "Would you like something?"

"Not right now, thanks."

The theater was crowded but they found two seats together on the end of the last row.

Lily was acutely aware of Raedan's presence when he settled into the seat beside hers. She was used to being around men who radiated power, but nothing quite like this. She flushed when he caught her staring, felt a shaft of heat go straight to the very heart of her when his gaze met hers.

A moment later, the lights dimmed and the first trailer came on.

Lily stared at the screen, wondering what had just happened. She felt that same warmth when he reached for her hand, his fingers twining with hers.

He smiled at her, his teeth very white in the darkness.

She wondered, suddenly, if she should have listened when Ava warned her to stay away.

She was only vaguely aware of what transpired on the screen, but acutely conscious of the man beside her, each breath he took, the press of his knee against her own, the way she found it suddenly hard to breathe whenever he glanced in her direction.

⚜ ⚜ ⚜

"Would you like to go out for a drink?" Raedan asked as they left the theater.

Lily hesitated a moment, then nodded.

There was a small tavern on the next block. Raedan guided her toward a booth. She slid onto the seat, hoping he wouldn't sit beside her, relieved and disappointed when he didn't.

"Did you enjoy the movie?" he asked.

"Very much," she said, although for the life of her, she couldn't remember what it had been about. She had been all too aware of the man beside her, the way her heart skipped a beat whenever they touched. Even though the auditorium had been crowded, she had felt like they were alone, just the two of them in the dark. Time and again, she had wondered if he would steal a kiss, not knowing if she was sorry or relieved when he didn't.

"You are afraid of me, aren't you?"

"Of course not."

The look in his eyes told her he knew she was lying. "What did your great-grandmother tell you about me?"

"She said you were a dangerous man. Are you? Dangerous?"

"I can be." His gaze caressed her. "But not to you, sweet Liliana."

He ordered a glass of red wine from the waiter. Lily asked for white.

"What shall we drink to?" Raedan asked when their drinks arrived.

"Truth?"

He smiled wryly. "Do you think I am lying when I say you are in no danger from me?"

"I don't know. You *are* a vampire, after all."

"And yet you still agreed to meet me."

She shrugged. "I know a lot of vampires."

"Indeed?"

"My father comes from an ancient line of Hungarian vampires."

His dark eyes widened in surprise. "How can that be? They sire only males."

"It's a family mystery. My twin brother is a vampire."

"But you are not." He might have thought she was lying, but the power he sensed radiating from her bore no hint of vampire. How could she and her brother be twins, yet so different? He could understand it if they were both vampire *and* witch, but they were not. She was a mystery, indeed, all wrapped up in a lovely package.

"Turnabout is fair play," Lily said. "Tell me about you."

"What would you like to know?"

"How old are you?"

"Thirty-seven, in mortal years."

"And in vampire years?"

"Nine hundred, give or take a decade."

Lily's eyes widened. Nine hundred! He was even older than her great-grandfather, Andras, who had lived for eight centuries. She wondered if they knew each other, but thought it highly unlikely, since each side hated the other. Too bad, she mused. Imagine the stories they could share!

"Are you going to tell me I am too old for you?" he asked, one brow arched in amusement.

Lily laughed in spite of herself.

And he laughed with her.

She loved the sound of it, so rich and deep and sexy. "Can I ask you something that's none of my business?"

"If you wish."

"When we met, I asked if you were married, and you said, 'not anymore.' Were you a vampire then?"

"Not the first time."

"You've been married more than once?"

"A few times."

She stared at him. A few times? Well, duh, she thought. Any man who had lived as long as he had was bound to have been married more than once or twice. How many times, wondered a little voice in the back of her head. Once every hundred years?

Raedan watched the play of emotions chase themselves across her face.

After a moment, she asked, "How many is a few?"

"Four," he replied candidly. "Though of course, there were other women in-between."

"Of course," she said dryly. He was a healthy male, after all.

"Did you think me another Bluebeard?"

Lily grinned. Bluebeard was the main character in a French tale of a wealthy man who had many, many wives, all who died by his hand, and whose bodies were kept in his castle.

"Trust me, none died by my hand."

"Are you reading my mind again?"

"There is no need. Your lovely face is very expressive. You must learn to hide your emotions."

"Would it do any good?"

"Perhaps."

"It's getting late," Lily said. "I should go."

He took her hand as they left the tavern. "I will walk you to your car," he said. "It is not safe for a young girl to be out alone this late."

"But who's going to protect me from you?"

Raedan laughed softly. "No one could. Will you go out with me again?" he asked when they reached the parking lot.

"Ava will know I was out with you tonight. She'll probably lock me in my room and throw away the key. Or send me back home to Savaria."

His gaze searched hers. "Tell her I will surely follow you if she sends you away."

Lily stared up at him. His words should have frightened her. Why didn't they?

"Would you object if I kissed you good night?"

"No," she whispered, suddenly breathless. "I've been hoping you would."

She sighed as his arms went around her, strong but gentle. Murmuring her name, he lowered his head to hers. His lips were cool and firm and the first touch kindled a fire deep inside of her. She leaned into him, her hands clutching his shirt front as his tongue found hers. The world fell away and there was only Raedan, his mouth hot on hers, his arms holding her tight, as if he would never let go.

He lifted his head a moment, murmured, "I knew you would be sweet," and kissed her again.

"Liliana!" Ava's voice, filled with barely suppressed rage, broke the stillness of the night. "Let her go, vampire!"

Raedan looked up, but didn't release Lily.

"I said let her go," Ava repeated, her voice several degrees below freezing as she stalked toward them.

Raedan glanced at Lily.

"Please," she said, "don't make things worse."

Reluctantly, he released her. "Good night, Liliana," he said quietly, and vanished from sight.

"What the hell are you doing?" Ava demanded. "Didn't I tell you to stay away from that man? Do you have any idea what he is?"

"What do you mean?"

"He's a demon!"

Lily stared at Ava. "A demon?"

"Yes."

"No," Lily said adamantly. "I don't believe it. I won't believe it."

"I called your grandfather before I came here. As far as anyone knows, there's only been one vampire-demon in all of recorded history. The man is a notorious monster, feared by other demons, witches, and vampires alike. Now that I think about it," Ava said, frowning, "I remember my great-great-grandmother telling me about such a being when I was a child. He was supposed to have been destroyed by a priest over two centuries ago."

"Then it can't be him, can it?"

Ava shrugged. "Better to err on the side of caution, child."

"Even if it's true, even if it *is* him, how can he be a vampire *and* a demon? I've never heard of such a thing."

"Me, either," Ava admitted. "And I've been around a long time. But that doesn't mean it's not true. After all, anything is possible. Your very existence is proof of that, child. Come on, let's go home."

"How did you find me?" Lily asked as she unlocked her car.

"Whatever walls you erected in your mind to block me came tumbling down. I'm guessing that happened when he kissed you."

Lily blushed furiously as she slid behind the wheel. A vampire-demon, she thought as she started the engine. How on earth was that even possible? She glanced to the left as she pulled out of the parking lot.

And saw Raedan standing in the shadows, watching her as she drove away.

Raedan swore under his breath. So, the woman claimed she knew what he was because Lily's grandfather had told her so. Fools! It was old news, at best, and Liliana's grandfather knew only half the story.

And then he smiled as he recalled how vigorously Liliana had defended him. Heaven bless the girl, her fighting spirit had glowed like that of a warrior priestess of old. There had been damn few—mortal or vampire—who had ever come to his defense, or given a damn if the accusations against him were true or not.

Whistling softly, he continued down the street until he came to a middle-aged woman waiting at a bus stop. Drawing on his preternatural power, he called her to him and took her in his embrace. Bending his head to her neck, he bit her, his eyes closing with pleasure as her blood flowed over his tongue, infusing him with warmth and power. What would Liliana taste like, he wondered, as he sealed the wounds in the woman's throat. Would she be sweet? Or bitter, as witch blood tended to be?

Someday, he thought. Someday soon, he would find out.

CHAPTER SIX

Lily sat at the breakfast table, an untouched bowl of cereal in front of her. Ava had gone back to Portland this morning to see how her friend's husband was doing, but had assured Lily she would be home before dark.

Lily grunted softly. Obviously, her great-grandmother didn't trust her to stay away from Raedan. Ah, Raedan, she thought with a sigh. The mystery man. Was he trapped in the dark sleep during the daylight hours like others of his kind? Did he kill those he preyed on? It occurred to her that that was the first question she should have asked him. Her father's people rarely killed except in self-defense, but Transylvanian vampires were a blood-thirsty lot, often draining their prey dry.

She sighed as she glanced out the kitchen window. Hours until sundown.

Pouring the cereal down the sink, she rinsed the bowl and placed it in the dishwasher, then went to her room. Pulling her scrying mirror from her suitcase, she sat on the bed and held it up in both hands. After summoning Raedan's image to mind, she began to chant the words Ava had taught her. "Powers of earth, wind and fire, reveal to me what I desire. Show me the vampire, Raedan."

When nothing happened, she chanted again, "Powers of earth, wind and fire, reveal to me what I desire. Show me the vampire, Raedan."

Slowly, the mirror grew dark and then brightened. Vibrant colors swirled across the surface, gradually fading, coalescing, until his image appeared.

He was stretched out on a double bed. She could see him clearly even though the room he rested in was dark. He wore a pair of black sweat pants and nothing more. The muscles in his arms and chest were sharply defined. His feet were bare. Asleep, he looked less harsh, less dangerous. Nothing else in the room was visible.

For a moment, she simply stared at him. Although he wasn't Hollywood handsome, he was still the sexiest man she had ever met, his body hard and well-formed. She wondered if he worked out and then laughed softly as she imagined him lifting weights in a gym, muscles rippling as he put the puny efforts of mere mortals to shame.

She was about to murmur the words to close the vision when she suddenly found herself staring into his eyes. Startled, she dropped the mirror on the floor and the image vanished.

Lily blew out a breath. Things like that were *not* supposed to happen! How on earth had he known she was watching him?

After some consideration, she called her brother.

"What?" he asked gruffly.

"Oops, sorry. I forgot you'd probably still be asleep."

Dominic grunted. "What do you want?"

"I met a guy."

"Yeah?"

Dominic was wide awake now, she thought. "He's a Transylvanian vampire."

"What the hell, Lily? Are you out of your mind?"

"That's not the worst of it."

"I'm not sure I want to hear the rest," he said dryly.

"Ava said he's also a demon, although I don't know if that's true."

Silence on the other end.

"Dom?"

"Are you sure?"

"Well, Granny seems to be."

"Any point in my telling you not to see him again?"

Silence on her end.

"Lily?"

"He's the first man I've ever really liked, Dom. I don't care what he is."

"He's not a man, Liliana. Hang on a sec."

Lily tapped one fingertip against the back of her cell phone. A minute passed. Two.

"You still there, Lily?"

"Yes."

"I just texted Dad."

"Why would you do that?"

"Is this guy's name Raedan?"

She hesitated a moment. "Yes."

"Dad said he's ancient. Older than grandfather. Very few in the vampire community even believe he's still alive, or have any idea of how dangerous he really is."

"I know."

"You know! How?"

"Ava told me."

"Dad says..."

"I can imagine what Dad says. I never should have called you!" she exclaimed. And ended the call. When her phone rang, she turned it off, summoned her power, and blocked her family from contacting her telepathically. Darn it! Why couldn't Dom just keep his big mouth shut? Yet even as the thought crossed her mind, she knew it was partly her fault. She should have made him promise up front not to tell anyone.

But it was too late now, she thought, groaning. No doubt the whole family would descend on her and demand that she return to Savaria immediately. And Dominic would side with them. And so would Ava.

What to do? What to do? Arguing would get her nowhere. There was only one thing to do, she decided—usc her power to shield her presence and leave town until things cooled down. And then she frowned. That wouldn't solve anything. How would Raedan know where to find her? They hadn't exchanged phone numbers. Or blood.

She'd worry about that later, she thought. Right now, she needed to get out of New Orleans as fast as she could before the Falconer family descended on her like a duck on a June bug.

Ava muttered an oath as she listened to Quill voice his concerns about Lily. She was back in New Orleans before the call ended. But she was too late. Lily had already gone. Oh, lord, had she run away with the vampire-demon?

She spent the next hour trying every location spell she knew, including a few she had never tried before, but to no avail. It was as if Lily had disappeared from the face of the earth.

Raedan stared up at the ceiling, troubled by what had happened earlier in the day. His little witch was far more powerful than he had first thought. All that supernatural power wrapped up in a beautiful, desirable package. An incredibly dangerous package, if she could locate his lair—thereby putting his safety at risk, something no one else, hunter, witch, demon, or vampire, had ever been able to do. If she turned on him, if she told those seeking his head where he took his rest... Damn! It didn't bear thinking about.

But the question remained—what was he going to do about Liliana? Had it been anyone else, he would have destroyed them without a qualm. He had killed others to protect his existence. But he couldn't snuff out her life. He told himself it was because doing so would bring the whole Falconer clan down on his head, but that had nothing to do with it. He liked her too much to take away her life, her future.

Raedan grunted softly, thinking his feelings for Liliana Falconer were far more dangerous to his continued survival than anything else.

Lily surveyed her new surroundings. After some consideration, she had gone to California, figuring it was as far away from New Orleans as she could get without leaving the country.

After conjuring a fake driver's license, she paid cash for a suite in a five-star hotel across the street from the beach. The rooms were lovely and there was a view of the ocean from the bedroom window. Thanks to a generous allowance from her father, money was no object and she had withdrawn a healthy amount of cash from her account before leaving Ava's.

In her hurry to leave New Orleans, she hadn't packed much and the first order of business was shopping for a bathing suit.

Grabbing her handbag and the keycard, she left the hotel, bound for a small shopping center located a few blocks away.

This was California and bathing suits were plentiful—everything from suits with skirts to the skimpiest bikinis she had ever seen. It took close to forty-five minutes to find a one-piece that she liked. It was black, with red roses twining down one side. She picked out a red cover-up that caught her fancy, as well as a flowered beach towel, a floppy-brimmed white hat, a pair of black sandals, and a pair of sunglasses.

In the dressing room, she slipped the cover-up on over her bathing suit, put on the hat, the sandals, and the sunglasses and then draped the towel over her shoulder. Next, she magicked the clothes and the shoes she had been wearing to her hotel room so she wouldn't have to carry them, then went up front to pay for her purchases.

Outside again, she strolled along the sidewalk. There were people everywhere—some in bathing suits, some in shorts and tank tops, a few in dresses and three-piece suits, others in jeans and t-shirts. Everyone seemed to have a cell phone in hand and be in a hurry to be somewhere else. She passed a gaggle of laughing teenagers, an old man slumped against the side of a building, a young mother trying to quiet a screaming child.

Crossing the street, she walked along a concrete path, then angled to the right and made her way down to the beach. After a few steps, she pulled off her shoes and walked barefoot in the sand.

Finding a vacant spot, she spread her towel on the sand and sat down, She had never spent much time at the beach. Taking a deep breath, she drew in the salty scent of the ocean, the heavy smell of sea weed, the faint scent of suntan oil. The sun and the sand were warm, though a faint breeze kept it from being too hot. Sea gulls called back and forth as they soared overhead. Way off in the distance, she thought she saw a porpoise, or maybe a seal.

Sitting there with the sun on her face, she realized it was the first time in her life that she had been free. Truly free. There was no one to tell her what she could and couldn't do, no one to remind her that she was Hungarian royalty, or to remind her to be demure and polite lest she bring shame to the house of Falconer. Free. It was a heady feeling, to know she could come and go as she pleased, say what she really thought, do whatever caught her fancy.

Lying back on the blanket, she threw her arms wide.

Free.

⚜ ⚜ ⚜

It was near dark when Lily returned to the hotel. She had spent most of the day at the beach. From there, she had gone for a long walk, then out for an early dinner at a seafood restaurant, where she splurged on a lobster dinner.

Riding up in the elevator, she decided to take a long soak in a hot bath, put on her nightgown, order a hot fudge sundae from Room Service, and spend the rest of the evening watching TV.

She came to an abrupt halt when she opened the door to her room and stepped inside, all her senses warning her that she wasn't alone. Turning, she reached for the light switch, let out a shriek when a hand closed over her shoulder.

"Liliana."

"Raedan!" Relief whooshed through her as she pivoted to face him. "What are you doing here? How did you find me?"

"How do you think?" A faint smile tugged at his lips. "I am a vampire. And a demon. He told me where you were."

"How did he ... it ... know?"

"I have no idea."

Heart pounding, she nodded. She told herself there was nothing to be afraid of. Hadn't she run away so she could see him again? But now that he was here ... He loomed over her, a man more powerful than anyone she had ever known. Perhaps she should have listened to Dominic.

"I told you before. I mean you no harm, Liliana. Do you believe me?"

She looked up, her gaze meeting his. His eyes were dark and beautiful, almost hypnotic. "Yes, but ... vampire or not, I don't understand how you found me. We have no blood connection."

"It is a demon thing. I cannot explain it."

He was here, she thought. How he had found her didn't matter. She was only glad that he had.

His gaze moved over her like an invisible caress and everything feminine within her responded. Too fast, she thought, this was happening way too fast.

Slipping past him, she settled on the sofa, her arms folded across her chest. She couldn't think when he was so close.

He regarded her a moment, then dropped into the adjacent easy chair. "Why did you run away?"

"My brother told my father about you and I knew that my parents would show up to take me home, and I ... " She lifted one shoulder and let it fall. "I don't want to go."

"Because of me?"

"Yes."

"Why?" His gaze searched hers. "You should be afraid of me like everyone else. Why are you not?"

"I don't know."

"You are the only one who isn't."

She didn't miss the faint note of bitterness in his voice, the centuries of sadness in his eyes. "The only one?"

He nodded.

"That's terrible," she murmured. But she could understand it. Surely he was one of a kind. The demons wouldn't trust him, the vampires and the witches would fear him. Why didn't she?

Lily bit down on her lower lip when he reached for her hand and felt his touch flow through her. She waited, her heart beating double-time as he leaned toward her. *He's going to kiss me.* The thought had no sooner crossed her mind than his mouth was on hers. It was the lightest of touches, tentative, gentle. And wonderful.

And she was lost. The world fell away. Right or wrong lost its meaning. And there was only the two of them. At that moment, she would have given him anything he asked for. She felt bereft when he lifted his head.

"I should go," he said gruffly.

"Go? Why? You just got here."

His gaze slid to her throat and lingered there. "I find you far too tempting," he admitted quietly. "And I fear I am not strong enough to resist you at this moment. But I should very much like to see you tomorrow night." *After I've fed.* "Will you trust me with your cell phone number?"

"If you'll give me yours."

"My pleasure."

He lingered a moment more after they exchanged numbers. Just being near him was exhilarating, Lily thought. He made her feel vital, alive. Desirable. Sexy, even.

"Tomorrow night," he murmured, his voice husky. "At seven."

Lily nodded, her eyelids fluttering down as he leaned forward and kissed her again.

When she opened her eyes, she was alone.

Raedan cursed his need for blood as he stalked out of the hotel. Many vampires required less blood to survive as they grew older, but he wasn't one of them. The blood-demon within him demanded to be fed at least once a night. To refuse to do so often had fatal consequences for his prey. It was only one of the many undesirable things about being possessed by the demon.

His nostrils flared as he caught the enticing scent of prey, the need to hunt momentarily driving every other thought from his mind.

Until he sank his fangs into the tender flesh of the woman's throat and wished it was Liliana in his arms instead.

CHAPTER SEVEN

In the morning over breakfast, Lily did some serious soul-searching. She was attracted to Raedan, there was no doubt about that. Fascinated. Intrigued. She knew she should be frightened of him—and she was. And yet she wasn't. He could easily have hurt her, killed her, even, yet he hadn't made any threatening moves or suggestions. Last night, he had been totally honest in his reason for leaving. She understood how dangerous a hungry vampire—Transylvanian or Hungarian—could be. She had seen it first-hand. Raedan had been a vampire for nine hundred years. Surely, by now, he could restrain his impulses—whatever kind they might be.

But what if he lost control? She would be as helpless as a mouse caught in the jaws of a tiger. She wasn't fool enough to think that her magic would save her. She had talent, yes, but she still had a lot to learn. And he was powerful as only the very old vampires could be.

She knew Dominic thought she was being foolish, and maybe she was. But it was her life.

It was close to noon when Lily donned her bathing suit, tucked a beach towel and some sunscreen into a tote bag, grabbed her keycard, hat, and sunglasses, and headed for the beach.

It was a beautiful clear day, postcard perfect. Being in the middle of the week, the beach wasn't overly crowded.

She found a suitable place to spread her towel and sat down. She smiled as a toddler let out a shriek when the water tickled his feet, watched a couple of teenage boys who probably should have been in school tossing a Frisbee back and forth. Further down the beach, a freckle-faced young girl was building a sand castle. The child let out an angry cry when a boy with the same freckles—probably the girl's older brother—purposely knocked it down.

With a sigh, Lily stretched out on her back, closed her eyes and listened to the sound of the waves, the whisper of the surf, the call of the gulls.

An hour later, she woke with a start. A glance at her phone told her it was after four. Rising, she walked along the shore before retrieving her things and leaving the beach. She stopped at a fast food place to grab a bite to eat, then hurried back to the hotel, her excitement at the thought of seeing Raedan again growing with every passing minute.

A shower and a shampoo were the first order of business when she returned to her rooms.

Feeling like a schoolgirl getting ready for her first date, she spent an hour fussing with her hair, putting it up in an elaborate do, then taking it down and letting it fall over her shoulders. Most men liked long hair, so she left it loose. She applied her make-up, brushed her teeth, then spent thirty minutes trying to decide what to wear. A dress? A skirt and blouse? A sweater and jeans?

In the end, she decided to go casual with a pair of white slacks and a hot pink sweater with a square neck. She pinned the left side of her hair back with a sparkling old-fashioned barrette Ava had given her, and stepped into a pair of white sandals. Blowing out a sigh, she looked at her reflection in the mirror and hoped Raedan would like what he saw.

Big, fat butterflies did somersaults in the pit of her stomach when she heard his knock at the door.

Raedan sensed Liliana's nervousness as he waited for her to let him in. She had been on edge around him before, but this was different. Not quite fear, he thought. Not exactly anxiety. Perhaps it was just a normal female reaction to dating a man she hardly knew—a man her family had repeatedly warned her to stay away from.

She was a vision, he thought as she opened the door. The pink sweater matched the flush in her cheeks, the clip in her hair rivaled the sparkle in her eyes.

"Come in," she said, taking a step back. Odd, she thought, that hotel thresholds didn't repel vampires the way they did in private homes. Perhaps it was because tourists didn't own the rooms, but only rented them.

"I thought we'd go out." His gaze moved over her. "Dancing, perhaps?" It would give him a perfect excuse to hold her in his arms. "And dinner, if you haven't eaten."

"That sounds nice," she agreed. "Just let me grab my purse."

Lily's eyes widened when she saw his car—a royal blue Audi RS 5. "Did you just buy it?" she asked when she saw the paper license plate. She wasn't much of a car buff, but she had recently seen this very car advertised in a TV commercial.

"I bought it last night, as a matter of fact," he said as he held the door open for her.

"Oh?"

He shrugged. "We had a date and I needed transportation."

"So, you bought this just to take me out?"

He grinned at her. "Maybe I wanted to impress you," he said as he closed her door.

"You could have rented a car for a lot less."

"Not one like this one."

She watched him walk around the front of the Audi. He moved like a jungle cat, she thought, all taut muscle and danger wrapped up in a beautiful hide.

He opened his door and slid behind the wheel. "So, are you impressed?"

"Very. It's gorgeous!" And must have cost a fortune, she thought.

"Then it served its purpose." When the engine purred to life, he pulled out of the hotel parking lot and turned left.

"Where are we going?" Lily ran her hands over the dark-gray leather, which was buttery-soft to the touch.

"What are you in the mood for?"

She hesitated a moment, then said, "I'm not really hungry."

"No?"

She fidgeted in her seat. "I know you don't eat, so … "

"But you do. Unless dining with me will make you uncomfortable."

"I thought it might make *you* uncomfortable," Lily said. "Watching me. Or maybe you don't miss it after so many years."

"I don't, and watching you dine will not bother me."

"Well, I haven't had dinner."

"So, what are you in the mood for?" he asked again.

"Italian, I guess." It was always her first choice.

"I know a little place not far from here. They have a small dance floor in the back."

"Sounds perfect." She watched him out of the corner of her eye as he drove, noting the easy way he handled the car, the clean cut of his profile, the way oncoming headlights cast silver highlights in his dark hair.

A short time later, he pulled into the parking lot of charming Italian restaurant. A discreet wooden sign proclaimed they were at *Mamma Sardino's*.

Raedan parked the car, then came around to open her door.

"Have you been here often?" Lily asked as he reached for her hand.

"Once or twice."

She was dying to ask who he'd been with but stifled the impulse.

The restaurant was dimly lit. Red-and-white checked cloths covered the tables, candles flickered in wrought-iron wall sconces. There was a bar to the left, tables and booths to the right, and beyond that, a doorway that led to what Lily guessed was the dance floor.

"Would you like a drink before dinner?" Raedan asked.

"No. Maybe later."

They didn't have to wait long for a table. A waiter seated them in a booth near the back and handed them menus. Another waiter brought a basket of warm bread sticks and two glasses of water.

Lily opened her menu. Everything sounded wonderful but she finally decided on lasagna. Raedan ordered a bottle of chianti.

Suddenly tongue-tied, Lily reached for a bread stick.

Raedan smiled inwardly. She was so young, so vulnerable. So beautiful with the candlelight dancing in her hair.

The beat of her heart so tempting. "You went to the beach today," he remarked.

"How do you know that?"

"I can smell it on you."

"Really? Even after I showered?"

He nodded. "Also the scent of your soap and your toothpaste."

"I don't know why I'm surprised," Lily said, with a shrug. "I come from a family of vampires, after all." She had learned early in life that it was very nearly impossible to keep a secret in a family of vampires and witches.

She glanced up as a waiter came with their wine and two glasses.

Raedan nodded his thanks as the waiter filled the goblets. "To us," he said when the waiter stepped away. "May we spend many evenings together."

"To us," Lily murmured, her gaze meeting his over the rim of her glass.

Lily experienced a moment of self-consciousness when her dinner arrived. She didn't remember ever eating in front of someone who wasn't also dining and it was a little disconcerting at first.

"I can make you think I'm eating a big plate of spaghetti and dripping Marinara sauce down the front of my shirt if it will make you feel more at ease," Raedan remarked, sensing her discomfort.

His words had the desired effect. With a laugh, she said, "Please, don't."

They made small talk over dinner—their likes and dislikes in movies and music, favorite books they had read.

When dinner was over, Raedan paid the check, then led her to the dance floor. There were only two other couples in the room. The lighting was low, the music soft and romantic, the man beside her ever so sexy.

Lily shivered with anticipation as Raedan took her in his arms. She was acutely aware of his nearness, his scent. Even relaxed, she could feel his power. Although he was much taller than she was, they fit together well, her body nestling against his. She had never been more aware of being a woman. Time lost all meaning and there was only the two of them, slowly swaying back and forth, her cheek resting against his chest, his arms warm around her.

Raedan brushed a kiss across the top of her head, his nostrils filling with the scent of her hair, her perfume. Her desire. She wanted him and the thought filled him with delight. And terror. Her blood sang to him. The demon within urged him to bury his fangs in her soft flesh, to taste her blood on his tongue, to feel the warmth of it flowing through his veins, sweeter than honey, chasing away the eternal cold of his existence.

He closed his eyes as he called on every ounce of self-control he possessed to resist the terrible hunger that engulfed him.

The blood-demon roared in his ears as he sensed he was losing the battle.

"Raedan?"

The sound of Lily's voice drove the demon away. Relieved, Raedan opened his eyes to find her watching him, her brow furrowed, his expression worried.

"Are you all right?" she asked, her gaze searching his.

He took a deep breath and blew it out in a sigh of relief. "I am now."

One last drink, one more dance, and he drove her back to her hotel. He held her hand in the elevator and as he walked her to her suite.

"I had a wonderful time," Lily said as she unlocked the door.

"As did I. Perhaps we could do it again tomorrow night?"

"I'd like that," she said with an impish grin. "After all, I don't know anyone else in town."

"I would be happy to make sure you never get lonely," he said, drawing her into his arms.

Lily closed her eyes, happiness bubbling up inside her as his mouth closed over hers. She was breathless when he lifted his head.

"Sweet dreams, Liliana," he murmured.

"You, too," she said, and then frowned. "Do you dream when you're at rest?"

His dark gaze caressed her face. "I will tonight." He kissed her one more time. "Until tomorrow, pretty lady."

With a nod, she closed the door, then stood there, unable to stop smiling.

She was falling in love, she thought. Feeling like she was walking on air, she went into the bedroom to get ready for bed. She had just changed into her nightgown when her cell phone rang.

"I wanted to hear your voice one more time before I retire," Raedan said when she answered the phone, though it would be hours before he sought his rest. "Good night, sweet Liliana."

"Good night." She ended the call and hugged the phone to her chest, her heart so full of happiness she thought she might burst. "Definitely love," she murmured, and turned out the light.

CHAPTER EIGHT

D ominic paced the living room floor in Ava's house. "What the hell are we going to do? Lily's been gone for days and no one's been able to get in touch with her. Not even me! For all we know he could have killed her by now!"

"Calm down, boy," Ava chided. "Thinking the worst isn't going to help. Even though she's blocked you, I'm sure you'd feel it if something had happened to her." Twins had a bond unlike any other.

"I hope you're right." He slumped into a chair. "My parents are ready to come back here. Mom's going out of her mind with worry. Dad threatened to rip the guy to shreds if he ever gets his hands on him."

"We're all worried, but I have to believe she's all right." Ava shook her head ruefully. "I had no idea she was powerful enough to block the whole family. I certainly never taught her any such incantation. And she never learned it from my grimoire, or any of my spell books. I know, because I've searched every one of them." She frowned thoughtfully for a moment, and then shook her head.

"What are you thinking?" Dominic asked.

"Raedan."

"What about him?"

"He's an extremely old and powerful vampire."

"Yeah, so?"

"And he's also a demon."

Dominic stared at her, and then cursed softly. "You think he's worked some kind of demon magic to mask her presence from the rest of us, don't you?"

"I don't know," Ava replied, her voice grim. "But I intend to find out."

CHAPTER NINE

I n the morning, Lily sat down at the small mahogany desk in the hotel bedroom and wrote her brother a letter. A text would have been faster, but that could have been traced.

Dear Dom:

I know you're worried about me, but I'm fine. For the first time in my life, I'm free to do as I please, when I please, with whom I please. Raedan is not the monster everyone thinks he is. Nothing untoward is going on between us, I promise. He's been a perfect gentleman. Please call Mom and Dad and tell them I'm fine and that I'll be returning to New Orleans soon. I just needed a chance to be on my own for once. Give Ava and Maddy my love and hug the baby for me. Love ya, Lily.

She folded the letter, slipped it into an envelope and addressed it to her brother, careful not to add a return address. She frowned as she sealed the flap. The postmark would let them know she was in California.

And then she smiled. She was a witch. She didn't need the United States Post Office to deliver her mail. She would send it Air Lily.

She spent the day at the beach again—walking along the shore, building a sand castle, lying in the shade of a rented umbrella, reading a paperback book she had bought in the hotel gift shop, and indulging in a king-sized Snickers candy bar.

Later in the afternoon, she bought a hot dog and a coke from a street vendor, then took another walk. She loved the scent of sea and sand, the way the waves rushed endlessly to the shore. She wondered about Raedan. Was he trapped in the dark sleep of his kind during the day? Or was he ancient enough that it was no longer necessary? Did he have to feed often? She knew some vampires fed less as they aged. And some fed often just because they liked it. Hungarian vampires were more human than the other kind. They didn't have to rest during the day, though most did, simply because they preferred the night. They were able to consume regular food, though they did require blood from time to time. They didn't kill their prey. Raedan had been a vampire a very long time. It bothered her to know he had probably taken many lives in the course of his existence.

And then there was the demon thing. How did that affect him, exactly, and how had he become infected with a demon in the first place? She had never even known such things as blood-demons existed. Of course, if there were witches and vampires, why not demons? There were stories in the Bible of people being possessed by evil spirits, but Raedan didn't act like a man controlled by some demonic, malevolent being. Could she live with him if he was?

The thought brought her up short. She was falling in love with him, of that she was sure. But did she want to spend the rest of her life with him? Of course, it was a moot point at the moment. For one thing, he hadn't asked her. And they had only known each other a matter of days. Maybe what she felt wasn't love at all, just infatuation for the most remarkable man she had ever met. How was she to know? There hadn't been very many men in her sheltered life. Her father and her brother had seen to that.

As the air cooled, she headed back to the hotel. She had plenty of time to worry about the future, she mused as she took the elevator to her room. If it was love, it would last. If not, she would enjoy it while she could. But there was no time to worry about it now. She had a date in a couple of hours.

Raedan showed up promptly at seven. As usual, she couldn't help staring at him. He looked runway model handsome in a pair of black jeans and a dark-blue jacket over a white pullover.

He grinned at her expression. "I think you look great, too."

"What? Oh! You're reading my mind again!"

"Sorry. Force of habit."

"Well, stop it!" Lily glared at him, wondering, as she did so, how she could have forgotten that vampires had that ability when she had been surrounded by them her whole life? Oh, lordy, had he read her thoughts the night before?

"If you're not too angry with me, where would you like to go tonight?"

"I don't know. I hadn't really thought about it."

"A walk? A movie? A moonlight swim? Dinner, if you haven't eaten."

"I called room service earlier. I'm not sure about swimming at night."

"You would be perfectly safe."

"I don't know. Maybe a movie, instead."

"Whatever you wish."

She flushed as his gaze met hers, because he was what she wanted. And she was sorely afraid he knew it.

It was Friday night, the latest superhero flick had just opened, and the movie theater was crowded. They managed to find two seats together about ten rows from the front. A little too close for Lily's liking, but she didn't care because Raedan was beside her, his muscular thigh brushing hers, his shoulder, too, if she leaned just a little to the left.

As the lights went down, he reached for her hand.

It was hard to concentrate on the screen when he was so close. His thumb caressed her palm, his masculine scent tickled her nostrils. They should have gone swimming, she thought. Because right about now, she could use a splash of cold water to cool her off.

When she risked a glance at Raedan, she found him looking back at her. His teeth flashed in a knowing grin as he leaned toward her and whispered, "I want you, too," before he claimed her lips with his.

"Raedan, not here," she whispered, pushing him away.

"No one can see us," he assured her. "We're in our own little world." He lifted the arm of the seat between them so it was out of the way and then he kissed her again, lightly, and when she didn't protest, he deepened the kiss, his tongue finding hers as his arm curled around her shoulders, drawing her body closer.

Our own little world, she thought as he kissed her again and yet again, each one a little longer, a little more intimate, than the last. She forgot where they were, forgot there was anyone else in the theater. There was only Raedan, his arm around her, his lips evoking feelings and sensations she had never experienced before, never dreamed existed. Sensations she never wanted to end.

She slid the fingers of one hand into the silky hair at his nape while her other hand clutched his arm, afraid if she let him go, she would slide out of her seat and land on the floor at his feet, a helpless bundle of longing.

She blinked at him when he lifted his head, felt a rush of embarrassment when she realized the movie was over and the lights were on.

Taking her by the hand, he lifted her to her feet and put his arm around her waist. "You okay, my sweet Liliana?"

She looked up into his dark eyes and feared she would never be the same again.

Raedan drove her back to the hotel, accompanied her to the door of her room, waited while she unlocked it.

"Thanks for tonight," Lily said. "I had a wonderful time."

"As did I."

Her cheeks warmed under the heat of his eyes, and the memory of how eagerly she had gone into his arms.

"Maybe we could do it again?" he said.

His voice, low and seductive, filled her mind with shadowy images of candlelight and the two of them lying entwined in each other's arms amid rumpled sheets.

When she met his gaze, she knew he was aware of her every thought, every doubt.

"Do you trust me enough to invite me in?"

She licked her lips. Would he be offended if she didn't? But surely he knew her reasons. He was far too sexy and she was feeling far too vulnerable.

Grinning, he brushed his lips across hers. "You are wise beyond your years," he said. "Can I see you tomorrow night?"

She was playing with fire, Lily thought. He was centuries older than she was, not only in years but experience. Compared to him, her powers were practically non-existent. Ava would not approve. Neither would her parents. Or Dominic. And yet she couldn't bear the thought of not seeing him again. Her voice trembled when she said, very quietly, "Yes."

"Same time?"

She nodded.

He leaned toward her and when she didn't back away, he kissed her, ever so gently. "Until tomorrow," he murmured.

Tomorrow, she thought as she watched him walk away. How could she wait until tomorrow?

After leaving Liliana, Raedan willed himself to Hollywood. Spending time with the lovely witch tended to rouse his hunger, and since he didn't want to think of her as prey, he sought satisfaction elsewhere. Hollywood was an interesting place, even late at night. Drunks and druggies wandered the dark streets. Hookers of every stripe lingered in alleyways, hoping for one more trick before calling it a night. The shrill sound of a siren bruised the quiet of the night.

He passed several people strolling along the sidewalk— tourists, whores, addicts looking for one more hit—but found none of them appealing.

Not willing to settle for anything unappetizing, Raedan willed himself back to his lair at the beach. Maybe he would have better luck tomorrow night.

And if not, maybe you can coax the fair Liliana into giving you a taste.

"No!" he roared. "Not Liliana! Damn you, demon, leave me the hell alone!"

CHAPTER TEN

Dominic thrust Lily's letter into Ava's hand. "What do you make of this?"

Ava frowned when she saw there was no return address. "Smart," she murmured. "No way to tell where she is." She might be able to work a reverse location spell, but she was pretty sure Lily—or Raedan—would have planned for that and conjured the spell accordingly.

Ava read the missive, and then read it again before returning it to Dominic. "When did you get this?"

"Last night."

"And you waited until now to show it to me?"

He shrugged as he returned the letter to the envelope. "Do you think she went with him of her own accord? Or is she under some kind of vampire-demon compulsion?" All vampires possessed the innate ability to appeal to the opposite sex. It was a preternatural gift that made it easier for them to attract their prey.

"It's possible, I suppose."

Dominic muttered an oath as he paced the floor. "If so, what's his motive?"

"I have no idea. Certainly not money. I've yet to meet an ancient vampire of any sort who wasn't already rich enough to buy a small country."

"Blackmail?"

Ava shook her head. "To what end?"

"I don't know! Dammit, my sister's in danger and I can't do a damn thing about it!"

"We don't know that she's in danger," Ava said, hoping to calm him, and reassure herself at the same time.

"I've tried a hundred times to locate her. This has to be his doing. She might be able to block the rest of the family, but we're twins. She's never been able to block me before."

"It may not be him, although I'm certain it must be. Still, she might have found a book on Black Magic somewhere. Maybe in one of the shops in New Orleans."

"And maybe in your collection," Dominic said, his voice thick with accusation. "I haven't forgotten that you used Dark Magic not so long ago."

"This is no time to rehash the past," Ava snapped. "Give me the letter."

"Why?"

"It usually takes Black Magic to break Black Magic. The letter, please."

Dominic hesitated a moment and then thrust the envelope into her hand. "Let me know if you find out where she is."

"Of course. Give Maddy my love."

With a nod, he left the house.

Ava spent the next two hours working every spell she knew on Lily's letter in an effort to determine her location, but to no avail. Frustrated by her failure, she slammed her fist against her work table. There was no way Lily should have been able to conjure such a powerful spell, Ava thought, her irritation growing stronger with every passing moment. She didn't have the knowledge or the skill.

But the vampire-demon possessed both.

Ava muttered an ancient, very unladylike oath. As she had feared, it wasn't Liliana who was blocking the family from finding her.

It was Raedan.

CHAPTER ELEVEN

"This is getting to be a habit," Lily murmured as Raedan slipped his arm around her shoulders. They had decided not to go out tonight. Earlier, she had ordered room service and a bottle of red wine. Now, with a fire burning low in the hearth and soft music coming over the sound system, she sighed with contentment.

His knuckles brushed her cheek. "Are you getting tired of me?"

"Of course not! I've never been happier."

"Nor have I." He drew her closer, thanking whatever Fate had brought her into his life.

"Tell me about your past. I know so little about you. What was your life like before you were turned?"

"I am not sure you want to hear it, my sweet. It is filled with ugliness."

"Tell me."

Gazing into the fire, he said, "I was just an ordinary man, the oldest of six brothers. We grew up on a small farm in a town outside Brasov that no longer exists. My father raised horses. My mother died in childbirth delivering her seventh child. A girl that didn't survive. Eventually, my brothers married and moved away. I married Cristobel, a girl from the neighboring farm."

"Did you love her?"

"No."

"Did she love you?"

"No. It was a marriage of convenience, more or less, but we got on well together. She gave me a son and a daughter and then, like my mother, she died in childbirth and the infant with her. Life went on. I hired a housekeeper to look after the children and the house."

He paused, a faraway look in his eyes. "It was late on a snowy night when the vampires came. They killed the housekeeper. One of them, a woman, found my children hiding under their beds and carried them away. I never saw them again. The other vampire, also a woman, came after me. I fought her off as best I could, but I was no match for her strength. When she bit me, I feared she was never going to stop. The world turned gray. I could feel her drinking my blood, feel the strength leaving my body. And then, as I began to sink into oblivion, she pried my mouth open. I cried out, afraid of what she was going to do next, but she did not kill me. Instead, she bit her own wrist and forced some of her blood into my mouth. It burned my tongue like hellfire, but I was too weak to spit it out. And then...then I did not want to.

"I don't remember much of the rest of that night. There were men, I do not know how many. They killed the vampire and left me for dead. I know now they were vampire hunters, just as I know they would have killed me, too, if they had known what she had done.

"I woke in agony the next night, certain I was dying." He laughed, a cold, bitter laugh. "Little did I know I was already dead. Hunger drove me out of the house. My horses were gone, stolen by the hunters, no doubt, so I walked to the village and attacked the first man I saw." He shook his head with the memory. "I drank him dry, and in the process, the demon that had infected him was somehow transferred to me." Again, that cold, bitter laugh. "As if becoming a vampire was not bad enough."

He glanced at Lily, who was staring at him, transfixed. "Have you heard enough?"

She shook her head.

"The country was at war then and I became a soldier. No one questioned where I went during the day. I fought at night, sometimes behind the lines, attacking anything and anyone who got in my way. I was indestructible. I lost count of the men who fell to my sword. And of the men who fed my hunger." A muscle throbbed in his jaw. "I was no fit companion for man or beast," he said, his voice harsh. "And I am not sure that has changed. Good night, Liliana."

"Raedan, wait..."

But he was already gone.

He never should have told Liliana of his past, he thought as he stalked through the night. He had thought his hatred for himself, for what he had done in the past, buried and forgotten, but it rose now, thick and hot within him—the memory of the lives he had taken with no thought of anything but the need to kill, to feed on the hot, fresh blood of his victims. He had known, in some deep recess of his mind, that it was the demon driving him so relentlessly, but he had lacked the strength to fight it.

It shamed him to know that he had reveled in the shedding of blood, in the taste of it on his tongue, in the power it gave him. It had taken him centuries to learn to subdue the creature, to feed without killing. Centuries to learn to pretend he was human, to blend in with humanity, to make love to a woman without taking her life.

He had to leave Liliana now, before his affection turned to something stronger, deeper. Before leaving became impossible. Before he succumbed to the demon's constant urging to sink his fangs into her sweet flesh and drink and drink until there was nothing left.

A whispered word broke the demon-spell he had woven around her to prevent her family from locating her whereabouts.

And then he fled the city.

Lily paced the floor, totally confused by Raedan's behavior. Why had he left so abruptly, with no explanation? Was it something she'd said? But how could that be? She had listened, transfixed, as he told her of his past—a terrible past, to be sure, one she had trouble reconciling with the man she knew. True, she hadn't known him that long. She knew he was a powerful being. But he had been nothing but kind to her. Gentle. Tender. Loving. He had done horrible things in the past, but then, he'd had horrible things done to him.

Hope flared within her when she heard a knock at the door. Hoping he had returned, she hurried to answer it. Only it wasn't Raedan.

"Granny! What are you doing here?"

"Where is he?" Ava brushed past Lily, her gaze darting around the room.

"He's not here," Lily said as she closed the door. "How did you find me?"

"It wasn't your spell keeping you hidden from us," Ava said grimly. "It was his."

"I don't understand."

"It was a demon spell. He cast it around you so we couldn't find you. Your parents and Dominic are half out of their minds with worry. Are you all right, child?"

"Of course I am."

"He hasn't… he didn't… ?"

Lily stared at her great-grandmother. "Didn't what?" she asked. And then blushed from head to foot. "Of course not! He's been a perfect gentleman the whole time. How could you even think such a thing?"

"Lily, use your head. The man is a vampire, possessed by a demon. I credited you with more sense than to get involved with such a creature! Get packed, I'm taking you home."

"What if I don't want to go?"

"I'm not asking."

"I like it here. I like being free to do as I please. I don't want to go back to Savaria. And if you make me, I'll just leave again."

"Lily…"

"I've been a prisoner my whole life and never realized it until I came here, to America."

"Your parents…"

"They love me, I know that. But they don't trust me enough to make my own decisions. I'm twenty-five years old and I've never been allowed to go anywhere without a bodyguard or one of the family."

"It's for your own safety, Liliana. Your family has enemies, even in Savaria, men who are jealous of your grandfather's power and position."

"They didn't keep Dominic locked up! They sent him here to look for the Elder Knight."

"That was more my doing than his, though he doesn't know it."

Lily's eyes widened. "What do you mean?"

"I knew how much your brother wanted to be out on his own," Ava said, with a shrug. "And so I arranged it."

"Then why can't you do the same for me? Please convince Dad to let me stay here, with you. I should be safe enough," she said, blinking back her tears. "Now that Raedan's gone."

"What do you mean?"

"He left just before you got here. Left without any explanation at all. "

"Maybe he had a good reason," Ava said, and wondered why she was suddenly defending the man.

"It felt like goodbye," Lily murmured, and burst into tears. "I don't... think I'll ever... see him again."

First loves were always painful, Ava mused as she gathered Lily into her arms. Sadly, sometimes the hurt never went away.

⚜ ⚜ ⚜

Dominic was waiting at Ava's house when they returned. "Thank heaven you're all right," he exclaimed, giving Lily a hug. "Do you know how worried we've all been? How could you run away without a word?"

"I sent you a letter," she said, her voice flat. "I was never in any danger."

"It was thoughtless of you. Mom and Dad have been worried sick."

Twisting out of his embrace, she said, "I'm going to bed."

"Lily..."

"Let her go," Ava said. "She needs to be alone."

"What's to keep her from leaving again?"

"I've warded the house with the strongest incantation I know. She's not going anywhere."

Eyes narrowed, Dominic crossed his arms over his chest. "Dad wants her home."

"I know. But now is not the time. Lily's feeling trapped, just the way you did. Your parents are going to have to give her some freedom or they're going to lose her, maybe for good."

Dominic dropped onto the sofa and cradled his head in his hands. "I told them they were keeping her on too tight a rein," he muttered. "But you can't blame them. She's the first—the only—female ever born to the family. There are those who want to know how it was possible. And not just our people. There are rumors that the Transylvanian vampires are also curious about her birth. Did you know that?"

"No." Ava sank into the easy chair across from the sofa. Transylvanian vampires were unable to reproduce. No wonder they were interested in Lily. No doubt they wondered what would happen if one of their men mated with her. Would it produce a child? And would that child be vampire or human or both?

"What should I tell the family?" Dominic asked.

"Tell then I'll bring Lily home in a few weeks. In the meantime, I'm going to check into these rumors and see if they're true."

"How are you going to do that?" Dominic queried as he stood.

"Don't worry about it. Give Maddy my love."

He nodded. "I imagine you'll be getting a phone call from Dad right quick."

Ava smiled serenely. "I imagine so. Good night, Dom."

With a rueful shake of his head, he left the house.

❦ ❦ ❦

As expected, the phone rang ten minutes later.

"Hello, Quill," Ava said cheerfully. "How nice to hear from you."

"This isn't a social call," he snapped. "I want my daughter home, and I want her here now. I knew it was a bad idea to send her to the States."

"Calm down. She's fine. Did you listen to anything Dominic said?"

"A lot of nonsense about Lily needing her freedom."

"It's not nonsense. She's not a child any longer, she's a grown woman, and you and Callie have to start treating her like one."

Silence.

"You've got to let Lily make some decisions on her own," Ava said quietly. "It won't end well if you force her to come home. She'll hate you for it if you do."

"It's dangerous for her there."

"In one way or another, life is dangerous for everyone, Quill. Even you. With the old Elder Knight dead, the Brotherhood is no longer a threat in New Orleans. I can handle the Transylvanian vampires."

Quill grunted, neither approval nor denial. "And the vampire-demon?"

"From the way she's sobbing in her room, I'd say it's over between them."

"And what if you're wrong?"

"Then I'll call for help."

"I'm trusting you with my daughter's life," Quill said flatly. "Don't let me down."

CHAPTER TWELVE

Claret frowned when she entered her favorite club and found a strange vampire with blond hair, and eyes such a pale blue they seemed almost colorless, sitting in her booth. He looked her up and down as she approached, his gaze both appreciative and disdainful.

"So," he said. "You're the Master of the City."

"And you're in my booth. So move your ass."

"Feisty, too. Let's talk."

She hesitated a moment, but curiosity won. "Who are you and what do you want?" she asked as she slid into the booth across from him.

"Information."

"Why come to me?"

"I think you can help me."

"Not until I know who you are."

"Varden. You may have heard of me?"

"I may have." Most Transylvanian vampires knew about Louis Varden. He claimed most of Mississippi as his domain. "So, what can I do for you? And what are you planning to give me in return?"

"I've heard some interesting things about a family of Hungarian vampires, including the fact that you're acquainted with them."

"I might be. What's your interest?"

"I heard that one of them married a witch and the witch presented him with twins. And that one of them was a girl."

Claret shrugged. "So?" He was talking about Lily Falconer, she thought.

"So," Varden went on, "I'm wondering if the daughter of that witch could mate with one of us and produce offspring."

"I have no idea. Nor do I care."

"But you know who I'm talking about?"

"Perhaps."

Eyes narrowed, he stared at her as he unleashed his power.

He was strong. She would give him that. But, thanks to the lingering effects of Dominic Falconer's blood, so was she. Smiling faintly, she countered Varden's power with her own.

Surprise flickered in his eyes. And then he smiled. "You're full of surprises, *cherie*."

"You have no idea," she said, baring her fangs. "What are you willing to pay for this information?"

"What do you want?"

"The blood of a Hungarian vampire."

Varden laughed softly. "Don't we all?"

"That's my price."

"You drive a hard bargain," he said.

"Take it or leave it," she said. "Now get your ass out of my booth."

Eyes narrowed, Claret watched Varden stride out of the club. She had no loyalty to the Falconer family, but she did have a soft spot for Quill and Dominic. Perhaps, if she went to Metairie and warned Dominic that his sister was in danger, he would reward her with a sip or two.

❧ ❧ ❧

"What the hell!" Dominic exclaimed when he opened the door and saw Claret standing on the porch. "What are you doing here?"

"Is that any way to greet an old friend?"

Dominic snorted. "Friend? Hardly the description I'd use."

"Oh, I'm sorry. Maybe I should leave. You obviously don't care that your sister is in danger."

He frowned at her. "Is that vampire-demon back in town?"

"No. Someone in New Orleans is looking for her."

"Who?"

Claret's gaze rose to his throat, her tongue darting out to lick her lips. "It will cost you."

"Gee," he muttered dryly, "I wonder what you want."

"Just a sip or two. My information is worth it."

"Fine. You first."

"There's a vampire named Varden looking for Lily."

"Never heard of him."

"He's an old one, perhaps four hundred years. He thinks if one of our males mates with Lily, they might be able to produce a child."

Dominic stared at her. "Where the hell did he get an idea like that?"

She stared at him as if he wasn't too bright. "Where do you think?"

"Right."

"He thinks that because your parents—a witch and a vampire—produced young, there's a chance that if one of the Transylvanian men mated with Lily—vampire and witch—she'll conceive. He didn't say as much, but I'm convinced he intends to mate with her himself."

"It won't work. He's the wrong kind of vampire."

"He doesn't care. He's determined to try." Her gaze lingered on his throat again. "I didn't have to come here and warn you, you know."

Dominic grunted softly as he stepped out onto the porch and closed the door firmly behind him. "Don't get carried away," he cautioned. "I'd hate to have to break that pretty neck."

With a seductive smile, Claret went up on her tiptoes—and sank her fangs gently into his throat.

Maddy would have a fit if she knew what he was doing, Dominic thought ruefully. After a few moments, he placed his hand on Claret's shoulder. "That's enough."

A low growl rose in her throat as she sank her fangs deeper into his flesh.

"Enough!" he hissed.

With a reluctant sigh, she backed away, licked a bit of his blood from her lips, and smiled. "Just as good as I remember," she murmured, and vanished from the porch.

Dominic stared after her, his thoughts troubled as he stared into the darkness and debated his next move.

CHAPTER THIRTEEN

Ava rapped on Lily's bedroom door. The girl had stayed in her room for the last five days, only coming out when Ava insisted she eat something. "Lily?"

"Go away."

"You've been moping long enough, child. You hardly knew the man."

Ava stepped back as the door opened. Lily's eyes were red and swollen and filled with such pain, Ava's heart went out to her. "You've been crying again." Pulling a tissue from her skirt pocket, Ava wiped Lily's eyes. "As far as I'm concerned, he's not worth a single one of your tears."

"I guess you're right," Lily said. "But I thought he cared for me and I ... I thought I might be falling in love with him."

Ava drew Lily into her arms and hugged her. "I know you don't believe it, but in time, the pain will pass. Why don't you go wash your face and change your clothes and I'll take you out for dinner. You've hardly eaten enough to keep a mouse alive in the last five days."

"I'm not hungry."

"Maybe not for dinner," Ava said. "But how about a banana split with double hot fudge and extra whipped cream?"

Lily sniffed. "If it'll make you happy."

"It will," Ava assured her with a wink. "It's just what you need."

Lily had to admit it felt good to be out of the house. Ava drove them to the city's biggest ice cream parlor. The lights were bright, the walls papered in a red-and-white stripe. The tables and chairs were white wrought-iron, the tables covered with cloths that matched the wallpaper.

Ava ordered a banana split for Lily and a hot fudge sundae for herself. They took a table for two by the front window.

"I talked to your father," Ava remarked after a moment.

Lily looked at her. "And?"

"I convinced him to let you stay here for a while."

Relief whooshed out of Lily in a sigh. "Thank you."

"I understand your need to make your own decisions, but you have to promise me that you'll tell me where you're going when you go out. Like it or not, you have to remember that you're a rare gift. A miracle. Others in the supernatural world are curious about the details of your birth. Your parents and Dominic are naturally concerned for your safety."

Lily stared at her. "People are interested in *me*? That's why my dad never let me go anywhere alone?"

Ava nodded. "You don't realize what a miracle your birth was. I'm not trying to scare you. I just want you to be careful. Be aware of your surroundings. Pay attention to your instincts."

"You don't think that's why Raedan was seeing me, do you?"

"I don't know. But if it was, he probably wouldn't have left."

Lily glanced out the window, let out a gasp when she saw a tall, dark-haired man standing outside staring at her.

"What's wrong?" Ava asked.

Lily leaned forward, her gaze probing the darkness. "I thought I saw Raedan."

"I don't see anyone."

"He's gone now." Lily sat back, her shoulders slumped. "I probably just imagined it."

Raedan cursed softly as he vanished into the night. He hadn't intended for Liliana to see him, but he missed her so damn much, he didn't know how much longer he could stay away. He had needed to see her, to assure himself that she was all right. But seeing her again had been a mistake. One look and he was smitten all over again. He had known hundreds of women in the course of his existence—old, young and in-between. Pretty or plain, rich or poor, all had been the same. He had cared for some, made love to many, but the love of his life had been his last wife—until he met Liliana Falconer. He didn't know what there was about her that intrigued him so, but his need for her was unlike anything he had ever known. It was as if she had soothed an ache he hadn't known he'd had until he left her.

He swore softly as he ghosted through the darkness. Leaving her had been the right thing to do. The noble thing. The unselfish thing. He knew it without doubt. And yet the thought of spending the rest of his existence without her was more than he could bear. Without her, he felt lost, empty inside. Adrift in a world in which a creature such as himself didn't belong. Would never belong.

What was worse, the blood-demon inside him knew it, too. The demon's voice whispered to him constantly, urging him to give in to his vampire nature, to surrender to the hunger that burned inside of him, to glut himself on the warm, rich, blood of his prey.

It's what you are, the insidious voice taunted him night after night. *Submit to your true nature. Satisfy your lust and your thirst. You know you want to.*

"Shut up!" he roared. "Just shut the hell up!"

And inside his head, he heard the echo of the demon's mocking laughter.

At home later that night, Lily stood at her bedroom window and gazed out into the night. Raedan was out there somewhere. Did he miss her at all? Was he sorry he had left her? Or had he already found someone new? Was everything he had said to her a lie? Had he ever really cared for her?

With a sigh, she crawled under the covers. Closing her eyes, she whispered, "Raedan, come back to me."

A moment later, she was asleep.

And he came to her there, in the dark recesses of her mind.

Liliana, my love, how I miss you.

Why did you leave me?

It was for the best.

Not for me. She held out her arms and he stretched out beside her.

I am no good for you or anyone else. His knuckles caressed her cheek. *You are inherently good and kind and gentle, my lovely Liliana. You deserve someone better, someone who can offer you the kind of good, decent life you deserve. The kind I can never give you.*

She gazed into his eyes, eyes filled with pain and loneliness. *I don't want anyone else.*

He groaned low in his throat. *You will never be safe with me. The demon inside me... "*

She pressed her fingertips to his lips. We'll defeat him together.

Do you think I have not tried?

Shh. Removing her fingers from his lips, she drew his head down and kissed him, her hands moving restlessly over his broad back, threading into the dark hair at his nape while she pressed her body against his.

Liliana! Lost in her nearness, in the warmth of her body, the heat of her lips, he crushed her close...

Lily woke with a start when the bedroom door flew open and the light came on. Heart pounding, she glanced around, searching for Raedan. But he was nowhere in sight. Tears stung her eyes as she realized it had only been a dream.

"Where is he?" Ava asked, her voice sharp.

Lily blinked against the light. "What?"

"Where is he?" Ava asked again. "I know he was here."

Eyes wide, Lily stared at her great-grandmother. Maybe it hadn't been a dream at all.

Raedan blew out a sigh as he willed himself to his lair. Right or wrong, he vowed he would see her again, do everything in his power to win her trust. And her love. Having held her in his arms again, tasted her sweet kisses once more, how could he ever leave her for good? She was the light to his darkness. The goodness of her soul strengthened him, acting as a buffer between himself and the demon.

Her scent was carried to him on every indrawn breath. The memory of her kisses made him smile as he tumbled into oblivion.

Lily woke with a smile on her lips. What she'd thought had been a dream the night before had been reality. Ava's sense of Raedan's presence in the house proved it had really happened. He had been there in bed beside her, holding her in his arms. Where was he now? When would she see him again?

She was still smiling when she padded into the kitchen, drawn by the mingled scents of coffee and bacon.

Her smile faded away when she saw the look on Ava's face. "What's wrong?"

"We need to talk."

"Are you breaking up with me?" Lily asked, hoping to lighten the sudden tension in the room.

"This is no laughing matter," Ava said, setting a plate of bacon and eggs in front of her. "You're in danger, child. And not just from your vampire-demon."

"What do you mean?"

Ava took the chair across from Lily. "Your brother called me earlier. He had a visit from Claret late last night."

"Claret!" Lily exclaimed. "What on earth did *she* want?"

"You remember I told you people were interested in you because of the circumstances of your birth?"

Lily nodded as she reached for her fork.

"Apparently there's a vampire looking for you."

"Someone you know?"

"No. This vampire went to Claret seeking information. He believes if he mates with you, it will produce a child."

Lily laid her fork back on the table. "That's ridiculous."

"Apparently he's determined to try."

"But… everyone knows only Hungarian vampires can successfully mate with humans. And even then, it doesn't always work."

"As I said, this one is determined to try."

Her appetite gone, Lily pushed her plate away. "Are Transylvanian vampires stronger than our kind?"

"Hungarian or Transylvanian, a vampire's strength grows more powerful as they age. But a vampire's sire also affects their power. The stronger the sire, the stronger the fledgling. Your grandfather was sired by a powerful vampire and that strength has been passed down through your family. Transylvanian vampires, old or young, turn mortals indiscriminately, with no thought of power. But a few of them have been turned by old ones. And some, like Claret, have gained power merely by surviving." Or by drinking Hungarian blood..

"And Raedan?"

"He is unique, one of a kind. Perhaps the strongest of them all."

Lily sipped her coffee, her thoughts chaotic and tinged with fear. A vampire was hunting her, not for her blood, but because he hoped to mate with her and produce a child. It had never occurred to her that any of the Transylvanian vampires would want children. They seemed to have no interest in home or family or anything other than blood and death. Personally, she had never given children much thought, either. She had just assumed that the day would come when she would marry and have a child or two like the rest of her family.

She frowned, struck by a new thought. Could Raedan father a child? Not that she was thinking about marrying him or anything. But was that possibility the reason everyone was so upset about her dating him? No sooner had the idea occurred to her than she saw her newly won freedom being taken away from her again "for her own good." How she hated those four words! She had heard them her whole life.

Lily looked up to find Ava watching her. "Am I being sent home?"

"Not at the moment."

"But?"

"I wouldn't be surprised if your father came after you. I'm sorry, child."

"I wish I'd never been born," Lily exclaimed, pushing away from the table.

"Liliana, you don't mean that!"

"I'm going to my room."

Knowing Lily needed time alone, Ava made no move to stop her, trusting that the wards she had set around the house would prevent the girl from leaving.

Upstairs, Lily paced the floor, her anger and frustration growing with every passing moment. It was her life. If she wanted to spend it with a vampire-demon, it should be her decision. How was it any worse than her father, a vampire, marrying a witch?

She threw herself on the bed and pounded her fists into the mattress. And when that didn't help to ease her anger, she scrambled to her feet and went to the window. It wouldn't open, of course. Ava had seen to that.

Picking up a heavy bookend, she hurled it at the glass. It bounced off the window as if it was made of rubber.

Fighting tears of frustration, she sank down on the floor and buried her face in her hands.

"Liliana."

"Raedan?" Lifting her head, she found herself staring at a pair of black-clad legs. "Raedan!" She took the hand he offered, let him pull her to her feet and into his arms. "How did you get in here?"

"Through the window."

She glanced past him, eyes widening when she saw the curtains fluttering at the open window. "How?"

He caressed her cheek with his knuckles. "Why are you so surprised, love?"

"But…Ava…she warded the house…"

"To keep you in," he said, lightly tapping his finger against the tip of her nose. "Nothing can keep me out." He had also cast his own spell to keep the old witch from sensing his presence.

Sighing, Lily rested her cheek against his chest. She had known him such a short time, knew so little about him, how could being in his arms feel like coming home? When he stroked her hair, she felt like purring.

Putting a finger under her chin, he lifted her head, his dark eyes filled with an emotion she couldn't decipher. Her heart skipped a beat as he slowly lowered his head to claim her lips with his. It was the lightest of touches and yet it sizzled like heat lightning all the way down to her toes.

"Liliana, my love, you are driving me crazy."

"Am I?"

"In ways you cannot imagine." His hands slid up and down her bare arms, sending shivers of delight up and down her spine.

Feeling suddenly weak, she leaned into him.

"Where do we go from here?" he asked, his gaze searching hers.

"I'm not sure what you mean."

She was so young, he thought. So damn young. He had no business involving her in his life. He was about to tell her so when she went up on her tiptoes, her hands cupping his cheeks as she pressed her body against his and kissed him.

What started as the mere brush of her lips over his soon turned into something far more intimate, far more passionate. Her feminine scent awakened his desire, the whisper of her blood enflamed his hunger and roused the demon.

With a groan, he wrapped his arms around her in a vice-like grip.

Lily surrendered to the desire blazing between them, only gradually realizing that his kisses had grown more urgent, his arms like iron bars around her. She stilled when his tongue laved her neck, knew a moment of stone-cold terror when she felt his fangs graze her throat.

With a cry, she twisted out of his arms and bolted across the room.

Raedan clenched his hands at his sides, his whole body rigid. "Forgive me," he hissed between clenched teeth.

"It's...it's all right," she said, her voice shaky. "I...I understand."

"Do you?"

"I come from a family of vampires, remember? I know all about hunger and thirst and the need to feed."

His brows rushed together in a frown. "Why do you not run screaming from my presence?"

"Well, you let me go, and since you don't seem to be out of control now..." She shrugged. "I'm sorry. I think maybe I over-reacted."

Raedan stared at her as if he had never seen her before. She was the most amazing, surprising woman he had ever known. "I should go," he said, hearing Ava's footsteps on the stairs.

"Will you come back later?"

"If you want me to."

"You know I do."

He planted a quick kiss on her cheek and disappeared through the window, closing it behind him, just as her bedroom door opened.

Ava glanced around the room. "Are you all right, Lily?"

She shrugged. "I'm sorry I got mad at you, Granny. I know you're just worried about me."

"I made some hot chocolate and cinnamon rolls."

"Sounds wonderful," Lily said, smiling, and sailed out the door.

Ava stared after her, wondering at Lily's sudden change of heart. She glanced around the room again. Then, feeling certain she had missed something, she followed Lily downstairs.

CHAPTER FOURTEEN

In the course of the following week, Ava regarded Lily's changed attitude with mingled confusion and suspicion. At worst, she had expected her great-granddaughter to be rebellious or angry. At best, she had prepared herself for a week or two of the sullen, silent treatment. Instead, the two of them had spent their time in her workshop, with Lily eager to learn new spells and enchantments, charms and potions. She had cheerfully agreed to go out to dinner and to the movies. They had taken long walks together, gone shopping for shoes and handbags, made a trip to the hair dresser.

But it was Lily's obvious happiness that worried Ava the most. As far as she knew, Lily hadn't been able to sneak out of the house for any midnight meetings with Raedan, yet she had the unmistakable glow of a woman in love. It was most perplexing and worrisome.

Hoping to find some clarity, Ava called Dominic after Lily had gone to bed that night.

"What are you afraid of?" Dominic asked. "The vampire's gone. Lily doesn't hate you for breaking things up. Seems like the problem solved itself."

"I'm missing something," Ava said. "I can feel it. She doesn't look or act like a girl who's broken-hearted."

"Maybe she wasn't as crazy about him as you thought."

"I can't shake the feeling that they're still seeing each other. But I know she hasn't left the house on the sly because I'd feel it if she broke the wards I set."

"It seems obvious to me that he's been coming there," Dominic said.

Ava frowned. Was that possible? And why hadn't she thought of it? "Why don't you and Maddy come to dinner tomorrow night? Maybe you'll sense something I'm missing."

"Sure. What time?"

"Around six-thirty?"

"We'll be there."

After disconnecting the call, Ava sat back, her brow furrowed. Was it possible the vampire-demon had found a way into the house without her knowing it? The mere idea sent a chill down her spine. If that was true, if Raedan had breached her wards without a trace, he was even more powerful than she had feared.

In her room, with Raedan's arms around her, Lily frowned as he related the details of Ava's conversation with Dominic. She felt a little guilty about his eavesdropping on what should have been a private call, but after hearing what had been said, her guilt dissolved with the realization that Ava was still determined to keep her and Raedan apart. What right did her great-grandmother have to make decisions for her? Ava had been married twice that Lily knew of, once to a member of the Knights of the Dark Wood. If her great-grandmother could wed a Knight, a man who had sworn an oath to destroy Hungarian vampires, where did she get off warning Lily away from the man she loved? At least Raedan wasn't out to destroy Lily's family.

"I should have known she'd get suspicious when I didn't stay angry," Lily muttered irritably. "But it's hard to pretend to be mad when I'm so happy." How could she be anything else, she wondered, when Raedan came to her room every night? When they spent hours in each other's arms exchanging kisses that grew increasingly deeper and more intimate as they got to know each other better. He told her of exotic places he had visited, of life in centuries past, of famous men and women he had known in the course of his long existence. He had dined with the kings and queens of England, ridden to hounds with noblemen, fought duels, and done a hundred other things she had only read about. She loved hearing about his past even though it sometimes made her jealous. She had never really done anything memorable or remarkable, never met anyone famous. Of course, he had been born in far more colorful and romantic times than she had, and he had hundreds of years of existence and experience behind him.

Reading her thoughts, Raedan tightened his arms around her. "I count it a blessing that you were not born in my time," he said, "because you would not be here now, and I never would have met you." He nuzzled her neck, his breath warm against her skin. "I have waited for you my whole life."

"That's sweet of you to say."

"I mean it, love. I knew from the first night that I saw you that you were what I had been waiting for, searching for, these past centuries. I have never believed in one man for one woman, or that people were made for each other, but I believe it now." Cupping her face in his hands, he brushed a kiss across her lips.

Lily looked up at him, stunned by his declaration. Before she could think of anything to say, he was kissing her again, his tongue a flame dancing against her own. She shivered with delight as he rained heated kisses along the side of her neck. The ecstasy thrumming through her ended abruptly when his fangs grazed her skin.

With a curse, he released her, his jaw rigid. "Forgive me."

She stared at him, speechless. Like Hungarian vampires, the eyes of Transylvanian vampires took on a faint, red glow when the hunger was upon them. But Raedan's eyes had gone black and Lily knew she was seeing the blood-demon for the first time.

Raedan rose effortlessly to his feet, hands clenched tightly at his sides. He had fed well before coming here and still he craved her blood, every warm, sweet, red drop.

The demon within him laughed.

"Raedan…"

"Good night."

"Will I see you tomorrow?"

"I cannot say." He closed his eyes and took a deep breath. "Liliana," he said, his voice raw. "I must go before it is too late."

And he was gone.

Lily fell back on the bed, tears burning her eyes. She was in danger every night she spent in his arms. How much longer could he fight the demon inside him, resist his innate nature to feed? Would he be able to take just a taste? Or would one taste tempt him beyond his power to resist? The wrong choice could leave her dead, or changed for life. She had thought she understood him, but she now realized she had been sorely mistaken. He wasn't just a vampire with a need for blood, he was possessed by a demon with a lust to take it all. How much longer could the vampire keep the demon at bay?

She desperately needed someone to talk to, but there was no one she could trust.

Raedan stormed through the night, his hatred for what he was like a stake in his heart. He had been a fool to think he could continue to fight the demon and win. Every hour he spent with Liliana made his desire for her blood and the demon's relentless hunger to taste her, grow stronger. How much longer could he fight the creature?

How much longer could he fight his own hellish thirst?

Liliana didn't try to fight the tears that poured down her cheeks. She had a terrible feeling she might have seen the last of Raedan. She didn't doubt his affection for her. She knew he had left so abruptly because he was afraid of hurting her. And because of his concern for her safety, she might never see him again.

Ava frowned as she glanced at the clock. It was almost noon and Lily still hadn't come downstairs. She had heard Lily sobbing in her room last night and while she had no way of knowing for certain, she was sure it had something to do with the vampire-demon. It seemed obvious that the two of them had found a way to be together in spite of the wards she had set around the house. Had something happened last night to put an end to their ill-fated romance? It was the most logical explanation.

Going to the foot of the stairs, she called, "Lily, lunch is ready."

Silence.

"If you don't come down, I'm coming up."

Another long silence and then she heard the door open and Lily's footsteps on the stairs.

Ava stifled a gasp when she saw the girl's face. Her eyes were swollen and red-rimmed, her face pale, her hair uncombed. "Oh, Lily, what's happened?"

"Nothing. I had a bad night, that's all."

A bad night? The girl looked as though her best friend had just died.

"I don't want anything to eat."

Ava nodded. "I'll fix you a cup of hot chocolate."

Not bothering to argue, Lily went into the living room and curled up in the easy chair in the corner.

A few moments later, Ava handed her a cup of hot chocolate liberally sprinkled with miniature marshmallows, and a small plate holding two slices of buttered toast. "You have to eat something, child."

With a sigh, Lily forced herself to drink the cocoa and eat a slice of toast.

"Talk to me, Lily," Ava said. "I can't help you if you won't confide in me."

"I've been seeing Raedan," she said, dully. "I think he loves me. And because he does, he's left me. Again. No doubt for my own good." She slammed her hand on the table beside the chair. "I'm sick and tired of people making decisions for my own good!"

Ava remained silent, waiting for her to go on.

After stretched seconds, Lily said, "He almost bit me last night. I know it's not him. It's the demon driving him." She looked at Ava through eyes dark with pain. "Isn't there some way to destroy the demon without hurting Raedan?"

"I have no idea. I've never heard of a vampire being possessed. With mortals, sometimes a priest can exorcise a demon, but I'm not certain that an exorcism would work on a vampire. It might do more harm than good."

Feeling as though all hope was gone, Lily sank deeper into her chair.

"I can make you forget him," Ava said quietly.

"No! No."

"I invited Dom and Maddy over for dinner tonight. Would you like me to cancel it?"

Lily nodded. She loved Dom and his wife, she was crazy about the baby, but she wasn't in the mood for company or anything else. "I'm going for a walk."

"I'll go with you."

"I'd rather go alone."

"Liliana..."

"It's broad daylight! I'll be fine."

Knowing that arguing with Lily would only make her more determined, Ava clamped her lips together and nodded.

Chapter Fifteen

The man's head snapped up when the front door opened and the woman he had been sent to find stepped out. She paused on the porch a moment before descending the stairs and heading for the sidewalk, where she turned to the left.

He waited until she was a block ahead of him and then, thanking his lucky stars, he followed her.

Had she lingered inside one more day, it would have cost him his life.

Lost in thought, Lily didn't realize she was being followed until it was too late. She froze when a hand closed on her upper arm. She whirled around, her instincts taking over when she saw the stranger behind her. When he lifted his other hand to press a cloth over her nose and mouth, she uttered a quick enchantment. Too frightened to concentrate, the spell meant to turn her assailant into a cat malfunctioned and the man turned into a fat, brown rat, instead. Before she could undo the spell, the creature darted under a hedge.

Focusing her magic, Lily murmured the words of undo-ing, but the rat must have continued running because the man didn't appear.

Shaking badly from the experience, she turned and ran back into the house and slammed the door.

"Lily, what's wrong?" Ava exclaimed. "You're white as a ghost."

"A man … on the sidewalk … he accosted me … and … "

Ava's gaze ran over Lily from head to foot. "Are you hurt?"

"No, but…" Still shivering, she wrapped her arms around her waist.

"Lily, calm down and tell me what happened."

"I was so scared, I tried to turn him into a cat to make him let me go, and…and I used the wrong word and he turned into a rat and ran under a hedge." Lily paused to catch her breath. "I chanted the words of undoing but nothing happened. I think he ran farther than my spell could reach."

Ava blew out a breath. "Serves him right," she muttered. "Had you ever seen him before?"

"No. But, Granny, we have to do something."

"What would you suggest?"

"Can't you find him and reverse the spell?"

"Not without knowing his name or where to find him. I can't just unleash a spell and hope it finds the right culprit."

"Who do you think he was?"

Taking Lily by the hand, Ava pulled her toward the sofa and sat down. "My best guess is he was under the compulsion of the vampire hunting you. His name is Varden and he seems determined to … to have his way with you."

Lily stared at her great-grandmother, wide-eyed with fear and disbelief. "You really think this Varden sent the man who approached me?"

"I'm almost certain of it."

Lily sat back, too stunned to reply. The vampire she yearned to be with didn't want her, but a stranger did. How bizarre was that?

"Lily?"

"Would it work?"

"What?"

"If the vampire had managed to get me in his power, would he have been able to father a child?"

"No."

"Why not? Aren't both kinds of vampires basically the same?"

"You know they're not."

Lily shook her head. "They aren't that different. They both need blood to survive. Both are capable of killing, changing shape, turning into mist. Both prefer the night. It seems to me the only real difference is that my father's kind can consume mortal food and be awake during the day. And after a few hundred years, even some very old Transylvanian vampires are able to endure the sun's light for a brief time."

"The other very big differences are that your father's kind only kill out of necessity and they can impregnate mortal women. No Transylvanian vampire has ever accomplished the latter."

"Have you ever met the one called Varden?"

"No. Nor do I want to. I think I'd better call your father and let him know what's going on."

"No!"

"Lily, he has a right to know."

"He'll take me home!"

"Would that be so bad?"

"If I go home," Lily murmured, her voice barely audible, "I'll never see Raedan again." Curling up on the sofa, she closed her eyes. A moment later, she was asleep.

Ava sighed as she rose and left the room. Lily was going to hate her for what she was about to do, but she felt duty-bound to let Quill and Callie know what was going on.

Lily dreamed she heard her father and Ava arguing, only to wake up in her room in her father's house and realize it hadn't been a dream at all. Sitting up, she glanced at the familiar surroundings—the book case that took up most of the wall across from her bed, the corner fireplace with its white marble mantel, the antique dresser, the pale blue curtains fluttering at the window that overlooked the Hungarian stronghold that stretched away as far as the eye could see. The home of her grandparents, a primeval castle from which the Falconer family ruled the people, stood in the center of the walled city. Everything within the city had been built around that castle—homes, schools, shops, museums, theaters, parks, and a lake. It was ancient and beautiful.

Feeling betrayed, she swung her legs over the edge of the bed and went to the window. Ava had called her father while she slept and he had whisked her home. She glanced at the small clock on the side table. A little after eight. It would be dark soon.

She wanted to be angry, but what was the use? Feeling resigned and heavy-hearted, she made her way down the winding staircase.

"Lily!" Her mother hurried toward her, arms open wide. "I've missed you so much!"

"I missed you, too," she replied, though there was little animation in her voice. Looking over her shoulder, she met her father's gaze.

"I'm sorry, Liliana," he said. "But I couldn't leave you in harm's way."

Callie released Lily and took a step back, her gaze meeting Quill's as he closed the distance between them. For a moment, father and daughter regarded each other and then Quill enfolded his daughter in his embrace.

Lily resisted for the space of a heartbeat, then wrapped her arms around his waist and burst into tears.

Raedan felt Lily's absence from the city the moment he woke from the dark sleep. Rising, he yanked on a shirt and a pair of pants, stepped into his boots, and willed himself to Ava's house.

She opened the door before he knocked. "She's not here."

"I know. Where is she?"

"Back home, where she belongs."

He stared at her, his eyes narrowed in disbelief. "She went home?"

"Her father came after her."

"Because of me?"

"It's none of your business," Ava said, her hand curled around the edge of the door. "Go home."

He put his foot in the way, preventing her from shutting him out. "Is she all right?"

"Yes. Goodbye." When he made no move to leave, she began to chant softly, only to stop when his eyes went black.

"Your witchcraft won't work on the demon," he said, his voice low and filled with menace.

Ava took a quick step back, a trickle of fear icing her spine. Before she could say or do anything else, he was gone.

Heaving a sigh of relief, Ava closed and bolted the door. She had done the right thing in notifying Quill, she thought. The vampire-demon was the most fearsome creature she had ever encountered.

Chapter Sixteen

Varden swore under his breath as he followed his thrall's scent trail from the witch's house. It led to a sidewalk, continued across a stretch of green grass, and then disappeared under a hedge.

Summoning his power, he leaped effortlessly over the hedge, only to come to an abrupt halt when he saw the chewed up remains of a large, brown rat. A rat that carried the same scent as the human who had been under his power. And mingled with that scent was the lingering signature of magic.

Witch magic.

Hell and damnation! It had taken him weeks to find a vampire willing to point him in the right direction—weeks and a good deal of persuasion. Mesmerizing a human to spy on the woman for him had been far easier.

But at least he now knew where the girl lived.

Varden chuckled softly. So, capturing that little Hungarian witch wasn't going to be as easy as he'd thought. But what the hell. He had always loved a challenge.

Raedan arrived in Savaria with the setting of the sun. He had been to Hungary several times in the last few centuries.

There was something about the place that appealed to him, though he wasn't sure what it was, or why. Perhaps it was the presence of so many vampires who lived together in peace. He had seen the walled compound where the Master Vampire resided though he had never met the man. Stories of his family were legendary, as was his power.

But he wasn't interested in the Master Vampire now. Only Liliana. And even though he had never tasted her blood, the demon had no trouble following her scent across the wooded hills.

Raedan drew up short when it led him to the walled city where the leader of the Hungarian vampires made his home. He swore under his breath. Liliana had told him she came from a long line of vampires, but Falconer was a common name. What were the odds that she was related to the Master Vampire himself?

He grinned into the darkness. Andras Falconer was rumored to be a powerful creature. What would it be like to face one almost as ancient as himself? He had contended against numerous Master Vampires in his time and defeated them all. And then he swore softly. If Liliana were related to Andras, defeating the vampire would not endear him to her.

Ghosting forward, he placed his hand on the high stone wall that surrounded the compound, only to yank it away as preternatural power scorched his palm and radiated up his arm.

Opening his senses, he searched the compound. There were many vampires within the walls. One was extremely powerful.

But the Master Vampire was not in residence.

CHAPTER SEVENTEEN

Callie sighed as Liliana poured out her feelings for the vampire-demon, Raedan, and then burst into tears.

"I love him," Lily sobbed. "And nothing any of you can say or do will change that."

Slipping her arm around her daughter's shoulders, Callie held her while she wept. Was there anything more painful, more heartbreaking, than the loss of your first real love? Quill had talked to Lily but Lily had refused to heed his advice, just as Lily had turned a deaf ear to everything Callie had said. And who could blame her? Callie thought glumly. She and Quill had married in spite of the odds against them. They had been through hell and back, but their love had only grown stronger. Lily was a grown woman. She had every right to make her own decisions, or she would have, if she were a mere mortal. But her decisions didn't affect just her but the entire Falconer clan.

Callie blew out a sigh. Andras was away from the compound, and they had not yet informed him of Lily's return or of her liaison with the vampire-demon Raedan.

Easing out of her mother's arms, Lily stood and wiped her eyes. "I'm going for a walk. Is that okay?"

"Of course it is."

"Just thought I'd check, now that you and Dad are making my decisions for me," she said bitterly, and stalked out of the room. The slamming of the back door followed her departure.

"Didn't go so well, huh?" Quill said, peering around the door frame.

"You could say that."

Crossing the room, he sat on the sofa beside her. "What are we gonna do now?"

"Wait for her to get over it, I guess."

"What if she doesn't?"

Callie shrugged. "Pray?"

"Maybe we shouldn't have brought her home without talking to her first."

"Maybe," Callie agreed.

"I guess I just panicked when I heard Raedan's name," Quill admitted gruffly. "He's a monster, even if Lily refuses to see it."

"What's your father going to say?"

Quill shook his head ruefully. "I don't even want to think about that."

"You should probably call him and let him..." Callie froze in mid-sentence as power unlike anything she had ever experienced washed over her, and then was gone.

Quill bounded to his feet. "What the hell was that?"

Callie sent a worried glance in his direction. "Are we being attacked?"

"Stay here. I'm going after Lily." Rising, Quill hurried out the back door, only to come to an abrupt halt when he saw Lily in the arms of a tall, dark-haired man. "Raedan." The name hissed past his lips.

The vampire-demon lifted his head, his hostile gaze meeting Quill's over the top of Lily's head.

It took all of Quill's self-control not to look away as Raedan's preternatural power slammed into him, threatening to drive him to his knees. And then Callie stepped outside and the vampire-demon's focus divided. But it didn't weaken.

Tugging on Raedan's arm, Lily said, "Stop it!"

Murmuring, "Forgive me, love," he withdrew his power.

Quill forced himself to stand his ground when all he wanted to do was sink to his knees. Without taking his gaze from Raedan, he reached for Callie's hand when she moved to stand beside him. As always, her nearness strengthened him.

"You're trespassing," Quill said. "All you had to do was knock on the front door."

An insolent smile curved Raedan's lips. "I wasn't sure of my welcome."

"So you climbed over the wall like a thief in the night," Quill said, his voice thick with contempt. "What do you want?"

"I should think that would be obvious," Raedan said dryly. "I love your daughter, and I intend to have her, with or without your permission."

"Is this the kind of man you want, Liliana?" Quill asked quietly. "One who has no regard for common courtesy or for the thoughts and feelings of your family?"

"Your family has made your thoughts and feelings about me quite clear," Raedan said. "Had I asked permission to date your daughter, I'm sure the answer would have been an emphatic no."

"Can you blame us?" Quill cocked his head to one side, his expression thoughtful. "What would you do if she was *your* daughter?"

Raedan's eyes narrowed ominously.

Quill felt his insides go cold as the vampire-demon put his arm around Lily's shoulders. He took a step forward, only to feel the vampire's power wash over him again. Dammit, the man was going to take Lily and there was nothing he could do to stop him.

Time stood still as Raedan bent his head and kissed Liliana, long and slow.

And then he was gone and Lily stood there alone, silent tears tracking her cheeks.

Raedan stalked the dark countryside outside the compound, Quill's words echoing in his mind—*What would you do if she was your daughter?* Raedan swore softly. He would never father a child, but if he had, he wouldn't hesitate to destroy anyone who dared harm a hair of her head. Of course Lily's family was concerned. Their only daughter had been secretly dating a monster.

Throwing back his head, he howled his anger and frustration to the uncaring moon, and in the distance, he heard an answering cry.

Filled with a sudden need to surrender to the beast within him, he shifted to wolf form and ran in search of the pack. He could shift to any form he desired, but the wolf was the only other form he had ever taken.

He found the pack in a forest several miles away.

The alpha let out a warning growl as he walked stiff-legged toward Raedan, his hackles raised.

Raedan stood his ground as the alpha circled him, then backed away. It was obvious the wolf sensed there was something different about the stranger among them. After a moment, Raedan sat back on his haunches and smiled a wolfish smile.

The alpha wagged his tail and let out a yip, then took off running deeper into the forest. The rest of the pack followed and Raedan fell in behind them.

He reveled in the kiss of the wind in his face, the feel of the earth beneath his paws, the sense of community with the wild ones. They ran for miles, jumping over deadfalls, leaping over a narrow stream, only to veer off when a buck crossed their path.

Raedan fell back as the wolves brought the deer down. He growled low in his throat as the scent of fresh blood teased his nostrils. He resisted as long as he could before easing his way between two females and lapping at the blood. He had only taken a little when he imagined Liliana's horror if she could see him now.

Backing away, he loped back the way they'd come. He paused at the stream to wash the blood from his muzzle, then shifted to his own form.

What if she was your daughter?

Like it or not, he owed Quill Falconer an apology.

"I hope you're happy," Lily said through her tears. "I'll probably never see him again."

"Lily…"

Dashing the tears from her eyes, she said, "I'll never forgive you for this. Never!"

"Ava Liliana Falconer," Callie said sternly, "you apologize to your father this instant."

Lily crossed her arms over her chest, her expression mutinous.

"I mean it," Callie said. "From the moment you were born, your father has never had anything but your best interests at heart. And so have I."

Lily took a deep breath and muttered, "I'm sorry, Father," in a frosty voice. Turning on her heel, shoulders back and head high, she returned to the house without a backward glance.

Callie blew out a sigh. "That didn't go very well, did it? Where do you think Raedan's gone?"

"He can't go far enough to suit me," Quill muttered.

"The more we're against him, the more Lily will defend him. You know how kids always want what they can't have."

"She's hardly a kid anymore."

"You know what I mean. She doesn't have a lot of worldly experience, especially with men."

"So what are you suggesting? That we give our daughter permission to date a vampire-demon? A guy who's likely the most powerful vampire in the whole damn world?"

"I don't know what to do," Callie confessed as she followed Quill through the back door and into the living room, where she sank down on the sofa. "I just don't know."

"As far as I can see, we've only got two options," Quill said, pacing back and forth in front of the hearth. "Either you put her under a sleeping curse, or we keep her locked up in the house for the rest of her life."

"That's not remotely funny," Callie retorted, kicking off her shoes and wiggling her toes.

"I know. I hate to admit it, but I think you're right. If we continue to object, he's liable to contact Lily secretly, maybe even talk her into running away with him."

"Or he could just spirit her away," Callie murmured. "And if that happens, we might never see her again." It was a distinct possibility, one that sent an icy chill down her spine. And then she brightened. "Maybe he won't come back. Lily certainly seemed to think he was gone for good."

"I hope she's right, but I doubt it. You heard what he said. He intends to have her with or without our permission." Quill blew out a sigh. "Girls are a lot of trouble, aren't they?" he muttered as he dropped down on the sofa beside her, only to throw up his arms in self-defense when Callie hit him over the head with a sofa pillow.

"Hey!" he exclaimed as he caught her in his arms and kissed her. "I was only kidding."

Lily wept until her pillow was damp and she had no tears left. Sitting up, she rested her head on her bent knees and contemplated going back to America. She didn't want to stay here. Her parents treated her like a child. Maybe she could stay with Ava again until she could find a job and afford a place of her own.

Liliana, your father is right.

Her head jerked up at the sound of Raedan's voice. She glanced around, expecting to see him in her room, but he wasn't there. "I don't believe that."

Think about it, love. If you stay with me, you will be an outcast. Your people will never accept me. My kind fear me. There is no place on earth that I can call home.

"We can make a place together. If you love me."

You know I do. That's why we cannot be together.

"That doesn't make sense!"

Ah, Liliana, you are so young.

"I'll get older."

His laughter sounded in her head.

"I'm going back to America to stay with Ava. Please come with me."

You must stay here! Have you forgotten there is a vampire hunting you? You will be safe here, among your own people.

"You could protect me."

Her words, softly spoken, struck a nerve.

Raedan took a deep breath, blew it out in a long, shuddering sigh. In that, at least, she was right. No one could protect Liliana the way he could. And it was the perfect excuse to stay close to her.

"Raedan?"

Silence.

"Are you still there?"

Yes.

"You're going to stay, aren't you?"

A low growl rose in his throat. She'd won and she knew it. He could hear it in the tone of her voice.

"Raedan?"

Lily's eyes widened in surprise when he suddenly materialized in her bedroom. They stared at each other across the width of the room, and then she was in his arms and he was crushing her close, murmuring that he loved her, that he would never let her go.

She stilled as someone knocked at the door.

"Lily?"

She looked up at Raedan, speechless.

"Open the door, daughter. I know he's in there."

"Why didn't you mask your presence?" she whispered.

"I intend to talk to your father."

"Are you out of your mind?" she exclaimed.

"Ava Liliana! Open the damn door."

There was no point in refusing, she thought. Her father would just turn into mist and slip under the door. She had found that amusing when she was a child. Taking a deep, calming, breath, she smoothed a hand over her hair before turning the lock.

Quill glared at Raedan. "I was hoping we'd seen the last of you."

"She's safer with me. Or have you forgotten there's a vampire hunting your daughter whose motives are far worse than mine?"

Quill muttered a pithy oath. "Of course I haven't forgotten. Which is why she needs to stay here."

"And if he follows her?"

"I can take care of my own."

"And I intend to help you." Raedan held up his hand when he saw the protest rising in her father's eyes. "I owe you an apology."

Quill raised one brow. "Is that so?"

Raedan nodded. "I want to court Liliana and I don't want to sneak around to do it."

Lily grinned at his use of such an old-fashioned word.

"And if I refuse?"

"Please, do not."

Quill raked his fingers through his hair as he weighed his options. "Very well. You have my permission to see Lily, but only within the confines of this compound. You will be welcome in my home, but *not* in Lily's bedroom."

Raedan inclined his head. "As you wish."

Quill looked at Lily, his expression bleak. "Don't make me regret this."

"I won't. Thank you, Papa."

Quill grinned inwardly at the use of her childhood name for him. With a curt nod, he left the room, leaving the door wide open.

"Looks like you got your way," Raedan said, taking her in his arms again.

She smiled up at him, then pulled his head down and kissed him, her tongue teasing his. He drew her closer, his mouth hot and hungry as he claimed her lips with his.

Abruptly, he put her away from him.

"What's wrong?"

"I am not supposed to be in your room, remember? And with good reason." Bowing from the waist, he said, "I will call on you tomorrow evening, Miss Falconer."

Lily grinned at his formality.

Taking her hand in his, he kissed her palm. "I love you, Liliana. Whatever happens in the future, always remember that I love you."

And with that, he left her standing there, her lips bruised from his kisses, her whole body aching for his touch.

CHAPTER EIGHTEEN

Varden wandered through New Orleans, his temper rising with every step. Where the hell had the girl gone? He had explored every residential area street by street, every shop, every restaurant, every damn place in the city and there was no sign of her.

Muttering an oath, he went in search of the pretty red-headed vampire he had spoken with before.

He found her in the same club, in the booth she claimed as her own.

She glanced up, one brow raised when she recognized him. "Still here, I see."

He grunted as he slid into the booth across from her. "Where'd she go?"

"Where did who go?" Claret asked, though she knew perfectly well who he was talking about.

"You know damn well who I'm talking about. I've looked everywhere for her. Where is she?"

"How should I know? We aren't girlfriends, you know. We don't share secrets."

His eyes narrowed ominously. "Don't play games with me."

"Don't threaten me, Varden. I don't like it."

They stared daggers at each other across the table.

"Do you know where she is?" he asked again. "I'll make it worth your while if you tell me."

Claret snorted. "You don't have anything I want. And even if I knew, I wouldn't tell you."

"Why the hell not?"

"Because I don't like you."

"You're siding with that witch family against your own kind?"

"So it would seem."

When he loosed a string of vile oaths, Claret threw her drink in his face. "Get out!"

Furious, he reached for her throat, only to draw back when half a dozen male vampires suddenly appeared around the booth, eyes sparking red, fangs bared.

"I'll find her, with or without your help, "Varden snarled, then vanished from sight.

Claret smiled at the vampires surrounding her. "*Merci, mon amis.* Tell Claude the drinks are on the house."

CHAPTER NINETEEN

Lily's heart skipped a beat when she heard Raedan's knock on the heavy oak door.

Running a hand over her hair, she ran down the stairs to let him in. "Hi!" she said breathlessly.

His gaze moved over her, the heat in his eyes warming her from the top of her head to the soles of her feet. "Good evening, love." He started to take her in his arms when Quill appeared.

"Where are the two of you going this evening?"

Raedan looked at Liliana.

"To the movies and then, maybe, for a walk around town."

Quill nodded. "What time will you be home?"

"Dad!"

"I'm sorry, Lily, but if you insist on putting your life in danger, I need to know where you're going and when to expect you back."

With an aggrieved sigh, she said, "No later than midnight, I guess. Is that okay?"

Quill nodded. "Have a good time, Princess."

Lily grabbed her coat, smiled when Raedan took it from her hands and held it for her.

Raedan glanced at Quill. "Stop worrying. I will take good care of her."

Quill grunted softly. Feeling as if he had just agreed to let his only lamb go out with a hungry lion, he closed the door behind them.

"Sorry about that," Lily said as they walked down the flagstone path to the sidewalk.

"He is your father, love. You cannot fault him for worrying about you."

"I guess not."

Raedan glanced around as they strolled hand-in-hand toward the town. The compound was laid out in concentric circles. The Falconer house, a huge, old mansion made of gray stone, sat in the middle, surrounded by smaller homes. Schools and playgrounds occupied the next ring in the circle.

Beyond the smaller homes and schools lay the town, a city in itself, he thought, as they passed restaurants, grocery stores, a post office, what looked like a government office of some kind, a shopping mall, hair salons and barber shops. The movie theater was located across from the shopping mall.

The streets were immaculate. Not a scrap of paper littered the sidewalks. There were no cans in the gutters. The buildings were all immaculate—no faded paint, no graffiti or cracked windows, no roofs in need of repair, no businesses boarded up. There were very few cars in evidence, but that was to be expected. When you could transport yourself anywhere you wanted to go with no more than a thought, why bother to drive?

They passed several people. The men, all Hungarian vampires, regarded him warily, then nodded at Liliana, who inclined her head in acknowledgement. The women were more friendly, nodding at him politely, openly smiling at Lily, who was obviously known and well-liked by the populace.

When they reached the theater, they took a place in line behind several dozen others. As the vampires caught Raedan's scent, they turned to look at him, their eyes filled with suspicion—until they recognized Liliana.

"Good thing you are with me," Raedan said dryly, "or I would have a fight on my hands."

"It always amazes me that vampires can tell one kind from another. I mean, you all look pretty much like ordinary people."

"Do you not recognize other witches?"

"Not always. Why do you and your kind hate my father's people?"

He shook his head. "I have no idea. The reason has been lost in antiquity." They were at the ticket window now. He bought two and they moved into the lobby. "Would you like something?"

"Popcorn and a small soda, please," Lily said.

Raedan nodded, his nose wrinkling in distaste as the scents of butter and salt, hot dogs and mustard, assaulted his senses, along with the thunder of so many beating human hearts, and the tantalizing aroma of blood. How did the Hungarian vampires stand it?

"Are you all right?" Lily asked. And then frowned. "It's the smell of all the food in here, isn't it? Do you want to go somewhere else?"

"No, it is all right." His gaze lingered on the hollow of her throat and the pulse beating there.

Lily didn't miss the faint flicker of red in his eyes as they turned away from the counter and entered the auditorium.

They found two seats toward the back.

"Do you think I'm really in danger from that vampire who's hunting me?" Lily asked when they were settled.

"Yes."

His curt answer sent a shiver down her spine. "I was hoping to go back to Ava's, but maybe it's not a good idea. At least not now."

"Would staying here be so bad?"

"Not as long as you're here with me."

He slipped his arm around her shoulders as the lights went down. "I will be here as long as you want me," he murmured. And even if she didn't, he intended to stay nearby as long as Varden was a threat.

It was hard to concentrate on what was happening on the screen with Liliana so close beside him. He likely would have enjoyed the film, since he got a kick out of super-hero movies, knowing he could easily do all the things they accomplished with green screens and computer images. But her presence distracted him on so many levels—the fragrance of her perfume tickling his nostrils, the beating of her heart, the faint whisper of the blood flowing so enticingly through her veins. The unique scent of the woman herself.

He was relieved when the movie was over. Outside, he took a deep breath. "Where to now, love?"

"A walk in the park?"

"As you wish."

The park was located two blocks from the movie theater. It was large and lush and green. Winding paths lined with tall trees led through a veritable forest of flowers and shrubs. The path they followed led to a large lake. Small sailboats were docked along the shore.

He had to admit, the Hungarian compound was one of the most beautiful places he had ever seen. But not as beautiful as the woman beside him. Unable to resist any longer, he pulled her into his arms.

Lily smiled up at him, her eyelids fluttering down as his mouth covered hers. As always, the mere touch of his lips sent shivers of pleasure coursing through her. She leaned into him as his hand slid seductively up and down her spine.

"Liliana." He groaned her name as desire and hunger flamed to life within him, fueled by his own need and that of the demon inside him.

She looked up at him, her eyes filled with doubt as his fingers lightly traced the line of her collarbone, slid around to the back of her neck to delve into the hair at her nape.

"Please," he whispered. "Just one taste."

"I'm afraid."

"I will not hurt you, I swear it on my life."

"One taste, you promise?"

"Yes." He groaned again as pain and need shot through him.

Praying she wasn't making the biggest mistake of her life, Lily turned her head to the side and brushed her hair out of the way.

Taking a firm hold on his self-control, Raedan lowered his head to her neck and bit her as gently as he could. The taste of her was like nothing he had ever experienced before. Her blood was like sunshine and it flooded his being with a sense of peace and contentment. And warmth. Ah, the warmth of it. He closed his eyes as it flowed through him, chasing the every-present chill from the depths of his being.

One taste led to two as the demon demanded more. Always more. He could control his own thirst, but not the demon's. It might be appeased, but it was never satisfied.

With an oath, Raedan jerked his head back. "Forgive me," he said, his voice filled with self-loathing.

Lily looked up at him in confusion. Forgive him? For what? Her whole being quivered with a longing for him to do it again. His bite had been the most sensual experience of her life.

"Liliana?"

"Will you bite me again sometime?"

Raedan stared at her. Was she serious?

"It was wonderful," she said dreamily. "I've never made love but I think it must feel something like that."

Somewhat taken aback by her remark, Raedan muttered, "I would be happy to show you." He had preyed on many women, but never lingered once the deed was done. He'd had no idea if his bite had been pleasant for his prey or not. Nor had he cared. Until now.

"Come on," he said. "I had better take you home."

"Will I see you tomorrow night?" she asked as they left the park.

"If you wish."

"You know I do." They walked hand-in-hand, pausing to kiss every now and then until they reached the front porch.

"Thank you for tonight," Raedan said.

"I should be thanking you for getting me out of the house."

Raedan shook his head. She had everything a woman could ask for, he thought. A family that loved her and worried about her, a beautiful home. She would never want for anything as long as she lived.

"Aren't you going to kiss me good night?" Lily asked with a teasing grin.

She was going to be the death of him, he thought, as he took her in his arms. But what a way to go.

❧ ❧ ❧

Not surprisingly, Lily found her mother waiting up for her. She took a deep breath as she prepared for the third degree. "Can we talk tomorrow, Mom? I'm kinda tired."

"I don't think so." Summoning her magic, Callie immediately sensed the change in her daughter. "What have you done?" she asked sharply, rising from the sofa.

"What do you mean? We went to the movies. You know that."

Eyes narrowed, Callie walked around Lily. "He bit you, didn't he?"

"How can you possibly know that?" Lily exclaimed, then clapped her hand over her mouth.

"Did you bite him?"

"Of course not!"

Callie breathed a sigh of relief. "Well, thank the good Lord for small favors."

"What's the big deal? I know Dad drank your blood. For all I know, he still does."

"But your father isn't possessed by a demon. Liliana, you are *never* to take Raedan's blood, do you understand? It could be fatal. You may think Raedan's in control of the demon, but I'm not convinced that's true."

Lily moved to the sofa and sat down, hard. Fatal? She had never even considered that possibility. But then, she had never considered drinking Raedan's blood, either.

"Have the two of you been intimate?" Callie asked after a moment's hesitation.

Lily stared at her mother, her cheeks flaming. "Of course not!" But they had come darn close. They might even have done the deed if Raedan hadn't backed off.

Callie sank down beside her daughter. It had been a mistake to let Lily date that man, she thought. Nothing good could come of it. If Lily drank from Raedan, there was a chance the blood-demon might infect her, too.

Or worse.

"It's late," Callie said after a moment. "Let's get some sleep."

Lily kissed her mother's cheek, then ran up to bed.

Callie stared after her, then picked up her phone and called Ava. She needed advice and consolation, and she needed it now.

Ava answered on the first ring. "What's wrong?"

Just hearing her grandmother's voice made everything seem better. As succinctly as possible, Callie explained her fears about letting Lily continue to see Raedan. "I don't know how to stop it. My magic isn't strong enough to thwart him, and neither is Quill's power. I'm not sure even Andras could defeat him. What are we going to do?"

"Perhaps what we need is a way to destroy the blood-demon," Ava suggested. "If Raedan were just an ordinary vampire, he wouldn't be so powerful or so dangerous."

"Have you ever encountered a blood-demon before?"

"No. Let me do some research. It might take a while."

"Thanks, Grams. Have you heard anything more about the vampire hunting Lily?"

"All I know is that he's searched the city from top to bottom. He's questioned Claret a couple of times, but so far, she hasn't told him anything."

"I don't trust her."

"I don't think she'll betray us," Ava said, a grin in her voice. "You know she has an insatiable thirst for Quill's blood."

"Yes, I know," Callie muttered. "And Dom's, too."

"Her obsession with Hungarian blood is our insurance," Ava said. "Try not to worry."

"Right. What's there to worry about? Except maybe the fact that Raedan bit Lily tonight. And will want to do it again as sure as the sun will rise in the morning."

"I can't argue with that."

Callie smothered a yawn with her hand. "Let me know if you discover anything," she said. "I love you, Grams."

"I love you, too, honey. I know it's hard, but try not to worry."

Good advice, Callie thought as she disconnected the call and went up to bed. But quite impossible for a worried mother to do.

Ava frowned as she put her phone aside. Going upstairs, she went into the room where she kept her spell books and magical implements and closed the door. She had rearranged the room not long ago for no other reason than she'd been bored. A long, narrow table stood in the center of the room. It held a variety of objects—a black cauldron, an athame, a silver dagger, a scrying mirror. Shelves held a number of beakers and bottles in assorted shapes and sizes. She had fashioned a new wand of elderberry wood. It rested beside a silver candelabra.

Going to the bookshelf, she searched for an ancient grimoire she had recently found at a yard sale, of all places.

Settling into the padded rocking chair in the corner, she opened the book, felt a rush of magical energy waft from the pages as she turned them one by one.

Time lost all meaning as she perused the ancient spells, some that she was familiar with, others that she had never heard of.

She paused when she came to a section labeled *Ancient Demons: Fact and Fiction.* Taking a deep breath, she turned the page, praying for enlightenment.

CHAPTER TWENTY

After leaving Liliana, Raedan strolled through the night, his hands shoved into his pockets, his thoughts, as always, on the woman. Her scent clung to his clothing, teased his nostrils, stirred his hunger.

She had enjoyed his bite. And then, to his utter astonishment, she had asked if he would bite her again. He shook his head, unable to believe she meant it. And yet, he would have known if she had been lying.

Curious, he willed himself out of the compound and into a distant city. He stepped into the first nightclub he saw. It was just what he was looking for, a dimly lit tavern with only a few patrons.

Taking a place at the bar, he ordered a glass of wine, then perused the crowd until he found a middle-aged woman sitting alone. She had been crying earlier, her eyes still a little puffy. Curious to know the cause of her tears, he read her mind. Her husband had walked out on her the night before, leaving her with two teenage daughters and no means of support.

Opening his preternatural senses, he called her to him. She hesitated a moment before coming to perch on the stool beside him. She was a pretty woman, with wavy brown hair and blue eyes.

His mind brushed hers again, searching for her name. "Relax, Reka," he murmured as he put his arm around her shoulders and drew her closer. You have nothing to fear."

She leaned against him, her eyelids fluttering down as his hand stroked up and down her arm. Trapping her in his thrall, he put his arm around her shoulders and bit her gently. Her blood was warm and filling, but nowhere as sweet or satisfying as Liliana's.

After sealing the twin punctures in her throat, he lowered his arm, his gaze searching hers.

She blinked at him, then lifted a hand to her neck.

"Did I hurt you?" he asked.

"No," she said in a dreamy voice. "I don't know what you did, but can you do it again?"

With a shake of his head, he reached into his pocket and withdrew a wad of cash. Slipping it into her coat pocket, he freed her from his thrall and sent her on her way.

All these years, he thought, and he had never known.

Whistling softly, he left the club. For centuries he had felt guilty for stealing the blood of his victims. And all the time he had unknowingly been giving them pleasure in return.

Throwing back his head, he looked up at the sky and laughed.

Chapter Twenty-One

Liliana woke with a smile. For a moment, she lay there, reflecting on the night before. She had let Raedan bite her. Why wasn't she appalled? Repulsed? Horrified?

Why was she so anxious for him to do it again?

She laughed softly. She knew why. She had never felt anything like it. She had expected pain and instead had received the most pleasurable experience of her life. How was that possible? Would he bite her tonight if she asked?

Throwing back the covers, Lily went to the dresser and peered in the mirror, searching for bite marks, but there were none. She stared at her reflection. If being bitten was so exhilarating, what would it be like to bite him in return? Would it be wonderful? Or disgusting?

Would it really put her life in danger? What if her mother was right and tasting Raedan's blood could infect her with the blood demon?

That thought alone was enough to change her mind.

Callie noticed the subtle change in her daughter the minute Lily stepped into the kitchen. She looked the same, but there was something different about her although she couldn't put her finger on it.

"Breakfast smells wonderful!" Lily exclaimed as she took her usual place at the table. "I'm famished." She frowned when she saw her parents exchange worried glances. "What is it? Is something wrong?"

"We're worried about you," Quill said flatly.

"Why?" Silly question, Lily thought.

"You know damn well why. You let that... that demon bite you. Do you have any idea how dangerous that was?"

"Raedan didn't hurt me. I feel fine."

Her father grunted softly. "That's what I'm afraid of."

Callie placed her hand on Quill's arm. "Let's not talk about it over breakfast."

"Let's not talk about it at all," Lily said. "I'm going for a walk."

Callie shook her head when she saw the look in Quill's eyes. *Let her go.*

He glared at her, but didn't say anything until Lily left the house. "I know I told Raedan he could date Lily, but I think it was a mistake. I think we need to lock her up until she comes to her senses. Or send her to live with my parents. My father should be able to keep her in line."

Callie shook her head. "It will only make her hate us, Quill. Is that what you want?"

"It's better than letting her ruin her life. How do we know he even cares for her? He might just be trying to put our minds at ease before he strikes."

"Quill—"

"And what if he somehow infects her with the demon? Or turns hers? Or kills her?"

Callie's shoulders slumped. "I hadn't really thought about that."

"Well, you'd better start thinking about it now before it's too late."

Rising, she rounded the table and sat in his lap. "Maybe Ava can do something."

Murmuring, "I sure hope so," Quill wrapped his arms around her, thinking he hadn't been this worried since he and Callie had been Claret's prisoners all those years ago.

Needing to think, Lily went to her favorite place in the park, a wooden bench beneath a flowering tree. She couldn't blame her parents for being worried about her. That's what parents did. They were convinced that being with Raedan put her life in danger. She didn't believe it, not for a minute. But what if they were right? And how was she to know? He was incredibly old and powerful, she knew that. She could feel it. But she couldn't believe he would ever hurt her. She remembered her mother saying that Raedan might not be in control of the demon. What if her mother was right? It was something to think about.

Lily huffed a sigh. Like it or not, her mother had planted the seeds of doubt in her mind and nothing she could do would uproot them.

She was about to go back home when Raedan appeared on the bench beside her.

Startled, she almost jumped to her feet.

"Sorry," he said, his deep voice like a caress "I did not mean to frighten you."

"Oh, that's all right. I like a good scare every now and then," she said, pressing her hand to her rapidly beating heart. "What are you doing here? And in the middle of the day?" Only then did she notice that he wore a long-sleeved shirt, jeans, black leather gloves, a hat with a wide brim, and dark glasses. "Shouldn't you be resting?"

"Your distress roused me." Taking her hand in his, he said, "No matter what your parents think, I would never hurt you, Liliana."

"I know you wouldn't, at least not on purpose." Her gaze searched his. "Have you ever lost control of the demon inside you?"

He thought of how hard it was to resist the blood-demon's demands when Liliana was near, as she was now, how difficult it was not to wrap her in his arms and drain her dry. "Not yet."

"That's not very comforting."

He grunted softly. He had left her twice before because he feared he would surrender to the demon's demands. What made him think he was any more resistant to the demon's influence now that he had tasted her blood? When he craved it more even now?

"Raedan, what are you thinking?"

"That your parents may be right about us."

Wide-eyed, she clutched his arm. "You don't mean that?"

He gazed into the distance, his voice a tortured growl when he said, "I do not know. All I know is that you are in danger every time we are together. If I ever hurt you…" He shook his head. "I have never loved anyone as much as I love you. Wanted anyone as much. Needed anyone the way I need you."

Cupping his face in her hands, she kissed him lightly. "We can make it work. I know we can."

"What if you are wrong? Are you willing to take that chance?"

"Yes."

"I cannot decide if you are the bravest woman I have ever met," he murmured, drawing her into his arms, "or the most foolish. All I know is that I do not want to live without you."

"Nor I without you." Anticipation spiked through her when his gaze shifted to her throat.

"Let me?"

With a nod, she canted her head to the side and closed her eyes as his fangs pierced her skin ever so lightly. She craved his bite, she thought, almost as much as he craved her blood.

One sip, two, and he lifted his head. "Are you all right?"

"I'm fine. I just wish it wasn't so dangerous for you to take more. It feels so wonderful." So wonderful she had no words to describe it.

"Maybe you would return the favor?"

"Why would you want me to do that?"

He shrugged. "I am curious to know if biting me would give you pleasure in return."

Lily stared at him, her mother's warning shouting in the back of her mind. *Liliana, you are never to take Raedan's blood, do you understand? It could be fatal.*

"Your mother told you that?"

She had forgotten he could read her mind. "Yes. Is it true?"

"I know not. I have never shared my blood with a witch." He had exchanged blood with other vampires on rare occasions, but witches were a totally different breed. "Probably best not to tempt fate."

She nodded in agreement, although she couldn't help wondering what his blood tasted like. And then she frowned. "What does my blood taste like to you?"

"Better than anything I have ever known. It lingers on my tongue, sweeter than the finest wine."

"That's odd. I've always heard that the blood of witches tastes bitter to vampires."

"I have also heard that," he said, stifling a grin. "Maye I should taste you again and see?"

"Ha-ha. No more for you today," she said, shaking her finger in his face. And then she smiled. "But maybe tomorrow."

"Until then," he said, and vanished from sight.

Back at home, Lily padded into the library and began to search through her mother's spell books, hoping to find something about vampire-demons—but there was no mention of them in any of the volumes she checked. There were numerous articles on demons—how to recognize them, how to summon them, how to exorcise them from humans. But no mention of how to drive them out of a vampire.

Discouraged, she sat back in her chair. There had to be a way to thwart the blood-demon and drive him away without harming Raedan, but she had no idea what it might be. Even if she found a way, perhaps, after all this time, it wouldn't work anyway.

Lily was about to replace all the books on the shelves when her cell phone rang. She smiled as she answered it. "Hi, Granny!"

"I've been thinking about you," Ava said. "Is Raedan still there? Is everything all right?"

"As all right as it can be. I've been searching for information about blood-demons but I can't find anything."

"What, exactly, are you looking for?"

"A way to drive it out of Raedan."

"From what little I have been able to find, it sounds impossible. They are also extremely rare, with only two confirmed cases of people being infected by blood-demons, and that was hundreds of years ago."

"What happened to the people?"

"They went mad. There's nothing in any of my books about blood-demons infecting vampires or werewolves or witches, or any other supernatural beings."

"Mom's afraid that drinking Raedan's blood might kill me."

"Merciful, heavens, child, why would you want to?"

"I don't, not really, but when I told Mom that he'd bit me, she said I was never to drink from him, that it might be fatal." Lily paused. "Do you really think it would kill me?"

"I think the more likely possibility is that it will infect you with some or all of the blood demon."

Lily quailed at the mere idea. "Is such a thing possible?"

"I have no idea. We're exploring unknown territory here."

Lily huffed a sigh. Why couldn't she have just fallen in love with a run-of-the-mill vampire?

"I'll do some more research," Ava said. "In the meantime, take your mother's advice."

"I will. Love you, Granny."

"I love you, too, child. Please, be careful."

Raedan stirred as Liliana's image appeared in his mind. What the hell? Vampires didn't dream.

But the blood-demon did. Held fast in the demon's clutches, he dreamed…and in his dream, Liliana was in bed beside him. Hounded by his yearning for her blood, half-mad with the desire to possess her body and soul, he sank his fangs into her sweet flesh as he made love to her. He gave no heed to her cries of pain, her pleas for him to stop before it was too late. Only when she went limp in his arms did he realize what he had done. But, by then, it was too late. He howled his anguish to the moon as the blood-demon laughed. And laughed...

Raedan bolted upright, his whole body damp with sweat as he glanced around the room. Only a nightmare, he thought, falling back on the mattress. Only a nightmare. But it shook him to the core of his being to know it could easily become reality.

After talking to Lily, Ava spent the next five hours concocting one spell after another in hopes of finding something that would protect Lily from Transylvanian vampires as well as the blood-demon.

After experimenting with dozens of different spells and enchantments, she fashioned a medallion similar to the ivory ones she had once created for the Knights of the Dark Wood to warn them when Hungarian vampires were near. This one, magicked from an ancient gold cross, would warn Lily whenever a Transylvanian vampire was nearby, thereby giving her time to invoke whatever spell she needed to cloak her presence or flee the area. Of course, the only way to know if it was effective would be to bring Lily back to New Orleans, since there were no Transylvanian vampires in Savaria or anywhere else in the country.

Bone weary, Ava made her way to her room, threw off her clothes, and crawled into bed. Tomorrow she would see if she could magick a spell to protect Lily against the blood-demon, although she didn't have much hope. Like she had told Lily, this was unchartered territory. It wasn't like making a simple medallion to alert her to the presence of a vampire. Ava had a sinking feeling that she might need the blood of the demon to concoct a spell to repel it. Few things frightened her anymore. She had lived a very long time, experienced all kinds of magic, both black and white and in-between. But the blood-demon frightened her on a level she had never known before.

It was hours before sleep found her.

CHAPTER TWENTY-TWO

Lily sat at the breakfast table with her mother, only half-listening to her plans for the day—something about meeting with the other wives of the members of the Hungarian Counsel, of which Quill was in charge while Andras was away.

"I know it sounds dull," Callie said, "but it's really just a way for us women to get together for lunch and gossip."

"Uh-huh." Lily knew most of them. They were all humans married to vampires.

"Lily, your face is turning blue."

"Sounds like fun, Mom," Lily murmured, then frowned. "What did you say?"

"I knew you weren't listening," Callie said, glancing at the clock.

"I'm sorry."

"You're thinking about him, aren't you?"

Lily nodded. "I talked to Ava last night."

"Oh?"

"I'm hoping she can find a way to drive the blood-demon out of Raedan."

"He'd still be a vampire, Lily. And not one of us."

"So, if Raedan was Hungarian, you wouldn't have a problem with him?"

"Not as much of a problem."

"Are you ever sorry you married Dad?"

"No, of course not!"

"I sense a 'but' in there somewhere," Lily remarked.

"I wouldn't change anything," Callie said. "But if I'd never met your father, I would have married an ordinary man, or a witch, and lived an ordinary life. Perhaps had more children."

"Why didn't you have more?"

"Even though it's possible, conception is rare."

Callie frowned. She had never really thought about it, but now that she was, she realized very few women married to the vampires had more than one or two children and all the kids were boys. Her frown deepened as she realized that if she married Raedan, she would never have any children. They could adopt, of course, but it wouldn't be the same as having a child conceived by their love for one another.

She shook the thought away. She hadn't known Raedan long enough to be thinking about marriage. Sure, she was in love with him, but their relationship was still new. She didn't believe in long engagements, but it certainly took longer than a few weeks to really get to know someone. There were still things she didn't know about him. Perhaps things she didn't want to know.

"Is there something going on with you and Raedan I need to know about?" Callie asked.

"No." Lilly held up her hand to stay the question in her mother's eyes. "We haven't done more than hold each other close and kiss, so stop worrying." And even if they did, there was no fear of getting pregnant out of wedlock. "I'm going out to soak up some sun." Pushing away from the table, she kissed her mother on the cheek. "Have a good time with the other ladies. I'll see you when you get home."

Callie was about to go upstairs to change her clothes when her phone rang. She smiled when she saw Ava's name. "Hi!"

"I need to see Lily," Ava said. "How soon can she be here?"

"Excuse me? What's this all about?"

"I've crafted a talisman that I hope will warn her when Transylvanian vampires are nearby. It works on the same principle as the medallions I made for the Knights. The thing is, we need to try it in the presence of a vampire to make sure it works."

'Why does she need one? There aren't any of the other vampires here."

"Better safe than sorry," Ava said. "What if Varden discovers her whereabouts and decides to come looking for her?"

"I doubt he'd be stupid enough to come here."

"I wouldn't put anything past him. The man is obviously mad."

"So bring one of them here." What was she thinking? Such a thing was strictly forbidden. The penalty for doing so was death. It had taken decades and a lot of bloodshed on both sides to clear the land of Transylvanian vampires. "Forget I said that."

"I know there's a bit of a risk," Ava said, "but if Raedan stays here with us, she should be safe enough."

"I don't know," Callie murmured. "I think the bigger risk is sending her back to the States. I'll have to discuss it with Quill."

"Of course, dear. I'm also working on an invisibility cloak she can wear that will make her invisible to all vampires but not to humanity. It's a little tricky, but I can think I can make it work. Anyway, call me as soon as you talk to Quill."

Muttering, "I will," Callie ended the call.

Quill was against sending Lily back to Ava's, as Callie had known he would be, but in the end, he agreed. She didn't like the idea, either, but she knew that, sooner or later, Lily would insist. There had been a strong connection between Lily and Ava ever since Lily was a little girl. At times, Callie had been jealous of their relationship, and yet she understood it, having felt the same bond with Ava when she had been a child.

Lost in thought, Lily sat on the grass in the backyard, her thoughts wandering—where did Raedan keep his lair here in Savaria? Or did he rest elsewhere? Were Dominic and Maddy enjoying their honeymoon in Hawaii? The last she'd heard, they had decided that instead of coming home next month, they were going to extend their honeymoon and visit Australia and New Zealand, and maybe some of the other islands.

Must be nice, she thought, to be able to go where you want when you want with the one you love, and have the time and the means to fulfill your every dream. J. D. would probably be walking and talking before her brother decided to come home.

She gazed up at the sky. Hours until the sun went down. Scooting under the shade of a willow tree, she fell back on the grass and closed her eyes ...

And Raedan was there. Dressed all in black, he loomed over her, his normally dark eyes blazing red, the fangs he usually kept hidden clearly visible when he smiled at her. A predator's smile.

She willed herself to move, to run, but his gaze held her immobile.

"I knew this day would come," he said, a thin layer of regret in his voice as he slowly knelt beside her and trapped her in the prison of his arms. "I cannot fight the demon any longer."

"Please, try," she gasped, her heart pounding with terror.

"Forgive me," he whispered, and sank his fangs into her throat.

There was no pleasure in his bite this time, only pain unlike anything she had ever known.

Just when she thought he was going to take it all, he bit into his wrist and held it to her lips. "Drink, Liliana!" he commanded, and she lacked the strength to refuse.

His blood was hot and thick and more repulsive than anything she had ever tasted. And just when she thought nothing worse could happen, she felt it…an alien presence that slithered into her, bringing darkness and an icy chill like death.

"No!" She screamed the word until her throat was raw…

"Liliana! Liliana, wake up!"

She woke abruptly to find Raedan kneeling beside her. With the nightmare still fresh in her mind, she scrambled to her feet and darted away from him.

He stayed where he was, his expression troubled. "It was just a bad dream," he said quietly.

Lily lifted a hand to her throat as she glanced around. The sun was still overhead. She could feel no bite marks on her neck, there was no blood on her skin. Just a dream. Pressing a hand to her heart, she dissolved into tears.

Rising effortlessly to his feet, Raedan moved slowly toward her, but not too close. "Do you want me to go?"

She shook her head, but when he started to move closer, she put her hand out to stop him.

"It was awful," she said, her voice shaking.

"It must have been, to rouse me. Do you want to talk about it?"

Taking a deep, shuddering breath, she wiped her tears away. "I dreamed that you came here. Your eyes were red. You…you drank from me. Drank and drank. And then…and then you…you forced me to drink from you."

A muscle throbbed in his jaw as he listened to her, afraid he knew what was coming.

"And then…" She began to tremble with the memory. "I felt the blood-demon crawl inside me. It felt vile and dark and cold…"

He knew exactly what it felt like. He longed to hold her, to comfort her, but he was afraid to touch her, afraid she would reject him. "Just a dream," he repeated quietly.

"But it could happen, couldn't it?"

He wanted to deny it, to assure her that it would never happen, that he would never *let* it happen, but how could he, when the very same fear haunted him whenever they were together? He remembered all too well his own nightmare. He squinted against the sun's light as it began to burn his flesh. He had left his lair in such a hurry, he hadn't taken time to grab any protective clothing. "I have to go. Can I see you tonight?"

She nodded uncertainly, and he was gone.

Lily's parents were seated at the kitchen table when she went back into the house. She glanced from one to the other. From their expressions, she wondered if someone had died.

"Sit down, Liliana," her father said.

She did so, reluctantly. Had they decided she couldn't see Raedan again? Were they sending her away? Had something happened to Dominic?

Folding her hands on the table top, her mother said, "I had a call from Ava."

"Is she all right?" Lily asked anxiously.

"She's fine. She's crafted a medallion for you, similar to the ones she once made for the Knights of the Dark Wood."

"Why? I don't need something to tell me when our kind are nearby."

"It's to alert you to the presence of Transylvanian vampires," Callie explained. "Like Varden."

"Oh." Lily frowned. What was the point? There were no vampires of his ilk in the country.

Callie blew out a long breath. "She wants you to return to New Orleans to see if it works."

"Oh!" Lily brightened immediately at the thought of going back to the States.

"I can see you're not opposed to the idea," Quill said dryly.

Lily shrugged one shoulder. "I love living with Granny."

Quill grunted, but said nothing.

"Can I go?" Lily asked.

Quill made a vague gesture with his hand. "I'm against it, but your mother has agreed. I'll take you whenever you're ready."

Jumping to her feet, Lily threw her arms around his neck.

Quill looked at Callie over their daughter's head. He had a bad feeling about sending Lily back to New Orleans, but they couldn't keep her locked up forever, he thought glumly, and wished for the days when she had been a little girl and he could keep her home, safe in his arms.

Later, in her bedroom, Lily let out a shout of joy, then twirled around the room the way she had when she was a little girl. She was going back to Ava's. No more castle walls to keep her inside. She would be able to come and go as she pleased again, albeit with Ava's approval. But there was so much to do in New Orleans, so many places she hadn't seen yet. She would have to be vigilant, of course, but if Ava's medallion worked, she would have plenty of warning whenever danger was near. With that and her own magic, she should easily be able to evade or out-maneuver anyone looking for her.

Grinning, she pulled her suitcase from the closet. While tossing her underwear inside, she wondered what Raedan would think when she told him.

When she finished packing, she spent the rest of the day with her parents. They went out to dinner at Lily's favorite restaurant, and then dancing. She had always loved to dance with her father, from the time she was little and she had stood on his shoes, until now. He was tall and handsome and she couldn't help noticing that all the women in the place stared at him.

"Does Mom ever get jealous?" Lily asked, "knowing all these women are drooling over you."

"I think she's used to it by now," he muttered. "And it's not really me, you know."

"Of course it is. Don't give me that vampire allure speech. Even if you were human they'd be staring."

"If you say so."

Quill walked her back to their table when the music ended and when a new song began, he led Callie onto the dance floor.

Lily smiled as she watched them. They made a beautiful couple, and they were so obviously in love.

As soon as they returned home, Lily called Raedan to let him know she was going back to Ava's. His cell rang a dozen times. She told herself he was out hunting, that he would return her call as soon as he could, but an hour dragged by, and then another.

Where could he be?

She waited as long as she could and then she tried again. And again.

She stared out the window as her imagination went into overdrive. He'd been hurt. Captured by hunters. Killed.

Or had he left her again? For her own good? He had done it twice before. She knew he was afraid of what the demon might force him to do.

She jumped when there was a knock at the door.

"Liliana? Are you ready?"

"Yes, Papa." She hated leaving without knowing where Raedan was, then shook her head. If he had decided to leave her, there was nothing she could do about it. If he wanted to know her whereabouts, he could find her easily enough. Forcing a smile, she opened the door. "Let's go."

CHAPTER TWENTY-THREE

Lily sat in her bedroom at Ava's house. It was a little after ten. Her father had brought her to New Orleans and he and Ava had spent over an hour locked in Ava's room before he returned to Savaria. Try as she might, Lily had not been able to eavesdrop on their conversation.

Staring out the window. Lily wondered what they had talked about for so long, but mainly she wondered about Raedan. Surely he knew she was no longer in Savaria. With the blood-demon's powers, he would know when she had left and where she was now. Why hadn't he contacted her? Why wasn't he answering his phone? Had his fears for her safety driven him away for good this time? Would he send her a letter saying it was the best thing for her? Funny, how many people thought they knew what was best for her when no one bothered to ask.

Yes, she had her own doubts and fears, but her love for him was stronger than all her misgivings.

"Lily, are you awake?"

"Yes. Come in."

Ava glanced around as she stepped into the room, relieved that there was no sign of the vampire-demon. "I've put the final touches on the medallion," she said, and withdrew it from the pocket of her apron. "Why don't you try it on?"

"It's lovely," Lily exclaimed as she reached for it. Crafted of gold, it fairly glowed in the lamplight as she lifted the braided silver chain over her head. The medallion warmed against her skin. "How does it work?"

"It will vibrate when a Transylvanian vampire gets close enough to be a danger to you."

Lily closed her hand over the pendant. She could feel the power vibrating within it. "Thank you, Granny."

"Of course, we won't know that it works properly until we test it."

"How will we do that?"

"I thought we'd take a walk down Bourbon Street."

"Right into the lion's den," Lily murmured.

"Indeed. We can wait until tomorrow night, if you'd rather."

"No, let's do it now."

Armed with magic and a couple of sharp, wooden stakes, Lily and Ava strolled down Bourbon Street. Most of the shops were shuttered for the night, though the bars remained open.

Lily clasped the medallion, her nerves on edge as they entered one of the clubs. No sooner had they crossed the threshold, than the pendant began to vibrate, softly at first and then stronger when Claret suddenly appeared before them. As usual, she wore a long, slinky dress that outlined every curve. This one was deep purple silk.

"Well, well," the vampire purred. "Look what we have here."

Ava glanced at Lily, one brow arched in question.

"It works," Lily said.

"What works?" Claret asked.

"Nothing that need concern you," Ava said.

Frowning, the vampire glanced from Ava to Lily and back again. "What do you want?"

"Nothing. We were just passing by."

Claret's eyes narrowed with suspicion and then she shrugged. "If you're smart, you'll go home. A few of my friends are watching you rather hungrily."

"We're going, but first, have you seen Varden lately?"

"Perhaps."

"I need to know," Ava said. "And it's in your best interest to tell me."

"Oh? Why is that?"

"Have you heard of Raedan?"

"Of course. Who among us hasn't?"

"He's a friend of ours. And he's in love with Lily."

"I don't believe you."

"It's true, nonetheless. It might be good for your health to be on our side. Especially if you ever hope for another taste of Hungarian blood."

Claret's eyes took on a faint red tinge as she stared at Lily. Muttering an oath, she said, "Last I heard, he was still searching for her. As were any number of mortal men he's mesmerized to do his bidding."

"Is he still here, in New Orleans?"

Claret shrugged. "If he is, I haven't seen him lately."

"You'll let me know if you do."

"Of course."

With a nod in the vampire's direction, Ava took Lily's arm and they left the club.

"She's watching us," Lily whispered.

"I know, dear. Don't look back. Just keep walking."

Ava rose early the next morning. While walking last night, they had passed a small shop tucked between two larger ones, a magic shop Ava didn't remember ever seeing before. Perhaps she had just never noticed, she mused. Or perhaps it was cloaked in magic during the day. Whatever the reason, she headed there now.

When she reached her destination, there was no sign of the shop, yet she detected a strong signature of dark magic. As she murmured an incantation of unveiling, the vague outline of a door gradually took shape. Taking a deep breath, she opened it and stepped inside.

The weight of black magic was oppressive. It settled on her like a heavy shroud. Glancing around, she saw shelves crammed with books, manuscripts, and ancient scrolls yellow with age.

"Who are you?"

Ava whirled around, her hand pressed to her heart. "You gave me quite a start."

"I asked you a question."

"Names have power," Ava said. "I don't share mine with strangers." Especially ones with the kind of power radiating from this woman. Clad in a long, colorful gauze skirt and a white shirt, she could have been anywhere from fifty to a hundred. Her hair was long and white, her eyes a vivid green. Her feet were bare. The tattoo of a two-headed snake wound around her left ankle.

A faint smile played over the witch's lips. "You also have power, else you would not have been able to enter my shop. What are you seeking?"

"I'm looking for a spell to cast out a blood-demon."

The woman's eyes widened. "They no longer exist."

"I'm afraid they do."

"You know one?" she asked, excitement coloring her voice.

"I know *of* one."

Turning away, the woman walked quickly toward a shelf on the back wall. A wave of her hand summoned a slim volume with a black leather cover. Power shimmered in the air as it came to her hand.

"I found this in a tomb in a cave in Egypt several decades ago. I have not been able to open it."

"Is it for sale?"

"Yes. But only because it is no good to me."

"How much are you asking?"

"Five thousand dollars, cash."

"Five thousand! For a book I may not be able to open?"

The witch shrugged.

"Very well." Turning away from the woman, Ava whispered a summoning spell. Within moments, the cash was in her hand. She offered it to the witch.

The woman took it and ran her hands over the greenbacks. Nodding, she handed Ava the book. "I wish you good fortune."

"Thank you." Heat crawled up Ava's arm as her fingers curled about the black book. "I think I'll need it."

Slipping the mysterious book into her handbag, Ava left the shop.

Lily had just finished a cup of green tea sweetened with honey when she went cold all over. Her skin prickled. Her stomach clenched with fear. Alarmed, she lurched to her feet as Ava stepped into the kitchen.

"What is it?" Ava asked. "You look like you've seen a ghost."

"Something's wrong. What evil have you brought home with you?"

"You can feel it?"

"Whatever it is, get it out of here."

Reaching into her handbag, Ava withdrew the black book and placed it on the table.

Lily felt a chill when looked saw it. "What is that?"

"I'm hoping it holds the answer to destroying the demon."

Lily stared at the book as if it was a bomb about to go off. There was no title on the cover. No decoration. Nothing at all. "Where on earth did you find it?"

"A little shop on Bourbon Street, one I've never noticed before." Ava quickly relayed her visit with the witch.

"Why couldn't she open it?" Lily asked.

Ava shrugged. "I have no idea. And no idea if I'll be able to open it, either."

"You spent five thousand dollars on a book and you don't even know if you can read it?

Ava shrugged. "To tell you the truth, I'm a little afraid to try."

"I don't blame you." Lily reached out a tentative finger, poked the book, and quickly withdrew her hand as power raced up her arm. "I don't think you should keep that thing in the house. And since Raedan is no longer part of my life," she said glumly, "I don't think we need it at all."

CHAPTER TWENTY-FOUR

Raedan rose with the setting of the sun, his whole being tense as he sensed the black magic emanating from within Ava's house.

Curious, he prowled the darkness. In Savaria, he had made the decision to leave Liliana. Although the thought of never being with her again was almost beyond bearing, it was the right thing to do. The demon had been teasing and taunting him, urging him to give in to his vampire nature and devour her blood and her life and move on. He had tossed his cell phone in a dumpster to keep from calling her, had closed the blood link between them. But he didn't need it to find her. The demon could locate her easily enough.

Try as he might, he couldn't stay away from the house where she resided. He needed to feel her presence, inhale her familiar scent, listen to the sound of her breathing, hear her voice as she spoke to Ava. By day, he rested in the earth in the witch's backyard; by night, he left long enough to feed and then he returned to Ava's, his presence masked from one and all.

He frowned into the night. What the hell was causing that insidious, dark miasma that hovered over the house?

Creeping up to the living room window, he peered inside. Ava and Liliana knelt on either side of the coffee table, a thin black leather book between them. It reeked of dark magic and ancient evil. Where on earth had they found that accursed book?

The blood-demon stirred to life within him. *Mine,* he hissed.

Lily stared at Ava across the coffee table, her nerves humming with tension, her brow furrowed and damp with perspiration. "Maybe we should just throw it away."

"I've got five thousand dollars invested in that little black book," Ava said, regarding the item in question through narrowed eyes.

"It's evil!" Lily exclaimed. "Can't you feel it?"

"Books can't be evil, child. Although I'm sure whatever spells or incantations are inside are capable of doing great harm in the wrong hands."

Lily bit down on her lower lip as Ava picked up the slim volume. When Ava tried to open it, bright purple sparks danced up and down her arm.

With a startled cry, Ava dropped the thing on the table. "What the hell! I've never felt anything like that in my life."

"Throw it away!"

"I can't do that. What if Varden got hold of it? Or Claret?"

"What makes you think they could open it?"

"I don't know that they could, but are you willing to take that chance?" Ava stared at the book. "It's obviously not witch made," she murmured, thinking aloud. "I suppose it could be vampire made, but I think it's more likely demon made."

Lily's eyes widened. "I never thought of that." The mere idea sent a cold chill down her spine. There were all kinds of demons, though they were rare. Most were really imps who caused mischief—flat tires, broken water pipes, computer glitches. A few were violent, like the ones mentioned in the Bible. They inhabited humans and drove them mad. The blood-demon was a law unto itself. Where it had come from no one knew.

Lily glanced at Ava. "Do you think it holds the key to destroying the blood-demon?"

"Possibly. Or someone might have imprisoned another one within its pages."

"Oh, Lord, I hope not."

Moving tentatively, Ava picked up the book again. "I'm going to lock this thing up until we decide what to do with it," she said, gaining her feet. "You're not planning to go out, are you?"

"No way."

"Good. When I come back downstairs, we'll make s'mores. Nothing like chocolate to soothe one's frazzled nerves."

Raedan frowned as he listened to the exchange between Ava and Lily. Ava had been right. The book had been demon-made and only a demon with the necessary powers could open it. At the blood-demon's command, he had been poised to burst into the house and grab the book from Ava's hands had she been able to open it. He didn't know what kind of information it contained—the demon had never seen fit to share it with him, but he was certain the book contained the evil incantations and spells necessary to create a blood-demon.

And the secret to how to destroy one.

Lily couldn't sleep that night. Every time she closed her eyes, she saw those hideous purple sparks race up Ava's arm, felt the evil that lurked between the leather covers of that black book. Where was Raedan? If Ava was right and the book was demon-made, would he be able to open it? And if so, would he be able to banish the blood-demon? And if he did, would it destroy him, too?

Head throbbing, she pulled the covers up to her chin, only to lie there, wide awake and staring at the ceiling.

"Raedan," she whispered. "Where are you?"

She heard no answer. Instead, the quiet strumming of a guitar filled her mind and lulled her to sleep.

CHAPTER TWENTY-FIVE

"You found her?" Varden's voice rose. "You're sure it's her?"

"Yes, master."

"Let's go."

"You wish me to take you there?"

Varden slapped the man across the face. "No, you stupid fool. Give me the address."

The man didn't blink, merely reeled off the house number in a toneless voice.

With a nod, Varden buried his fangs in the man's throat and drank until there was nothing left. Wiping the blood from his lips, he roused a half-dozen other thralls and sent them to the address he'd been given, with orders to bring him the girl.

"I have to go, Lily," Ava said, glancing at the clock over the mantel. "I won't be gone too long. I should be back before dark. Stay inside and keep the doors locked."

"Don't worry about me," Lily said. "I have my medallion and my magic. You've warded the house. The doors and windows are locked. So go and have a good time."

Lily grinned as Ava kissed her cheek and hurried out of the house. Life was full of surprises, she thought. This morning, Ava had received a phone call from a man she had known twenty-five years ago. At the time, they had been instantly attracted to each other, dated a few times, and then the trouble with the Knights of the Dark Wood had started and Ava had lost touch with him.

Laughter bubbled up inside her. Wouldn't it be something if Ava found love a third time after so many years?

With a sigh, Lily settled into the easy chair in front of the fireplace, her thoughts, as always, turning toward Raedan. Closing her eyes, she imagined he was there beside her, playing his guitar, whispering that he loved her...

Lily woke with a start, her heart pounding, as six men rushed into the living room. Before she could form a coherent thought, they held her down and pressed a dirty rag over her mouth and nose. Struggling only made it worse. Two deep breaths and the world receded into swirling blackness and then faded away into nothing...

Raedan came to an abrupt halt, the prey he had been pursuing forgotten as he felt Lily's panic. And then felt nothing at all. Muttering a vile oath, he transported himself to Ava's place, swore again when he saw the door had been forced open. Opening his senses, he tested the wards Ava had erected, swore again when he realized she had warded the house against any and all supernatural creatures but had apparently neglected to include ordinary mortals.

A quick glance inside told him everything he needed to know—except where they had taken Lily.

And where the hell was Ava? Expanding his senses, he followed the witch's scent to a classy restaurant in the heart of New Orleans. He brushed past the man at the door, his gaze searching the interior.

He found Ava sharing a booth with a tall, good-looking man of indeterminate age. A warlock.

Ava looked up, surprise and fear in her eyes when she saw him. "What's happened?"

"Varden has Liliana," he said, his voice tight. "I cannot sense her presence. Either she is unconscious, or under a spell of some kind. Or he has killed her." His hands clenched at his sides. If Liliana was forever lost to him, he had no reason to on living. He would hunt Varden to the ends of the earth and when he found him, he would rip the vampire's heart from his chest and burn the remains. And then he would end his own existence.

All the color drained from Ava's face. "How is that possible? My wards..."

"Were insufficient," Raedan growled. "Varden sent mortals after Lily."

Ava glanced at her companion as she grabbed her handbag and slid out of the booth. "Mason, I've got to go."

"Can I be of assistance?" he asked.

Ava glanced at Raedan, who nodded. "Perhaps you can."

Mason dropped a fifty dollar bill on the table and they hurried out of the restaurant. The sun was setting when Raedan transported the three of them to Ava's.

"There were six men," Raedan said. "He pointed at the rag on the floor. "They took her by surprise and drugged her." He picked up the rag and smelled it. "Damn Varden. Too much of this will kill her."

"He doesn't want her dead," Ava reminded him.

The thought of his Liliana, helpless and at Varden's mercy, filled him with rage.

"Can you tell what kind of magic he's using?" Mason asked.

Ava shook her head. "It isn't witch magic," she replied slowly. "Raedan, you don't think he has demon magic, too, do you?"

Raedan stared at her. *Demon? Is his demon magic?*

Malicious laughter rang inside Raedan's mind. *You'll never find her.*

You will help me, damn you, or I will open that damn book and destroy you!

More evil laughter. *You cannot. You do not know the words or have the power to do so. I alone can break the spell. You cannot live without me, but I can survive without you. I have inhabited hundreds of bodies in my time. And I will find another when you are gone.*

Raedan swore softly. What if the demon was telling the truth? *I need your help. I'll give you whatever you want.*

The woman's blood.

No!

Then the vampire will bed her.

A cry of denial and rage erupted from Raedan's throat.

Do we have a deal, vampire?

Raedan's anger was palpable. Ava clutched Mason's arm as a shiver of fear ran down her spine.

All right, dammit. Now help me find her!

Her blood. Whenever I want. Swear it.

I swear it.

"Raedan?" Ava tugged on his arm. "What's going on?"

"The demon has agreed to help me, for a price."

"What is it he wants?"

"Liliana's blood."

"He wants you to drink from Lily?"

"Yes."

"I thought you already had."

"He wants more than just a small taste."

Ava stared at him in horror. "He wants you to turn her?"

"No. He doesn't want it all. Just the right to drink it whenever he wants."

She shook her head. "You can't promise him that! What kind of life would that be for her?"

"Better than the alternative," Raedan growled, both hands tightly clenched at his sides.

"Varden can't father a child."

"But he'll be able to try as often as he wants." The words were torn from his throat.

Ava paced the floor. What kind of choice was this? Leave Lily in Varden's hands or subject her to a life of giving blood to a demon? And what if Raedan lost control and took it all? Filled with anguish, she cried, "How can I make a decision like that?"

"I've already made it," Raedan said, and vanished from her sight.

Ava collapsed on the sofa, hands clenched in her lap. She groaned deep in her throat. This was all her fault. She never should have allowed Lily to date Raedan. She should have sent her back to Savaria the night they met. What if the blood-demon couldn't find Lily? Her mind filled with horrific images of Varden venting his lust on Liliana over and over again in an effort to impregnate her.

Sitting beside her, Mason draped his arm around her shoulders. "Is there anything I can do?"

Ava blew out a sigh. She wasn't accomplishing anything just sitting here. Taking Mason by the hand, she led him up the stairs to her room where she picked up her scrying mirror. "Powers of earth, wind and fire, reveal to me what I desire. Show me the vampire, Raedan."

Colors swirled across the glass, shifting, fading until a faint image martialized.

Ava stared at his surroundings. He was standing in front of what looked like a tomb in the midst of a tangled mass of dead vines and leaves and crumbling headstones.

"Mason, can you combine your magic with mine?"

"I believe so."

"Good." Taking his hand again, she murmured, "Powers of earth, wind and fire, reveal to me what I desire. Show me Raedan's location."

His image vanished and a sign post appeared in its place. "I know where he is," Ava said. "Let's go!"

The blood-demon led him to an ancient tomb. Raedan shuddered as he imagined his innocent Liliana lying inside, at the mercy of another man. She hadn't been in Varden's clutches long. Had he already defiled her? His hands curled into claws as his fangs descended. "Varden," he hissed. "You're a dead man." *Demon, open the damn door.*

You remember your promise? It will not end well for you, or for the girl, if you betray me.

I remember.

There was a shimmer of power that rocked Raedan where he stood, a grinding sound as the heavy concrete door slowly opened inward. An open coffin sat on the dais in the center of the room. Dozens of stone shelves had been cut into the side. Each held an urn.

There was no light inside save the faint glow of moon-light that shone through the open doorway.

Afraid of what he might find inside, Raedan took a hesitant step forward and peered into the coffin.

Liliana lay inside, her eyes closed, her arms folded over her bare breasts, her hair like a splash of black paint on the smooth white satin.

Six men stood along the back wall, unmoving, their eyes open and unblinking.

Raedan's heart caught in his throat until he assured himself that she was breathing. "Liliana?" Leaning forward, he kissed her cheek. "Liliana, wake up."

She stirred, her eyelids fluttering open. She screamed when she saw him.

"Hush, love," he murmured. "You're safe now."

"But you're not."

Before he could turn around, Varden lunged forward and drove a stake into Raedan's back. Raedan staggered forward as pain speared through him. A snap of Varden's fingers and the six thralls surrounded Raedan, all of them attacking him with silver-bladed knives and sharp wooden stakes.

Liliana stared in horror at the nightmare scene before her. Raedan was covered in blood from head to foot and yet, miraculously, none of the attackers had found his heart.

She was trying to summon her magic when Ava and a stranger appeared in the doorway. Fingers entwined, they chanted softly and, one by one, the six men dropped to the ground, leaving Raedan and Varden standing a few feet apart.

Raedan looked at Varden, a malicious smile on his face. And then, in a blur of movement, he was on the other vampire, his hands curling around Varden's throat.

How was he still standing? Lily wondered. She had never seen so much blood. Unable to look away, she watched as

Raedan broke the vampire's neck, then picked up one of the wooden stakes. He drove it deep into Varden's heart and gave it a cruel twist. There was a hissing noise and then a hideous sound she would never forget as the vampire's body seemed to collapse in on itself and slowly turn to dust. A gust of wind swept through the crypt, scattering the remains.

Raedan stood there, breathing hard, his face as pale as the walls of the crypt, his eyes a hellish red.

Lily stared at him. She wanted to run to him, to hold him in her arms, but before she could move, Ava stepped into the tomb and laid a restraining hand on her arm. "Don't touch him. Let's go home."

"But…"

"He needs to be alone." Ava removed her coat and helped Lily into it before leading her out of the tomb.

CHAPTER TWENTY-SIX

L ily sat on the sofa, a thick quilt around her shoulders, a mug of hot chocolate cupped in her hands. A fire blazed in the hearth. Earlier, Ava had helped her shower and into her nightgown and robe. Try as she might, she couldn't stop shivering.

Ava sat beside her. Mason sat on the chair across from the sofa.

"Did he hurt you?" Ava asked quietly.

Lily stared at her, eyes haunted.

She looked like hell, Ava thought, but who could blame her? Kidnapped by a lunatic vampire. Held captive in a coffin in a tomb. "You can tell me, child."

Lily shook her head. "Don't ask me. Don't ever ask me again." A shudder wracked her body. "I want Raedan."

"I'm sure he'll be here as soon as he can," Ava said.

Lily stared into the mug in her hands. It wasn't chocolate she saw, but the mad gleam in Varden's eyes as he promised to get her with child no matter how long it took. Bile rose in her throat as she heard his words in her mind again, saw the lust in his eyes as he climbed into the coffin.

With a cry, she lurched to her feet, chocolate splashing over the rim of the mug as she dropped it on the table and ran for the bathroom.

Ava stared after her, her heart and soul aching.

Leaning forward, Mason reached for her hand. "If there's anything I can do ... "

"I know. Thank you for being here. She's had a traumatic experience, but it could have been so much worse. And it's all my fault. I never should have left her home alone."

"You can't blame yourself."

"Can't I? My wards were inadequate and Lily paid the price."

"Perhaps it's my fault for refusing to take no for an answer when I asked you out."

"It doesn't matter where the fault lies," Ava said. "The damage is done."

"She's young and resilient," Mason said quietly. "In time, she'll be able to put it behind her."

"I hope you're right." Patting his hand, Ava stood. "I'd better go look in on her."

Raedan lingered outside in the shadows. Filled with rage and a desperate need for blood, he had preyed on the six men in the tomb and left them there, barely alive. He had made a quick trip to his lair to clean up and change his clothes and now he stood outside Ava's house. Lily had screamed when she saw him inside the tomb. Had she mistaken him for Varden? Or had the presence of another vampire—even one who loved her desperately—terrified her?

And then he heard her whisper his name. He waited until she returned to the living room with Ava before he knocked on the front door.

Ava let him in. "I'm so glad you're here," she said quietly. "Lily needs you."

He nodded, then followed her into the front parlor.

Ava motioned to Mason and they quietly left the room. "Liliana?"

She looked up at him, her eyes like dark smudges in her pale face. "Oh, Raedan," she murmured, and burst into tears.

Crossing the room, he sat beside her and drew her into his embrace. "I'm here, now," he said, lightly stroking her back. "No one will ever hurt you again."

She snuggled against him, her tears wetting his shirt front as sobs wracked her body. He held her while she cried, his heart aching for her, for the terror she had undoubtedly felt when she woke and found herself inside a tomb, at the mercy of a monster. He wished fleetingly that he could destroy Varden again, that he had ripped the vampire to shreds before he destroyed him. Just killing him hadn't been enough by half.

Gradually, Lily's tears slowed and stopped. Her even breathing told him she had fallen asleep. Lifting her in his arms, he carried her up to bed, removed her robe, and tucked her under the covers. She looked like a wounded angel lying there, her pale cheeks stained with tears.

After removing his boots, he stretched out on top of the covers and closed his eyes.

Your promise, vampire. Remember? I thirst.

Not now, demon. She is too weak.

Now!

Raedan muttered an oath as pain ripped through him. Sitting up, he leaned over Lily and brushed the hair away from her neck. Hating himself for what he was about to do, he bit her as gently as he could. Exhausted as she was, she didn't stir.

Sweet, the blood-demon murmured. *Sweeter than life itself.*

Not wanting to face the world, Lily snuggled deeper under the covers and tried to go back to sleep, but it was no use. Memories of the time she had spent in Varden's clutches swirled through her mind. She felt again her fear, her terror when he dropped her into the coffin. Groggy from the drug they had given her, her arms and legs unresponsive, she could only lay there, waiting…

He gazed down at her, his eyes blood-red. "Mine," he said, as he climbed into the coffin, his fingers stroking her face. "All mine. No matter how long it takes, I will plant my seed in you. And you will give me a son!" He frowned when she didn't blink or respond, then unleashed a string of vile curses as he turned and berated the half-dozen men standing motionless against the wall. "Damn fools! I wanted her to be awake, aware of what's happening. There's no fun to be had in violating a woman who doesn't even know what's going on! Fools", he muttered. "You could have killed her."

Still muttering curses under his breath, he stormed out of the vault and closed the heavy door behind him, leaving her in total darkness, with only the sound of her own labored breathing and the foul scent of old death…

With a cry, Lily threw the covers aside and jumped out of bed. The house was quiet. Where was Ava? And Raedan? He had been here last night. held her while she cried. But of course he was gone now. The sun was up. She wondered how he had survived such a brutal assault, marveled at how quickly he had healed. There had been no sign of his injuries when he came to her.

Drawing her robe around her, she padded into the bathroom and splashed cold water on her face. "You look like death warmed over," she muttered to her reflection.

And that was how she felt, too. Drained. Weak. Tired, even though she had slept the clock around.

Maybe a cup of black coffee would help, she mused as she headed downstairs to the kitchen. She stopped in the doorway, surprised to see Ava and the same strange man she recalled seeing last night sitting at the table.

"Lily!" Ava started to rise, then sat back down. "Lily, this is my friend, Mason Balfour."

Lily nodded, wondering just how friendly they were, seeing as how both Ava and Mason were still in their night clothes. Moving to the stove, she poured herself a cup of coffee.

"Come, sit with us, child," Ava said. "We were up late last night, so I invited Mason to stay over."

Nodding, Lily pulled a chair from the table and sat down. "It's nice to meet you, Mr. Balfour."

"And you."

"How are you feeling, Lily?" Ava asked, her expression anxious.

"I'm fine." It was a lie and they both knew it.

"Can I fix you anything?"

"I'm not hungry." But, oh, so thirsty. She drank her coffee, then poured herself a tall glass of orange juice and practically inhaled it.

Ava's eyes narrowed as Lily poured herself a second glass. She heard Raedan's voice in her mind: *He wants more than just a taste.*

Raedan had stayed with Lily last night. And suddenly everything was clear. The reason Lily looked so pale. The reason for her thirst.

Raedan had fed the demon Lily's blood.

Lily frowned as Ava insisted she eat a big breakfast, even though she wasn't hungry and when breakfast was over, Ava urged her to go lay down on the couch and watch TV for a while, no doubt hoping some insipid television show would take her mind off last night's horror. As if she would ever forget it!

"All right, Granny, what's going on?" Lily asked as Ava ushered her toward the sofa.

"Sit down and I'll tell you."

Suddenly apprehensive, Lily dropped onto the couch. Clutching a throw pillow to her chest, she waited for an explanation.

Ava blew out a sigh. "I don't know how to tell you this, except to just say it. When Varden took you, I couldn't find you and neither could Raedan."

"But he did find me," Lily said.

"Only after he made a deal with the demon."

"A deal?" A cold shiver ran down Lily's spine. "What kind of deal?"

"The demon said he would find you, but only if Raedan agreed to give him your blood."

Lily stared at her great-grandmother in disbelief. "How could he make a promise like that? How could you let him?"

"I didn't *let* him, Lily. He agreed to it before he even told me. But, Lily, child, what else were we to do?"

"Couldn't you have used a location spell of some kind? Anything!"

"It would have taken time," Ava explained. "Raedan wouldn't wait. And there's no guarantee I could have found one before..." She swallowed hard. "Before Varden... before he had his way with you."

Lily sank back against the sofa. Would she really rather they had waited? Had they done so, she might still be in Varden's power, unable to fight him off, forced to endure his touch. Just the thought of him violating her even once made her stomach clench in revulsion.

"Lily?"

"Was the promise to give the demon my blood to be a one-time thing?" Lily asked hopefully.

"No."

"So, Raedan agreed to...to bite me whenever the demon says so? How could he do that? What if he loses control and...and..." She couldn't say it out loud. It was too horrible to think about. And what if one day she decided she didn't want to see Raedan anymore? It was unlikely, but anything was possible. Maybe he would tire of her. What kind of life could she have if she had to let him drink from her whenever the demon asked? What if she refused?

What if Raedan hadn't made a deal with the demon? What if she'd had to endure being Varden's prisoner for days while Lily and Raedan searched for her? Suddenly, feeding the demon didn't seem quite as bad as the alternative. She would much rather let Raedan drink from her than be Varden's prisoner, subject to his every repulsive whim.

Pressing her palms to her throbbing temples, she closed her eyes, thinking her life had suddenly turned into a living, breathing, nightmare.

CHAPTER TWENTY-SEVEN

Raedan woke with the setting of the sun, his first thought for Liliana. Opening his senses, he searched for her. She was in the kitchen, having dinner with Ava and the warlock, Mason Balfour. When his mind brushed hers, he detected worry, fear, depression, and confusion.

Damn. He showered, dressed, and went in search of prey, his own mind filled with guilt, and doubts about any future they might have had together. Had making a deal with the blood-demon destroyed her faith and trust in him? Could he blame her if it had? He had condemned her to a horrible fate. Perhaps he should have waited. Perhaps Ava and the warlock might have found a spell or incantation that would have guided them to Liliana's whereabouts. But how could he have waited, knowing Liliana was at the mercy of a vampire with only one thing on his mind? He couldn't bear the thought of her being raped time and again by another man.

Any man, human or otherwise.

He fed quickly, taking more than he usually did in hopes of placating the demon, but not enough to do the woman any harm.

Leaving his prey, he moved down the street, wondering if he would be welcome at Ava's house, if Liliana would be glad to see him, or if she would turn him away.

❧ ❧ ❧

Lily glanced at the clock as she magicked the dishes into the dishwasher. It felt good to be doing something so ordinary, so natural. Dinner had been pleasant. Mason had entertained them with stories of his youth in England, of his travels across the world as he perfected his magic. He had seen all the wonders of the world, known some fascinating people.

It was easy to see that Ava was totally smitten with him. Not that Lily could blame her. Mason was a very attractive man with a winning personality and an easy smile. The two of them had gone outside to be alone after dinner.

Sitting in the parlor, Lily tried to read, but she couldn't concentrate. She jumped at every sound. Putting the book aside, she paced the floor, her thoughts confused and fragmented.

She shivered when the doorbell rang, remembering the night past all too clearly. But it couldn't be Varden or his men. Raedan, then? Was he coming to visit her, to see how she was doing? Or to take her blood for the demon? What would happen if she refused to allow it?

Taking a deep breath, she opened the door. He was dressed in ubiquitous black, and it occurred to her that he was a part of the darkness, a part of the night itself. As always, his very nearness called out to her.

"Liliana, I know you probably do not wish to see me right now," he said quietly, formally. "I just came by to make sure you were all right and to tell you how sorry I am."

When he turned to leave, she caught his arm. "Don't go. We need to talk."

With a nod, he followed her into the living room, took the chair across from her when she settled on the sofa.

For a moment, they simply eyed each other warily.

"Tell me," Lily said, hands clenched in her lap. "What, exactly, did you promise the demon?"

"I swore I would give him your blood whenever he asked for it if he would lead me to you."

"And if you don't your word?"

"I do not know. I guess we will find out."

"What do you mean?"

"I saw what it did to you when I complied the other night. I felt its effect on the demon. It made him stronger and that is a bad thing. He is going to want more, and want it more often, and I am afraid ... "

"Afraid you'll take too much?"

"Yes." He raked his fingers through his hair. "I do not want to hurt you, love. Or worse, turn you against your will. But I cannot be sure I will always be able to stop before it is too late, or that I will not take too much. How can I put your life in danger like that?"

"But we have the demon's book. If we can figure out a way to open it ... "

Raedan shook his head. "He is the only one who can open it."

"What if that's not true? What if he's lying? Surely two witches, a vampire, and a warlock should be able to unlock whatever magic binds the book."

"Perhaps. But he will know what we are going."

Lily frowned. "Doesn't it ever sleep?"

"Usually when I do, though he is at rest now."

Lily smiled faintly. Then they would just have to work on a spell during the day, when Raedan and the blood-demon were at rest.

Raedan went still as the blood-demon stirred within him.

Could it be? Is that the woman's blood I smell?

Not now, demon.

You swore an oath, vampire. Feed me.

"What is it?" Lily asked as Raedan went suddenly still. "What's wrong?"

His gaze moved to the pulse throbbing in her throat. "He is thirsty."

Fear danced in Lily's eyes as she stared at him.

"Not to worry. I will not give him what he wants." No sooner had Raedan said the words than pain shot through him, hot, agonizing pain that burned through his veins like the flames of perdition. With a low groan, he doubled over, hands fisted, jaw clenched, his whole body rigid as the pain went on and on.

Blood!

He had to get out of here, Raedan thought, but when he tried to stand, his body refused to obey and he fell to the floor, a solid mass of misery. "Lily," he growled. "Get. Out."

Get out? How could she leave him in such agony? Dropping to her knees beside him, she held her arm out in front of him. "Drink, Raedan! Hurry!"

"No!"

"Please! I can't bear to see you like this."

When he still refused, she ran into the kitchen, pulled a knife out of a drawer and ran back into the living room. Kneeling again, she clenched her teeth, then dragged the tip of the blade across her wrist. Bright red blood immediately oozed from the shallow cut as she thrust her arm in front of Raedan again.

Lily's blood. Hot. Fresh. Groaning, he took hold of her arm and sank his fangs into her flesh.

"What's going on here?" Ava's voice, filled with revulsion and alarm.

Lily looked up, tears flooding her eyes, dripping on Raedon's hair. "The demon is torturing him. I have to make it stop."

Ava looked up at Mason. "Shouldn't we do something?"

The warlock shook his head. "I don't think that would be wise just now."

After what seemed an eternity to Lily, Raedan's body relaxed. A moment later, he ran his tongue over the shallow cut in her arm. It healed immediately, leaving no trace. When he lifted his head, his eyes were filled with regret. And gratitude. "I am sorry," he murmured. "So damn sorry."

"Are you all right now?"

"I will be, thanks to you."

"Please don't ever refuse him again. It's not worth it."

"Come on," Mason said, tugging on Ava's arm. "I don't think we're needed—or wanted—here."

Before Ava could protest, Mason urged her out of the room and up the stairs.

Raedan blew out a sigh, thinking he would rather cut off his arm than endure such pain again.

Rising, Lily offered him her hand. With a wry smile, he let her help him to his feet.

"I am sorry," he said again. "Are you sure you are all right?"

"I'm fine."

"You are a brave girl, to tempt a vampire like that," Raedan murmured, drawing her into his arms. "Or maybe just a very foolish one. But I love you the more for it."

"And I love you."

For a moment, he simply held her close, unable to believe she hadn't thrown him out of the house. Not only that, but she had willingly cut into her own flesh and offered him her blood to ease his pain and appease the demon. He didn't know where they were going from here, but for this moment, he didn't care. All he wanted to do was hold her close.

As the seconds ticked by, he realized that, although Liliana's blood had made the demon stronger, it had somehow done the same for him.

CHAPTER TWENTY-EIGHT

L ily woke smiling. Raedan had stayed with her until almost one in the morning. Sometimes they had made idle conversation, sometimes they had been content to just sit quietly close holding hands. He had told her a little of his more recent past, how he moved from town to town, state to state, every twenty years or so, partly so the few people he associated with wouldn't notice that he never aged, partly because of boredom.

It had never occurred to her that vampires might get bored with life, but it made sense when she thought about it. What would it be like to have been everywhere, seen everything? It must be a lonely life, too, she mused. You could never tell people what you really were, never confide in anyone for fear of betrayal. If you married, you would either have to trust your spouse with the truth, or pick up and leave when they started aging and you didn't. She tried to imagine what it would be like to never see the sun, to live only at night, to survive on a warm, liquid diet. Yes, it would be nice to never age, never get sick, heal in an instant, move faster than lightning, but when she thought of all she would have to give up, it just didn't seem worth it. How much worse must it be if you were turned against your will? And you were also infected with a blood-demon?

She would have to sacrifice a few things if she stayed with Raedan. Like having children. That would be hard. Even adoption didn't seem like a viable alternative. Being a witch, she would likely live much longer than average and if she didn't want to look old, well, she could always alter her appearance, the way Ava did. But she would never live as long as he would.

But that was a worry for another day, she thought as she threw the covers aside and swung her legs over the edge of the bed. She wasn't going to let what might or might not happen in the future ruin the present.

After breakfast, Lily followed Ava and Mason up to Ava's workshop, where they spent the entire morning studying spells and incantations, leafing through Ava's numerous grimoires and spell books, experimenting with fire magic and air magic, earth magic, and even a bit of dark magic.

"Don't we need demon magic?" Lily asked at one point.

But Ava shook her head. "I'm afraid demon magic might only make the creature stronger."

They took a break at noon and Mason decided to go search the voodoo stores in hopes of finding something new to try.

"You really like him, don't you, Granny?" Lily asked as they prepared tuna fish sandwiches for lunch.

"I guess it shows."

"I guess it does. Is it serious?"

"You could say so. He asked me to marry him."

"He proposed? And you didn't tell me?"

"It just happened last night."

"What did you say?"

"Yes, of course," Ava said, with a laugh. "I wasn't about to let him get away from me a second time."

"Is he as old as you?"

"Liliana! What a question!"

"Is he?"

"Not quite, but close enough that it doesn't matter."

"So, I guess that's not how he really looks, either."

"You know how men are. Some get better looking as they grow older." Ava placed their sandwiches on paper plates, added some chips, and carried them to the table. "How are things between you and Raedan?"

Lily shrugged. "As good as they can be, all things considered."

"Have you thought about what staying with him will be like, for you?"

Lily nodded. "All the time."

"Do you think it's worth it?"

"I don't know. I guess only time will tell. After all, we really haven't known each other very long. But I love him, Granny. I can't help how I feel."

"I know, dear. I can see it your eyes when you look at him."

Lily glanced frequently at the time as the sun dipped in the west. She had expected Raedan to arrive as soon as the sun went down, but an hour passed and then another and there was still no sign of him. Where could he be?

Raedan sat at the bar in one of the many nightclubs along Bourbon Street, a glass of wine in his hand as he perused the men and women around him. The place was crowded with tourists from all over the country. He noted that he wasn't the only vampire in the club. And then he grinned faintly as he recognized the Master of the City. She was a pretty thing, with her fiery red hair and a voluptuous figure shown off tonight by an off-the-shoulder gown of forest green. He had not seen her since she had confronted him one night soon after he arrived in New Orleans. He knew the very moment when she caught his scent. Her head snapped up, her eyes—so dark a brown they were almost black, narrowed as she searched the crowd. When their gazes met, he smiled at her.

Lifting one brow, she sashayed toward him. "Are you going to tell me your name this time?"

"Raedan. And you're Claret, Master of the City."

"Indeed." She frowned as she drew in his scent. "What are you?"

"Excuse me?"

"You're more than just vampire." She cocked her head to the side. "You're not a witch, but the scent of witch magic is all over you. How is that possible?"

"Perhaps because I spend a lot of time with witches."

Claret took a deep breath. "A Falconer witch. Liliana!" Her eyes widened. "You destroyed Varden, didn't you?"

"He needed killing," Raedan growled, and felt his rage surface anew as he remembered what the vampire had done to Liliana. "It gave me great pleasure to destroy him."

She made a vague gesture with one elegant hand. "He was quite insane. A danger to one and all."

Finishing his drink, Raedan placed the glass on the bar top. "A pleasure to see you again," he said.

"Do you know Quill?"

"We've met."

"Tell him hello for me should you see him again."

"I shall." Wondering how in hell Claret knew Quill, Raedan left the club.

Moments later, he was standing on Ava's front porch. It was Ava, herself, who opened the door. She frowned when she saw him. "What were you doing with Claret?"

"You know her?"

"We all do," she said, taking a step back so he could enter the house. "Like most Transylvanian vampires, she craves Hungarian blood." She looked at Raedan thoughtfully as she closed the door. "Do you?"

"No. She did ask me to tell Quill hello should I see him again."

"Yes, she's very fond of his blood."

"He shared it with her?"

"Yes, but not because he wanted to. It's a long story. You must ask him to tell you about it some time. Personally, I don't know why he didn't destroy her long ago."

Raedan grunted softly. He had never been an overly curious man but this was a story he had to hear.

"Raedan!" Lily flew down the stairs and into his arms. "I missed you!"

"I missed you, too, love," he said, his gaze caressing her.

She looked him over from head to foot. "Are you all right?"

"I'm fine, thanks to you." Raedan glanced briefly at Mason, who had entered the room behind Liliana. "Can we go out somewhere?"

"Sure, if you want," she said, smiling. "Just let me grab my coat."

Ava and Mason exchanged concerned glances as Raedan helped Lily into her coat.

"Don't be late," Ava called as Raedan opened the door.

Lily waved, and then they were gone.

❧ ❧ ❧

Lily blew out a breath, her eyes wide when she realized they were on a sandy beach somewhere. "How did you do that?"

Raedan shrugged. "A little vampire magic."

"I knew witches could move fast, but that…wow!" Glancing around, she asked, "Where are we?"

"A stretch of beach in San Diego."

"California?"

He nodded.

Lily took off her coat and spread it on the sand, then sat down. After a moment, Raedan dropped down beside her, his arm sliding around her waist to draw her closer.

"It's a pretty night," Lily remarked. The sky was dark blue and clear, sprinkled with stars. A quarter moon hung low in the sky. A small house stood alone a good distance away, the windows boarded up. All the world seemed quiet around them save for the gentle whisper of the waves caressing the shore.

"What are we doing here?" she asked.

Raedan shrugged. "I just wanted to be alone with you. Do you mind?"

"Of course not."

"Will you marry me, Liliana?"

She stared at him, eyes wide. "You want to get married?"

"Is the idea of marrying me so repugnant?"

"No! No, of course not. I just didn't…I mean, we really don't know each other very well."

"It's all right." Removing his arm from around her waist," he said, "Forget I asked."

Lily bit down on her lower lip. She was handling this all wrong. Taking his hand in both of hers, she said, "I love you, Raedan. You know I do. I just think we should wait a little while. If and when you ask me again, my answer will be yes. I just don't want to upset my family, maybe give them a little time to get used to the idea of you and me."

His gaze searched hers, as if he was looking for the truth. And then he leaned forward and kissed her lightly. "I'm not going anywhere unless you tell me to leave," he said, quietly.

"Oh, Raedan, I do love you so!" She threw her arms around him and he fell back on the sand. Drawing her down on top of him, he rolled onto his side, carrying her with him. He showered her with kisses—her brow, the tip of her nose, the hollow of her throat—before settling on her lips in a long, searing kiss she felt from the roots of her hair to the soles of her feet and everywhere in-between.

Breathless, she gazed at him. He was so beautiful, she thought, and she loved him beyond words.

"Beautiful?" he asked, stifling a laugh.

"It isn't polite to eavesdrop on someone else's thoughts."

"Sorry, love. I think you're beautiful, too." She was so close, her hair silky where it brushed his cheek, her scent intoxicating, her skin warm and smooth. And he wanted her. Wanted her with every fiber of his being.

There's no one else on the beach for miles, whispered the blood-demon. *You can take her body, take her blood, and wipe the memory from her mind. No one need ever be the wiser.*

No!

You want to. You know you do. Even now, the scent of her life's blood is calling to you, to me. To me," he chortled. *Remember your promise, vampire.*

Raedan tensed as he felt the demon's power unfold inside him, reminding him of the excruciating agony he had felt the last time. He couldn't face it again, he thought, nor could he ask Liliana to sacrifice her blood for him again.

And he couldn't make Liliana his wife, couldn't be with her night and day, not with the demon forever clamoring for her blood. Sooner or later, he would take too much and in so doing, he would kill her. And destroy his own will to live.

Pulling her to her feet, he transported the two of them back to Ava's front porch. "I must go."

"What?" Her gaze searched his face. "Why? What's wrong?"

"I will call you later," he said, his voice tight with pain as he vanished from her sight.

Lily stared into the darkness, wondering what had just happened. And then she knew.

He had left her rather than feed the demon her blood. He had left because he didn't want her to see his suffering.

Tears burned her eyes as she opened the door and stepped inside. One way or another, they had to find a way to destroy the blood-demon before it destroyed Raedan and the love they shared.

In his lair, Raedan writhed on the floor in blinding agony, his body contorted with pain and bathed in crimson sweat while the blood-demon screamed threats and obscenities in his mind.

CHAPTER TWENTY-NINE

Lily woke with a start as a sharp pain tore through her. She bolted upright, knowing immediately that the horrendous pain she felt was Raedan's. Flinging the covers aside, she ran to Ava's room and threw open the door, only to come to an abrupt stop when she saw that Ava wasn't alone in bed. Mason lay beside her, one arm curled around her shoulders. But there was no time to absorb that now.

"What is it?" Ava exclaimed, drawing the covers up to her chin. "Is the house on fire?"

"It's Raedan! The blood-demon is torturing him. I've got to go to him."

"Liliana, do you think that's wise?"

"No, but I can't let him suffer when I can stop it. I just wanted to let you know that I was going." With a last contemplative glance at Mason, Lily left the room and closed the door behind her.

Muttering under her breath, Ava slipped out of bed and into her robe. "I've got to help, if I can."

"I guess our secret is out," Mason drawled.

"Oh, shut up," Ava muttered, though there was no malice in her voice. "I guess I can't tell her to practice what I preach anymore."

⚜ ⚜ ⚜

Lily had assembled all of Ava's magical implements when Ava arrived stepped into the room. "Maybe you should do it," Lily suggested. "Your magic is stronger than mine."

Ava shook her head. "You're closer to him than I am. You should be the one to do it."

Gathering her power around her, Lily gazed into the mirror. "Power of earth, wind, and fire, reveal to me what I desire. Show me Raedan's lair."

She held her breath as the mirror's surface shimmered with bright colors that gradually turned to black and gray and midnight blue before separating to reveal a small house located on a narrow stretch of deserted beach. "I know this place," Lily murmured. "Raedan took me there the other night. Send me there, Granny. Hurry."

"I don't like the idea of your going alone."

"I'll be all right." Lily summoned her cell phone. "I'll call you if I need help. Hurry!"

Ava wove a spell around Lily that carried her where she wished to go. It wasn't as dramatic or as quick as being transported by a vampire but the results were the same.

She landed at the front door, only then remembering she was in her nightgown. But it didn't matter. She tried the latch. It was locked, of course. Pounding on it with both fists, she called Raedan's name.

A minute passed. Two. There was no response. She tried to magic the door open, but when nothing happened, she pounded on the door again, harder this time. "Raedan!"

The door opened with a squeak of hinges and he was there. Lines of pain bracketed his mouth. His brow was sheened with sweat that looked like blood. His eyes were red, his cheeks sunken.

"Lily...what...the hell...are you...doing here? Go home."

He doubled over, his hands clutching at his belly as a groan was ripped from his throat. "Go...home. You're not...safe...here."

Ignoring the voice of her conscience that screamed at her to get out of there as fast as possible, she pushed him inside and shut the door. He staggered toward the sofa and fell onto it, his body convulsing.

Lily followed him. Kneeling beside the couch, she offered him her arm. "Drink, Raedan."

"No." He groaned deep in his throat. "No."

"Don't argue with me. Don't you know I can feel your pain? If you won't do it for yourself, do it for me. Now drink!" When he still refused, she resorted to the same tactic she had used before. Conjuring a small knife, she made a shallow cut in her left wrist, then held her arm to his mouth.

He latched on to it like a hungry baby suckling at his mother's breast. Surprisingly, this time there was no pain, only a rush of sensual pleasure as he drank from her.

When she started to feel light-headed, Lily tugged her arm away, let out a little cry of denial when he refused to let her go. Only he didn't drink again, merely ran his tongue over the wound as he had before.

Murmuring her name, he lifted her onto the sofa and held her close to his side.

Lily sighed as Raedan's eyes closed. The tremors that wracked him gradually ceased as the tension went out of his body. They couldn't go on like this much longer, she thought bleakly. For his sake as much as hers, they had to find a way to destroy the blood-demon without killing Raedan at the same time.

There had to be a way. There just had to be.

❦ ❦ ❦

With the coming of dawn, Raedan slipped into the rest of his kind.

Lily eased out of his arms, yawned and stretched, and then went in search of something to drink, although she didn't have much hope of finding anything. And she was right. There was nothing in the house to eat or drink save for half a bottle of red wine.

Sitting at the small, round table in the kitchen, Lily conjured a loaf of bread, a jar of blueberry jam, a glass of orange juice, a cup of coffee heavily laced with cream and sugar, and a butter knife.

She ate leisurely, refusing to think of anything unpleasant. When she finished, she wandered through the house. All the rooms needed painting. The only furniture was the table and single chair in the kitchen, the sofa in the living room, and a double bed in one of the tiny bedrooms.

Curious, she opened the closet, noting that his shirts and pants were hung with care, his shoes and boots in a neat row on the floor. A shelf in the closet held his underwear and sox. A guitar case stood in one corner. Curious, she opened it and plucked the strings. Did he play when he was here, alone? Who had taught him? Would he play for her if she asked?

Closing the case, she peered into the bathroom. It held a couple of large towels and men's toiletries.

Why did he live here, she wondered, when he could live anywhere he wanted? He drove an expensive car, wore top of the line shirts, trousers, and boots. Surely he could afford a nice house, or at least a suite in a five-star hotel.

She should go home, she thought, returning to the living room, but she was reluctant to leave him. He looked vulnerable, lying there on the sofa. Helpless, although she knew he was neither.

She made a quick call to Ava, assuring her that she was fine and would be home later.

After ending the call, Lily glanced around, but there was nowhere to sit except the sofa. With a shrug, she conjured an easy chair, a book, and a candy bar, and spent the next two hours lost in a mystery written by one of her favorite authors.

Later, she changed out of her nightgown and into one of Raedan's t-shirts, picked up her book, and went outside to sit in the sun. Odd, she mused, that a vampire would choose to live at the beach when he could never stretch out on the sand and get a tan. Did he miss the daylight? Or had he lived in darkness so long he no longer thought about it?

When the sun grew too warm, she conjured a beach umbrella, stretched out on her belly, and took a nap.

Ava reclined in the easy chair in her work room. Mason sat on the floor, his back against the wall, watching her. She had been sitting there, staring into the distance, since Lily called. There was a faraway look in her eyes that made him wonder what she was thinking. He knew asking would be a waste of breath. She wouldn't tell him until she was ready.

Five minutes passed.

Ten.

"Mason, what do you know about the Knights of the Dark Wood?"

"Not much. I know they used to be hell-bent on destroying Hungarian vampires, but other than that..." He shrugged. "Last I heard, a powerful witch had pulled their fangs, so to speak."

"Indeed."

"That witch wouldn't have been you, would it?"

"Maybe," she replied, although there was no maybe about it. "The Brotherhood is ancient," she said, thinking out loud. "They go back to medieval times. I wonder..."

"I'm not sure I like that look in your eyes," Mason murmured. "It looks like trouble brewing."

"Decades ago, before Lily and Dominic were born, there were rumors that the Elder Knight had a library of grimoires and spell books that dated back a thousand years or more."

"Yeah?"

"Those books are passed from Elder Knight to Elder Knight."

Mason grunted softly. "I don't think I like where this is going."

"The new Elder Knight is young. No doubt he could be easily manipulated."

"Go on."

"I could go to visit him, sort of a good-will tour. Take him a gift, perhaps some new protection from Transylvanian vampires. Or perhaps I could put an enchantment on their swords so that they would strike true every time. What do you think, Mason?"

"And in exchange for this generous gift, you wouldn't want much. Just a tour of the Elder Knight's library."

Ava nodded.

"Don't look so smug," Mason chided good-naturedly. "What makes you think he'll agree to meet with you?"

"Oh, he will," she replied confidently. "Wait and see."

❧ ❧ ❧

Raedan woke abruptly, the transition from rest to consciousness happening within mere moments. He knew immediately where he was and that Lily was in the house. He sensed the couple swimming half a mile away and knew they posed no danger.

Rising to his feet, he went into the kitchen where he found Lily enjoying a spaghetti dinner with all the trimmings, including a bottle of chianti.

She looked up, her anxious gaze running over him from head to foot. "Are you all right?"

"Of course." His eyes narrowed. "Have you been here all day?"

She nodded. "Do you mind?"

"No." It was mostly true, but disconcerting to know she had been in his lair while he rested, something no one had ever done before.

"Would you like a glass of wine?" she asked.

"Yes, thank you."

She conjured a second glass and splashed some wine into it, conjured a second chair and handed him the glass when he sat down.

"Does Ava know you're here?"

"I called her this afternoon."

He grunted softly, surprised Ava had allowed her to stay. And then he grinned inwardly, thinking his Liliana was pretty good at getting her own way most of the time. "Have you no regard for your own safety? Don't you know I could have killed you last night?"

"But you didn't."

"You might not be so lucky next time."

"You're stuck with me, Raedan. Get used to it."

His laughter surprised her. It was a warm, full-bodied sound, one she hadn't heard nearly enough.

Pushing away from the table, he lifted her to her feet and into his arms. "I love you, witch woman," he murmured, and kissed her, his tongue dueling with hers while his hands skated up and down her spine.

She closed her eyes as she leaned into him, wanting to be closer, desperate for his touch, hungry for his kisses. Though his lips were cool, they lit a fire inside her that burned away every thought save the need to please him, to give him everything he wanted and more and in so doing, fulfill her every dream, her every desire, as well.

When she opened her eyes, they were lying side-by-side on a bed covered with furs in a white room she had never seen before. It had no doors and no windows. And no roof. Overhead, a million stars glittered against a blanket of black velvet. Soft music filled the room though she couldn't tell where the sound was coming from. A low table stood beside the bed. It held two crystal goblets and a bottle of red wine. A delicate vase held a single, blood-red rose." Where are we?"

"In my imagination."

Lily stared at him. "Are you kidding me?"

"No."

"I don't believe it. How is that possible?"

"The blood-demon brought us here."

A shiver ran down her spine. "Was it your idea? Or his?"

"Mine, darlin'. There is no need to be afraid."

"I'm not!" she exclaimed.

"Ah, my brave Liliana." He caressed her cheek with his knuckles, let his fingers slide down to settle lightly in the hollow of her throat. "Do you not know that lying makes your heart race?"

She swallowed hard. "Raedan, *now* you're scaring me."

"I know. I am sorry." He kissed her tenderly. "I love you, Liliana. No matter what happens between us, never doubt it or forget it." He held her close, but not so tightly she felt imprisoned. His breath was cool against her skin. His hand slid up and down her side, skimming the curve of her breast as he kissed her cheeks, her brow, her chin, the soft, tender place beneath her ear. "A taste?"

"I don't think that's a good idea at the moment."

"Just one, I swear."

Thinking it might be wiser to agree than to argue, she murmured, "Just one."

His bite was gentle and he took only a little. And still a rush of sensual pleasure flowed through her. Almost, she begged him to take more.

True to his word, he only took a taste. And then he kissed her again.

When she opened her eyes this time, she was alone on the front porch of Ava's house.

Raedan prowled a distant city searching for prey, his heart swelling with love for Liliana. He had taken her into his imagination partly to see if she truly trusted him, but mostly to see if he could trust himself—if he was capable of keeping the blood-demon at bay while she was at his mercy, helpless to fight him off, unable to call for help.

For the first time, he had hope that, between them, they would find a way to defeat the demon.

CHAPTER THIRTY

"Lily!" Ava threw her arms around her granddaughter and hugged her tight. "I've been so worried about you. I tried to call you. I tried to locate you. I tried everything to find out where you were. I've never been so scared! Where on earth have you been?"

"In Raedan's imagination."

"What?" Ava stared at her in open-mouthed astonishment.

"You heard me. And what an amazing and scary place it is."

"I've no doubt of that! Let's go in the kitchen and have some tea. Or maybe you'd prefer dinner?"

"No, I ate earlier tonight. But tea sounds good."

Lily sat at the table while Ava set out two flowered China cups, a bowl of sugar, a pitcher of milk, and a jar of honey before quickly conjuring a pot of dandelion tea.

"What did you do while I was gone," Lily asked. "Besides try to find me?"

"While I was worrying about you, an idea occurred to me."

"Oh?"

"The Elder Knight keeps a large, comprehensive library of ancient grimoires and spell books at the stronghold."

"Really? I didn't know that." Lily sipped her tea, her expression thoughtful.

"Few people do. I was thinking of paying him a visit and offering him a gift in exchange for a chance to search the library."

"What do you hope to find in there?"

"The secret to opening the black book, or, better yet, a way to destroy the blood-demon without also destroying Raedan."

"I'm game! When are we leaving?"

"Mason and I are leaving as soon as I can locate their new stronghold, which I'm hoping hasn't been moved since I gave them that new directive."

"You're not thinking of leaving me behind, are you?"

Ava's first thought had been to do just that, until she thought it through. Taking Lily with her was probably a far better choice than leaving her behind, alone with Raedan. "I was," Ava admitted. "But on second thought, I think you'd better come along. We'll leave as soon as I verify the location of the stronghold. You might want to gather your wand and whatever other amulets you think you might need. I'll be up in my workshop."

Lily finished her tea and magicked the cup into the dishwasher. Rising, she hurried up to her bedroom where she gathered her wand, a crystal amulet infused with power to ward off evil, and a bracelet that was capable of imbuing her wand with added strength. Lifting a hand to the medallion Ava had given her, she glanced around the room, thinking she could summon anything else she might need.

She was about to go up to Ava's workshop when Raedan materialized in the room. "I didn't expect to see you again tonight," she said, smiling. "But I'm so glad you're here."

"I came for a good-night kiss. Or maybe two."

"Or three?"

"As many as you can spare," he murmured, drawing her into his embrace. "Do I need to keep count?"

"Never." Lily closed her eyes as he bent his head toward hers. As always, warmth flowed through her as he kissed her again, and yet again, until her knees were weak. She moaned softly when he raised his head. "Don't stop."

"Ava is coming," he said, frowning. "Where are the two of you going?"

"What do you mean?"

"It's a simple question."

"We're going to see the Knights of the Dark Wood."

"Indeed?"

"Ava thinks they might have the answer to opening the black book, or maybe the secret to destroying the blood-demon without harming you."

"And you didn't think to tell me?"

"I just found out a little while ago."

He grunted softly, then released her when Ava knocked on the door.

"Lily, are you ready?" Ava called and then paused. "Is Raedan with you?"

"Yes. Come on in."

Lily felt the tension in the room go up a notch as witch and vampire regarded each other. Mason stood in the hall-way, behind Ava, his hand resting on her shoulder.

"I guess Lily told you what we're planning," Ava remarked.

Raedan nodded. "In a way. Are you leaving now?"

"Yes." Ava held up her hand. "Before you ask, the answer is no. Taking you along isn't a good idea. The Brotherhood still hunt your kind. If we show up with you in tow, they'll never believe that we've come peacefully. Their first instinct will be to destroy you and we don't want any bloodshed while we're there."

Raedan nodded slowly. "As you wish." Drawing Lily into his arms again, he kissed her lightly. "I will see you soon."

"I'll miss you."

"And I, you." He kissed her again, and then vanished from the room.

"I have a bad feeling about this," Ava muttered, wondering what the odds were that Raedan would stay behind. "Grab your things, Lily. It's time to go."

The Stronghold of the Knights of the Dark Wood was located in the Dark Forest in Connecticut, so named because it sat in the dark shadows of three mountains. Lily shivered as they made their way through the forest, which was rumored to be haunted, or so Ava had told her when they arrived. Lily had no doubt it was true. She could feel the lingering shadows of old death and decay, of sorcery and black magic. According to Ava, the place had once been known as Owlsbury, and had started as a small settlement way back in 1740. It had been a popular place until people and animals started disappearing without a trace. By the twentieth century, all the descendants of the town had died or moved away.

Ava had made no move to hide their presence so Lily wasn't surprised when a delegation of Knights was waiting for them outside the Stronghold when they arrived. Made of dark gray stone, the place resembled an ancient fortress, complete with turrets at the four corners.

"Who goes there?" demanded one of the Knights, his hand resting on the hilt of his sword.

"Please tell Jeremy 26 that Ava Morgana Langley wishes to speak to him."

The Knight frowned as he stared at her. "I know you," he said.

"And I know you, Arnold 18. Please be so kind as to deliver my message."

The Knight glanced from Lily to Mason and back to Ava. "Jason 30, advise the Elder Knight of their request."

With a nod, the designated Knight rapped on one of the large double doors. It opened immediately and he disappeared inside.

"This is a hell of a place," Mason remarked. "Do you really think he'll see us?"

"I'm sure of it," Ava said.

She had barely uttered the words when the door opened and they were ushered into a large, open area paved with stones. Twelve Knights were gathered there, all standing at attention.

A moment later, a Knight wearing a long white robe strode into the center of the opening. He was a tall man, somewhere in his mid-forties. Hair that had once been dark brown was now sprinkled with gray. His eyes were a sharp, a shade darker than his hair.

He inclined his head when he saw Ava. "Please, be seated," he said, gesturing at a long wooden bench.

"Thank you."

Lily and Mason sat on either side of Ava. Lily was filled with trepidation as she glanced around. There was strong magic in this place, both black and white.

At the Elder Knight's signal, two of the men disappeared into the nearest building and returned carrying a jewel-encrusted chair fit for a king. When the Elder Knight was seated, his gaze rested in turn on each of his guests. "Why have you come here, uninvited?"

"I have come to thank you for upholding the truce made years ago. And to offer you and your Knights a gift."

"A gift?" He lifted one brow. "Of what sort?"

"A spell for their swords that will insure that they always strike true."

"That would be welcome indeed," the Elder Knight acknowledged. "And what do you require in return?"

"A small favor," Ava replied. "I have in my possession a small black book that may hold the key to exorcising a blood-demon that has infected an acquaintance of mine. I was hoping you might grant me a few minutes in your library."

"What do you hope to find?"

"A companion book to the one in my possession, one that will tell me how to unlock the secrets of the black book and decipher whatever message it holds."

The Elder Knight stroked his jaw, his brow furrowed as he considered her proposal. "No outsider has ever been allowed access to our library."

"I am aware of that," Ava said, "but I was hoping you would make an exception for an old friend."

"And if I refuse?"

Ava made a vague gesture with her hand. "I cannot believe you would be that foolish."

The Elder Knight's jaw tightened at her thinly veiled threat.

Ava waited patiently. She knew he was remembering the last time she had come to the Stronghold and the mayhem that had ensued.

"I will allow you one hour," he decided.

"That is most gracious of you," Ava said, smiling.

The Elder Knight rose. "Please, follow me."

❧ ❧ ❧

The library was located underground, in a large cavern hewn from stone. Lily shivered as she crossed the threshold, let out a sharp cry as the Elder Knight closed the door behind them, leaving them in total darkness.

Shivering with unease, she called on her magic and summoned a lantern.

And nothing happened.

"Ava!"

"I'm here."

"Something's wrong."

"I know, child. The Elder Knight has betrayed us."

"What do you mean?" Lily's voice echoed against the damp, stone walls.

"When I knew the Elder Knight years ago, he possessed a small amount of magical ability. Since then, I fear he has been hard at work learning Dark Magic from a powerful black witch. Whoever she is, she has warded this room against any and all magic, both black and white and in-between."

"Are you saying we're trapped in here?"

"That depends on the Elder Knight's motives."

"It seems to me his motives are quite obvious," Mason said dryly.

Lily jumped when a deep voice behind her said, "Good thing I am not a witch."

"Raedan!" She cried his name as his arms folded around her waist. "I've never been so glad to see anyone in my life!"

"Be still." Summoning the blood-demon's power and drawing on his own, Raedan focused all his energy on opening the heavy iron door.

Lily buried her face against his back as waves of preternatural power swirled through the room. It caused her stomach to churn, raised the hairs on her arms. There was a harsh, grinding sound, a horrible scream as the door exploded outward, crushing the Knight who been guarding it.

Pale light poured into the cavern.

"Stay behind me," Raedan ordered.

Like good soldiers, Lily, Ava, and Mason followed him up the stairs and down a long, narrow corridor until they were outside again.

The Elder Knight was waiting for them, surrounded by his Knights. Lily noted there were many more than twelve now. If the Elder Knight was surprised to see Raedan, it didn't show on his face.

Moving faster than the eye could follow, Raedan darted behind the Elder Knight, one arm snaking around his chest to hold him immobile. Leaning down, he sank his fangs into the side of the Elder Knight's neck, but only for a moment. "Do you wish to become a vampire?" Raedan asked, his voice dark and deep and filled with menace.

"N...no." Wisely, the Elder Knight didn't move or struggle.

"Do you know the whereabouts of the book Ava is seeking?" Raedan's teeth grazed the Elder Knight's throat. Two thin lines of blood followed in the wake of his fangs. "Do not lie to me."

"Y...yes. I know."

"Send one of your men to fetch it."

"None of them know where to look."

"Tell them." Raedan licked the bit of blood from the Elder Knight's neck. "I advise you to hurry."

"Top shelf, Lance 33. Last bookcase on the right. It has a dark-red cover."

One of the Knights broke ranks and hurried away.

Ava stalked toward the Elder Knight. "What is the name of the witch who instructed you in the Dark Arts?"

"I dare not say." He flinched as Raedan's fangs pierced his throat again. "Hildegaard the Gray."

"Why have you betrayed me?"

"I read the old records and scrolls. I learned many things about the Brotherhood, things that sounded familiar as I read them. I found the witch and asked her if she could restore my memory and when she did, I knew why they sounded familiar. And I decided to return to the Old Ways."

Ava's eyes narrowed. "Pity."

The Knight sent to retrieve the book burst out of the corridor clutching a thin red volume in his hand.

"Give the book to the witch," The Elder Knight said between clenched teeth..

"But..."

"Do as I say!"

The Knight glared at Ava as he thrust the book into her hand, then rejoined his brothers. "We'll be leaving now," Ava said, slipping the book into her skirt pocket. "Raedan bring the Elder Knight."

"No. He is mine."

Ava stared at Raedan, but before she could say anything, he vanished, taking the Knight with him.

Lily let out a gasp as he disappeared. She had little doubt that the Elder Knight would survive the day.

"It seems we're going to need a new Elder Knight," Ava remarked after a moment. Her gaze and her magic moved over the Brotherhood, assessing them one by one. She finally settled on a small, wiry man with cropped blond hair and honest gray eyes. "You, Antonio 55, come to me."

Having no choice, the Knight moved toward her. "You are now the new Elder Knight." Magic swirled around them. "You and your kind will not, I repeat, *not*, hunt Hungarian vampires or white witches. The penalty will be death for all Knights. Do you understand?"

"Yes. I understand."

Gathering her power, Ava chanted softly, then unleased the spell that would make it impossible for any other witch to change or diminish the directive she had imposed. She moved slowly from Knight to Knight, chanting a similar spell to reinforce her words with each individual Knight, assuring their lifelong obedience.

When she was done, Mason slipped his arm around her, knowing that casting so many spells in such a short amount of time would have drained her.

"We can go now," Ava said, clinging to the warlock. "We have what we came for."

CHAPTER THIRTY-ONE

Lily rested in the easy chair in Ava's living room, her mind in turmoil. Mason and her great-grandmother sat on the sofa across the way, whispering to each other. Occasionally, Lily heard her name mentioned, and once, Raedan's. She felt a rush of jealousy as she watched Mason caress Ava's cheek. Where was Raedan? Didn't he know she was missing him? She wondered if he had drained the Elder Knight dry and immediately shied away from the obvious answer.

How could she live with a man who killed others? Even when she knew he had done it because of her? The Knight had put her life in danger and for that, he had to die.

"Lily. Lily?"

She looked up, realizing that Ava had called her name several times.

"We're going up to bed. We'll examine the red book tomorrow morning. I'm too tired to do it tonight."

"All right. Good night, Granny. Mason."

Ava kissed Lily on the cheek and then, hand-in-hand, she and Mason went up the stairs.

Lily stared after them, silent tears tracking her cheeks, her heart aching to be with Raedan.

How often had she sat alone, waiting, wondering where he was?

❦   ❦   ❦

Raedan paced the floor of his lair, pausing now and then to stare at the Elder Knight who cowered in a corner, watching his every move. He had intended to drain the man dry for daring to put Liliana's life in danger. And he had come damn close to doing just that, but as the man's heartbeat began to slow, he pictured the stark disapproval in Liliana's eyes when he told her what he had done. Filled with self-loathing, he had stopped before it was too late.

And the blood-demon had laughed.

Cursing, Raedan pulled the Knight to his feet and transported the two of them to a tavern where he bought the man a glass of orange juice and a glass of wine before he wiped all memory of what had happened from his mind.

When that done, he transported the two of them to Ava's house and rang the bell. Several moments passed before the door opened and Mason stood there, glaring at him. "Do you know what time it is?" the warlock growled. "What the hell do you want?"

Raedan opened the screen door and shoved the Elder Knight inside.

Mason reared back in surprise. "What am I supposed to do with him?"

"I really don't give a damn," Raedan growled, and vanished into the darkness.

Peering over the rail on the upstairs landing, Ava called, "Who was that at the door?"

"Raedan."

"Raedan! What did he want?"

"Come and see."

Holding her robe closed, Ava descended the stairs, only to come to an abrupt halt when she saw the former Elder Knight standing in the foyer, looking confused. "I don't believe it."

"What?"

"I don't believe this man is still alive. I was sure…" Ava shook her head. "Well, I've got to wipe his memory. I can't have him going back to the Brotherhood thinking he's still the Elder Knight."

Mason grunted softly. "No, I guess not."

Between them, they got the former Elder Knight settled on a chair in the kitchen. It took only moments for Ava to implant the new memories she wanted him to have.

"What do we do with him now?" Mason asked.

Ava shrugged. "Send him back to the Stronghold, I guess. We can't just turn him loose in the city. I'll take care of it in the morning." She glanced over her shoulder as Liliana padded into the kitchen.

Lily's eyes grew wide when she saw the Knight. "He's alive," she murmured, her voice filled with wonder.

"So it would seem," Ava said.

"I don't believe it." Lily stared at the Knight. He looked dazed and she realized he was under one of Ava's spells. "He didn't kill him." A slow smile spread over her lips. "I was so sure he'd…do you know what this means?"

"That he wasn't hungry?" Ava said dryly.

"No. Don't you see? It means Raedan was in control of the blood-demon." Humming softly, she floated back up the stairs to her room.

Ava stared after her granddaughter. Maybe there was hope for the vampire, after all.

Everyone in the house slept late the next morning. After a leisurely breakfast, Ava transported the former Elder Knight back to the Stronghold and left him there. It was almost noon when she returned.

"Well, that's done! I had to make a little change to the memories of all the other Knights to make them forget Jeremy 26 had once been the Elder Knight." Clapping her hands, she said, "Come on, we have work to do."

Lily and Mason followed Ava up to her work room. Mason conjured some padded stools and the three of them sat at her work table.

Ava summoned her magic, casting every spell of undoing she knew but to no avail. The red book refused to open. "Mason?"

"I can try," he said with a shrug.

His magic was different than Ava's, Lily thought. Not stronger. Not more powerful. Just different. Was it because he was a warlock? Or because he came from another country?

Mason shook his head. "I don't feel anything."

"Let me try," Lily said.

Ava and Mason exchanged glances, then Ava shrugged. "What have we got to lose?"

Closing her eyes, Lily placed her left hand on the cover, felt it grow warm beneath her palm. She jerked her arm back when there was a blinding flash of light and the cover flipped open. The first page was blank. The second page was filled with words in some foreign language hand-written by a delicate hand.

"I can't make heads or tails of it," Ava said. "Can either of you read it?"

"Not me," Mason said. "I've never seen anything like that."

"Nor I." Ava glanced at Lily, one brow raised.

Lily shook her head and then she focused her thoughts on Raedan. A moment later, she felt his presence in her mind. *I need your help.*

Are you in trouble?

No. We're trying to decipher the red book. It's written in a language we've never seen before. I was hoping maybe you could help us. Picking up the book, she was aware that he was seeing it through her eyes. It was the strangest sensation she had ever known. *Can you read it?*

Yes.

She heard him gasp with pain. *What's wrong?*

The demon… He was panting now, his voice tight. *The demon… he knows what we're trying to do. He wants me to stop.*

Lily felt Raedan's agony as the blood-demon clawed at his insides in an obvious effort to distract him.

It is in… the dragonian language.

Dragonian? she queried. *I've never heard of it.*

It is an ancient language, long forgotten. Raedan took several deep breaths. *If I am reading it correctly, it says you need to sprinkle the blood of a virgin on the pages.* A low groan erupted from his throat. *Once that is done, the words will be revealed.*

The blood of a virgin?

That's what it says. Do you know any?

Lily grimaced at the faint note of laughter in his voice, amazed that he could find humor when the demon was tormenting him. He meant her and they both knew it. *I might know one.*

You opened the book, did you not?

Yes. How did you know?

Only a virgin with a pure heart could do it. Another groan was ripped from his throat and he fell silent.

Ava tugged on Lily's arm. "Well?"

"I contacted Raedan. He said we need to sprinkle the blood of a virgin on the pages in order to decipher the writing."

Ava cleared her throat. "I hesitate to ask, but are you still...?"

Lily felt a blush rise in her cheeks. "Yes, Granny. I am."

"That explains why neither Mason nor I could open it," Ava murmured. "Well, shall we give it a try?"

"Let's get it over with."

Ava picked up her athame and made a small cut in Lily's palm, then, holding Lily's hand over the red book, she slowly turned the pages, letting Lily's blood fall on each one in turn. The drops hissed and smoked as they dripped onto the pages. As the blood sizzled and disappeared, the words were revealed one by one.

"It worked!" Ava exclaimed. She leaned forward, and then frowned. "I can't read it, Lily. Can you?"

"Yes. It says there is but one way to destroy a blood-demon. The one infected must fill a silver chalice with the blood of a black dragon, add seven drops of a virgin's blood, and a dash of nightshade, which the infected one must consume at the witching hour under a full moon."

"Is that all it says?"

Lily turned the page. "No. It says the words needed to unleash the spell are contained in the black book and will only be revealed when the necessary ingredients have been assembled and three drops of the virgin's blood have been sprinkled on the cover and three on the page."

"Is there more?"

Fingers shaking, Lily turned to the last page. All the color drained from her face as she read the next few words.

"What does it say?" Ava asked.

"If the virgin's blood is not pure, or if the one who drinks the potion is unworthy, death follows." Lily looked up at Ava. "There's a chance Raedan could die if he drinks it."

I'm willing to take that chance to be free of the demon.

But I'm not.

It is my *decision, Liliana. I have carried the demon for centuries.*

Lily gasped as she felt Raedan's agony engulf her. How did he endure it?

A harsh cry of pain escaped his throat. *I cannot bear it any longer.*

Knowing there was no point in arguing, Lily grasped at the only straw left. "Where are we going to find a dragon?" All she knew about dragons was what she had seen in movies like *The Hobbit* and *Harry Potter* and her favorite, *Dragonheart,* starring Sean Connery as the dragon. "Even if such creatures really exist, where on earth would we find one?"

"I have no idea," Ava said. "The only dragons I've ever heard about are in fairytales."

"Many fairytales are based on truth," Mason remarked.

I may know where to find one.

Lily's heart sank when she heard Raedan's voice in her mind. How could he be so eager to risk his life?

There were rumors of a dragon in the Southern Carpathian Mountains of Transylvania over three centuries ago. Whether it was truth or fiction at the time is anyone's guess. But if the rumors were based on truth, there is no one left to ask if the beast is still alive.

Discouraged, Lily repeated what Raedan had said.

"I guess we'll have to go to Romania and see for ourselves," Ava said cheerfully. "I haven't been there in years. We'll leave in the morning."

"What about Raedan?" Lily asked.

"I guess you'll want him to come along."

"I guess you're right."

"Ask him if he'll transport us," Ava said. "He can get us there a lot faster than I can."

Raedan had slipped out of Liliana's mind after agreeing to transport them to Romania. He closed his eyes as the blood-demon's insidious power gradually subsided. How many times had he thought of taking his own life to escape the demon's influence? To escape the agony of feeling as though his veins were on fire, as if his internal organs were slowly being ripped to shreds?

Thrusting the painful memories away, he turned his thoughts toward home. He had been born in a small town outside Brasov over nine centuries ago. Had spent his whole mortal life in Romania, and the first two hundred and fifty years after he had been turned.

The Carpathian Mountains were divided into three ranges, the Western Carpathians, the Eastern, and the Southern, sometimes known as the Transylvanian Alps. There had always been rumors of dragons in the Southern Carpathian Mountains, he thought, staring into the darkness of his lair, but he had never seen one, or known anyone who had. But that didn't mean one didn't exist, or that the existence of dragons was beyond the realm of possibility. Vlad Dracul had belonged to the Order of the Dragon. Some believed his son, named Dracula, which meant son of Dracul or son of the dragon, was the first vampire, although there were no historical facts to support that theory.

Romania. He had not been there in centuries. Had no desire to return. There were too many painful memories there, parts of his life after he had been turned that he preferred be left buried and forgotten.

But he could not, would not, let Liliana go without him.

CHAPTER THIRTY-TWO

They had agreed to meet just before sundown the following night, which would put them in Transylvania at four in the afternoon. Raedan arrived at Ava's wearing a long, black cloak with the hood up, gloves, and a pair of dark sunglasses. He found Ava, Mason, and Liliana in the living room.

"Are you ready?" he asked, glancing from one to the other.

"I think so," Ava said.

Lily smiled at Raedan. "Aren't you going to kiss me hello?"

He glanced briefly at Ava, then put his arms around Liliana and kissed her lightly.

"Is that the best you can do?" Lily teased.

"For now," he said, conscious of Ava's disapproval and Mason's amusement. Although Ava had stopped objecting to his courting Liliana, he knew she wasn't happy about it, and likely never would be. "Where are we going?"

Ava handed him a slip of paper with an address and a map drawn on it. "I rented a house in Transylvania."

Raedan nodded as he studied the crude map. The house was in the country outside the city itself. "Ready?"

His three companions each picked up a small suitcase.

"Now what?" Lily asked.

"Ava and Mason, come stand on my left and hold onto each other. Liliana, stand on my other side and put your arm around my waist." When they had done as instructed, Raedan put one arm around Ava's waist and the other around Liliana's. "This is going to take a minute or two. It will probably make you feel nauseous, maybe disoriented. Just close your eyes and hang on. Here we go."

Lily closed her eyes, her heart pounding with fear and anticipation. Raedan had transported her short distances before, but never so far. What if something went wrong? Would they be forever lost in some never-never land? She held Raedan tighter as her stomach dropped to her toes and the world went black.

When reality returned, they were standing outside a small, two-story farmhouse located on a swath of green grass. It was a darling place, Lily thought, built of white brick with a blue, peaked roof and matching shutters on the windows. The front door was white with blue flowers painted on it, the chimney was red brick. A white stone path led to the door.

"Everyone all right?" Raedan asked, his arm still around Liliana. She nodded, though she looked a little pale.

Ava clung to Mason. "I'd forgotten what that's like," she said, grinning.

The warlock looked a little green.

"The key is under a clay pot beside the front door," Ava said, staggering forward.

Raedan followed close on her heels, eager to get out of the sun.

Lily smiled as Raedan escorted her inside. The house was quaint, the furniture old-fashioned. A colorful braided rug covered the wooden floor in front of the hearth. Pretty lace curtains hung at the windows. A flowered sofa and two matching chairs stood in front of the fireplace.

"There are two bedrooms upstairs." Ava glanced at Raedan. "And a small, windowless attic."

Raedan nodded, a wry smile twisting his lips. The message was plain, he thought. He would be sleeping alone. But the attic was perfect; it would be dark during the day. Taking

Liliana's hand, he said, "I am going up to rest. I will see you in a few hours."

"All right."

He kissed her on the cheek, then headed up the narrow staircase.

Lily and the others spent the next several minutes putting their few belongings away and looking around the house. It was fairy-tale cute, Lily thought. She could easily imagine the seven dwarfs singing and dancing with Snow White in front of the fireplace.

In addition to the parlor, there was a small dining room, a bathroom with a claw-footed tub, a round sink, and an old-fashioned commode with a pull chain. No shower. The kitchen was fairly large, furnished with a table and four chairs, a stove, and a small refrigerator. Shelves and cupboards held an assortment of pots, pans, and dishes.

At length, they retired to the parlor. Ava and Mason settled on the sofa.

Lily sat in one of the chairs. "So, how do we go about finding a dragon? Do we just go hiking in the mountains and hope we get lucky? Ring a bell?"

Ava glanced skyward, as if seeking help. "Hardly. After dinner, we'll try our hand at a dragon location spell. I doubt we'll be successful, since we don't have skin or blood or bone of the creature to guide us."

"Maybe the demon can show us the way," Mason suggested.

"Maybe," Ava said, "but doubtful. I'm sure it knows what we're up to. I'm not even sure Raedan will be any help, since the blood-demon will likely thwart him at every turn. On the other hand, in fairytales, dragons sometimes defended the princess," she said, smiling at Lily.

"Maybe the dragon will come to us."

Lily stared at her great-grandmother, a shiver skating down her spine as she imagined a big, black, scaly dragon carrying her off to a dark cave in the Carpathian Mountains. "You're kidding, aren't you?"

"Of course, dear."

In spite of Ava's words, Lily wasn't reassured.

At five-thirty, Ava went into the kitchen and conjured dinner—spaghetti, meatballs, Caesar salad, a loaf of garlic bread warm from the oven, and a bottle of wine.

An hour later, as the sun was setting, Raedan appeared at the table. Lily felt a thrill of excitement when she looked at him. Had any man ever been as handsome, as sexy, or as beautiful as he was? Her insides turned to mush when he dropped into the ladder-back chair beside her and reached for her hand. The touch of his fingers entwining with hers made her heart swell in her chest.

"Good evening, love."

"Hi."

"We were wondering how to find the dragon if it exists," Ava said. "Do you have any ideas?"

"Since it is unlikely that the beast will come to us, I suppose we will have to go to him."

"You mean just go wandering around the mountains hoping we bump into it?"

Raedan shrugged. "Perhaps you can call him here, to you, although bringing a dragon into the countryside might not be the best idea."

"A good point," Mason remarked dryly.

With a wave of her hand, Ava cleared the table. A word summoned a detailed map of the Carpathian Mountains. After unfolding it, she said, "So, where do we look first?"

It was after midnight when Raedan kissed Liliana good night and left the house. Ava and Mason had gone to bed earlier, but it was hours until dawn and he needed to feed.

He sensed the others as soon as he stepped out the front door. He paused as a half-dozen male vampires materialized out of the darkness, fangs gleaming in the moonlight.

One of them stepped forward, unleashing his preternatural power as he did so.

The Master of the City, Raedan thought, come to assert his authority. Raedan smiled faintly as he unleashed his own power. It drove the Master of the City to his knees, though his head remained unbowed.

The others took a wary step back.

"What do you want?" Raedan asked, though he knew perfectly well why they had come.

"We want no trouble," the Master of the City replied, bristling at Raedan's tone. "It is my right to question those who come into my territory."

Raedan inclined his head. "It is, indeed. I have no wish to usurp your authority. But I warn you that if you harm those under my protection, you will not survive long enough to regret it."

"I understand."

"How are you called?"

"Bondurant. And you?"

"Raedan."

The vampire's eyes grew wide.

Raedan arched one brow. "You have heard of me?"

"Who has not?"

Raedan grunted softly as he gestured for the Master of the City to rise. Most vampires knew of him, and about the blood-demon that possessed him.

"Why have you come here?" Bondurant asked.

"My companions and I are looking for a black dragon. Have you seen one?"

"No."

"Do you know if one exists?"

"According to legend, a dragon lives in a cave high in the Carpathians. No one has seen it, only the blackened remains of those who didn't live to tell of their encounter with the beast."

"I thank you for your help," Raedan said. "I trust you will not object if I hunt in your territory?"

"And I trust you will not leave bodies in your wake."

"You have my word."

With a nod, the Master of the City melted into the shadows, and his companions with him.

Whistling softly, Raedan went in search of prey.

Lily tossed and turned in her bed after Raedan kissed her good night. She knew he had gone to feed. She knew it was necessary for his own survival, and to keep the blood-demon satisfied, as well, but she couldn't help worrying. Or missing him. They hadn't had much time alone together lately. Was he losing interest? Getting tired of her? With Ava and Mason in the house and their bedroom right next to hers, it was doubtful she and Raedan would get to have any private moments together in the near future.

Unable to sleep, she threw the covers aside and went to stand at the window. Outside, all was dark and quiet. There were no lights to be seen save for the millions of stars sprinkled across the indigo sky. Where was he?

I am on my way to you.

Raedan!

He appeared beside her in a shower of shimmering motes, his arms wrapping around her waist to draw her body flush with his as he bent his head and claimed her lips in a long, searing kiss that drove every thought, every doubt, from her mind. He kissed her again and yet again, his hungry hands caressing her, his tongue hot against her skin as he backed her toward the bed, lifted her onto it, and covered her body with his.

Breathless, she wrapped her arms and legs around him as he rained kisses on her brow, her cheeks, her eyelids, the curve of her throat.

"Let me." His voice was a low growl in her ear.

She wasn't sure what he was asking, but she didn't care. She had waited so long, wanted him so badly, she was willing to give him anything he desired.

She felt the gentle prick of his fangs at her throat, sighed as pleasure surged through her, warm and sweet and intoxicating. She writhed beneath him, then went still when he pushed her nightgown up over her hips. His hands were cool against her bare skin and she closed her eyes. He was going to make love to her, and she was going to let him.

Abruptly, he rolled away from her and sat up, his back toward her.

"Don't stop," she whispered. His back was rigid when she touched him.

"Believe me, I do not want to." He raked his fingers through his hair. "But we need a virgin, remember? And for now, you are the only one we have."

Lily stared at him, not knowing whether to laugh or cry. How could he think of *that* at a moment like this?

"I am sorry, Liliana," he said quietly. "Forgive me."

How could she not? He was fighting a demon, fighting for his very existence, for their life together.

Sitting up, she wrapped her arms around his waist and rested her cheek against his broad back. "There's nothing to forgive. I love you, Raedan."

Turning, he pulled her onto his lap and held her close. "Ah, Liliana, you are a rare creature, and more precious to me than you will ever know."

"Promise me we'll have time alone together when this is over."

"I promise," he murmured. She was so young, so foolish to put her trust in him. But then, he was equally foolish to think he could keep the blood-demon forever at bay.

In the morning, after breakfast, Lily, Ava, and Mason gathered around the kitchen table to discuss how best to find the dragon.

"We have to consider Raedan," Ava said. "I don't know how long or how often he can be exposed to the sun when it's at its hottest. Protective clothing might help, or we might have to start hunting later in the afternoon and on into the night. Or we can go without him. After all, he could come to us in an instant."

Lily shivered at the thought of being in the Carpathian Mountains after dark.

"It might take us days to find the thing," Mason said. "We also need to decide whether to camp out or return here every night."

"Fortunately, whatever we decide won't be a problem," Ava said. "We can conjure whatever we need whenever we need it."

Mason nodded. "True enough."

"We need to be mindful of bears and wolves," Lily remarked. She shrugged when Ava and Mason looked at her. "I did some research before breakfast. I guess both are plentiful in the mountains. Lynxes and wildcats, too."

"Good to know," Mason said.

"I'm pretty sure they won't bother us," Ava said. "Most animals shy away from vampires. And witches."

"I hope so," Lily murmured. "There's also deer, wild cats, and wild boars. And bison."

"I doubt if any of them are as dangerous as Raedan and the blood-demon," Ava said dryly. "Let's plan to leave late this afternoon. We'll decide whether to spend the night later."

With a nod, Mason slapped his hands on the table. "I need to get out and stretch my legs. Anybody want to come along?"

"Sounds good to me," Ava said. "Lily?"

Smothering a grin at their none-to-subtle desire to be alone, Lily shook her head. "You two go ahead. I think I'll read for a while. And maybe take a nap."

They were like a couple of horny teenagers, Lily mused as they hurried outside.

She sat there a moment, staring out the kitchen window, and then padded up the stairs to the attic. She hesitated outside the door, then turned the handle as quietly as she could and peered inside.

There was nothing in the room save for an old leather-bound trunk. And one very handsome vampire clad in nothing but a pair of black sweat pants. He rested on his back on the hard plank floor. No blanket. No pillow. She should have conjured a bed for him, Lily thought. Or at least a mattress.

She stood in the open doorway for several minutes, just looking at him, admiring the sheer masculine beauty of him, the unyielding line of his jaw, the sensuous curve of his lips, his fine straight nose, the symmetry of his bare chest, his muscular arms, and long, long legs.

"If you do not stop looking at me like you, you will have me blushing in a minute."

"Oh! I thought you were asleep!"

"I was." He turned his head and regarded her through eyes dark with amusement. "Sheer beauty?"

A rush of heat flooded her cheeks. "You're making fun of me."

"No, I am not." He held out his hand. "I am flattered."

She stepped into the room, reached for his hand, and sat beside him. "Aren't you uncomfortable on the floor?"

"No."

"Well, I am." She murmured a few words and a mattress sprang up beneath them, along with two fluffy pillows covered in blue silk cases. "There, that's better."

"Much," he agreed, and tugged her down beside him. "What would Ava say about this?"

Lily made a dismissive gesture with her hand as she rolled onto her side, facing him, her head resting on his shoulder. "She's out 'walking' with Mason. I'm pretty sure she isn't thinking about me."

He grunted softly as his hand stroked lightly up and down her thigh. "You are playing with fire, girl. You know that, do you not?"

"I'm perfectly safe," she said, her lips twitching in a grin. "I'm a virgin and off-limits, remember?"

"As if I could forget," he muttered. He turned onto his side so they were lying face to face, bodies aligned shoulder-to-thigh. "You are a wicked woman, Liliana Falconer. And too damn trusting for your own good."

"You won't hurt me."

"Are you so sure about that?"

"If I wasn't, I wouldn't be here."

"And the demon? Do you trust him, too? Even now, he is urging me to bury my fangs in your throat and drain you dry."

"But you won't," she said, her voice hoarse and uncertain.

"No, I will not." Lucky for her, the blood-demon was weak during the day, though no less hungry for her blood. His fingertips drifted over her lips, tracing their outline, before he covered her mouth with his.

Lily sighed as her eyelids fluttered down. She ran her hands over his bare back, feeling his muscles flex at her touch, hearing the quickening in his breathing as he deepened the kiss, his tongue dueling with hers, his hands bringing her body to vibrant life everywhere he touched.

Lily stilled when she felt the light scrape of his fangs at her throat. "Raedan."

"Just a sip, love."

She stared up at the ceiling as he drank from her, her whole body tense. He was right, she thought. She was indeed playing with fire.

Her breath whooshed out of her lungs in a sigh of relief when his tongue ran over the bites in her throat, sealing the tiny wounds.

"Thank you, my sweet Liliana. I need to rest if we are going dragon hunting later. Will you stay with me?"

"For a while, if you like."

"I should like it very much." It was a rare thing, resting with a woman beside him—a woman he loved more than his very existence. He brushed a kiss across her cheek, closed his eyes, and fell into darkness.

Lily stayed beside Raedan for an hour, content to lie there beside him, her head on his shoulder, her fingers playing in the dark hair sprinkled across his chest. He didn't seem to breathe while he was at rest. What would it be like to spend the remainder of her life with him? She had grown up with vampires, but her father's kind were different from Raedan in so many ways.

It didn't matter, she thought, as she gained her feet and tiptoed out of the attic. Nothing mattered but her love for him and his for her. Her parents had overcome numerous obstacles and survived. Why couldn't they?

Raedan slept until just after three in the afternoon. Rising, he pulled on a pair of black jeans, a long-sleeved navy-blue shirt, gloves, and a pair of boots, donned his sunglasses and left the house.

He transported himself to the nearest town and dined on a pretty, dark-haired young woman before returning to the rental house. He found Lily, Mason, and Ava gathered in the living room, munching on a plate of chocolate chip cookies and washing them down with glasses of milk.

"There you are!" Lily exclaimed. "I went upstairs to wake you a few minutes ago and you were gone."

Raedan glanced briefly at the cookie plate. "I went out in search of a snack of my own."

"I should have known," Lily said with a smirk.

"Well, now that we're all here," Ava said, "we should get going."

As he had before, Raedan gathered the three witches around him and transported them to the upper reaches of the Carpathian Mountains with its virgin forests and lofty peaks. He caught the scents of wildlife—red deer and wild cats, the stink of a long-dead carcass buried under a pile of dry leaves.

From this height, he could look out across the valleys below, lush and green at this time of year. A narrow swath of blue indicated a river far off to the north. A small herd of sheep grazed along the banks. The cliffs, the peaks, and the mountainsides were lush with wildflowers and plants, many of them medicinal. He had heard that traditional Transylvanian villagers still used the old mountain remedies.

It reminded him of an old Carpathian legend surrounding the polovraga plant that was said to date back to the Dacians. The ancient, elusive plant was purported to have the power to heal any sickness. Believers still came from all over the world to search for it.

Redan took a deep breath and let it out in a long slow sigh. Even after so many centuries away, it smelled like home.

CHAPTER THIRTY-THREE

The dragon stirred as his senses warned him that his territory had been invaded by humans from below. It had been over a century since anyone had dared to invade his domain. His lair was littered with the scorched, dry bones of those humans who had been foolish enough to travel here.

Moving to the mouth of the cave, he spread his massive wings. Perhaps it was time to show these puny humans the folly of encroaching on land where they were not wanted or welcome.

He lifted his head as the wind shifted and he caught a scent he had missed before.

The ancient, near-forgotten scent of demon blood.

Chapter Thirty-Four

L ily paused to take a deep breath. They had been wandering the narrow, twisting trails of the mountain for hours, searching for the dragon's lair, but to no avail. Small critters had scurried out of their path. Once, she had seen a stag lurking in the shadows. Another time she had seen a brown bear off in the distance. It had stared at her for a long moment before turning and lumbering away.

And now the sun was setting in a blaze of crimson and ochre and pink. A cool breeze blew out of the east, chilling the air around them.

Ahead of her, Raedan stopped and glanced over his shoulder. "Are you all right?"

"Just a little out of breath," she said. "We're awfully high up."

"We can rest if you like," he said.

"I think that's a great idea," Ava said, coming up behind Lily. "We've been walking for hours."

"How do you know we're going in the right direction?" Mason asked.

"I do not know for sure," Raedan admitted. "But when I was a child, all the stories I heard said the dragon lived somewhere in this part of the mountains."

"Well," Ava said, sinking down on a fallen log, "that's good enough for me."

Mason sat beside her. "I don't sense anything."

"I don't either," Ava said. "And yet…"

"What?" Lily asked.

"I have the feeling we're being watched."

Raedan slipped his arm around Lily's waist. "We are."

"Have you seen something?" Mason asked.

"No. The demon told me."

Lily shivered. "Is it the dragon?"

"Probably." He glanced up the mountain, shouted "Hit the dirt!" as a great black dragon swooped out of the sky and arrowed toward them.

A roar shook the earth as a blast of red-hot fire ignited a stand of timber only yards away from where Lily cowered on the ground in the shelter of Raedan's body.

Lying on her belly beside Mason, Ava uttered an incantation that extinguished the flames, leaving smoking, black trunks and branches behind.

"I think we found him," Lily said in a shaky voice. "Can we go home now?"

Moments later, Lily sat in a chair in their rented house, a cup of hot chocolate cradled in her hands, a blanket draped over her shoulders. She couldn't stop shivering. Never, in all her life, had she seen anything so scary, so ferocious. A great, horned dragon with shiny black scales, huge ebony-colored wings that cut through the air like a giant scythe, a whip-like tail, and foot-long talons. She might have thought it beautiful if the sight of it hadn't scared her half to death.

Raedan sat beside her, his thoughts obviously turned inward. He hadn't said a word since they left the mountain.

Ava and Mason huddled on the sofa, their heads together, making Lily wonder what they were plotting.

After what seemed like hours, Raedan stood and paced the floor. When he stopped, Ava and Mason looked up at him.

"I am going to the mountain tomorrow night," he declared. "Alone."

"Are you crazy?" Lily exclaimed. "He'll incinerate you!"

Raedan shrugged. "Better me than you. Besides, I am not sure your magic will have any effect on the beast. I felt his power as he swept by. His rage. But it was turned toward the three of you. Not me."

"I don't understand," Ava said. "You're the most dangerous one of us all."

"There is a link of some kind between the dragon and the blood-demon," Raedan said. "I do not know what it is, only that it is there."

"I won't have it," Lily said adamantly. "You can't go alone. I forbid it."

Stroking her cheek, he murmured, "Liliana, my love, you cannot stop me."

There was nothing more to be done that night. Raedan waited until the household was asleep before he went in search of prey. He needed to feed and feed well if he intended to face the dragon on the morrow.

He stalked the quiet streets of Transylvania, preying on any mortal foolish enough to be out and about so late— mostly tourists seeking excitement of one kind or another.

Curiosity and a morbid sense of humor had him following a young couple.

"Are you game to visit Dracula's castle tomorrow?" the young man asked his companion. "I bought a couple of tickets this morning. It might be fun."

"Why not? It isn't really the home of Dracula, you know," the woman said flippantly. "I mean, there's no such thing as vampires. Dracula is based on fiction, not fact."

"How do you know?" the man asked. "Don't you think the whole vampire thing would have died out years ago if there was no truth to it?"

His companion shrugged. "There are stories of Nessie and Big Foot, too, and no concrete evidence that either of them ever existed, either."

Raedan grinned as the couple turned down a shadowy street. Dissolving into mist, he moved ahead of them and then stopped beside an alley. He materialized when they were abreast of him..

The couple came to an abrupt halt. The woman let out a shriek as she grabbed the man's arm.

The man tried to speak, but the words wouldn't come.

"I hear you are going to Castle Dracula tomorrow," Raedan said, glancing from one to the other.

The woman nodded, her face pale, her eyes wide. "Who … who are you?"

"*I* am Dracula."

The woman stared at him, and then she laughed nervously. "Very funny. Come on, Jerry."

"You do not believe me?" Raedan asked.

"Of course not!" she exclaimed. She tugged on her boyfriend's arm, frowned when he didn't move.

Raedan let his eyes go red as he took a step toward her.

The woman gasped when she tried to back away—and realized that, like her companion, she couldn't move.

Raedan flashed his fangs. "Do you believe me now?" he asked, his voice silky-soft with menace.

She swallowed hard. "They … they could be plastic."

"They could be," he growled as he folded his hands over her shoulders. "But they are not."

She let out a startled cry as he sank his fangs into the soft skin of her throat. Her blood was warm but not so sweet or so satisfying as Liliana's. But he hadn't expected it to be.

When Raedan had taken as much as he dared, he turned to her partner. Ordinarily, he didn't drink from men, but there were no other people on the street and he needed to be at his most powerful tomorrow night.

When he lifted his head from the man's neck, he found the woman watching him intently.

"You really are Dracula," she murmured.

"A distant cousin, perhaps. Enjoy your visit to the castle." He released them from his thrall, bowed in the woman's direction, and vanished from their sight.

Raedan found Liliana sitting on the mattress in his attic room when he returned to the house. "What are you doing here?" he asked. "I thought you had gone to bed."

"Where have you been?"

He arched one brow in amusement. "Where do you think?"

A silly question, she thought. What else would he be doing in the middle of the night?

"It's late," he remarked. "You should get some sleep."

She grabbed his hand and pulled him down beside her. "Raedan, please don't go after the dragon by yourself. I'm afraid."

"I will not put your life or Ava's in danger," he said quietly. "I do not think the dragon intended to kill us today. I think it was merely a warning."

"And if it wasn't?"

"Liliana…"

She pressed her fingertips to his lips. "Please don't go." Falling back on the mattress, she tugged him down beside her, cupped his face in her hands and kissed him.

He wrapped her in his arms, holding her close, her body flush with his as he took control of the kiss, his tongue ravishing her mouth as his hands stroked over her body. She was warm and pliable, her lips sweeter than life itself, her hair like strands of fine silk against his skin.

He groaned softly as he rose over her, everything forgotten save his desperate need to possess this woman above all others, to make her his, body and soul.

Yes! Take her. Take her now! The blood-demon's voice, exultant, triumphant.

With a low growl, Raedan rolled to his feet and backed away from the bed. *No!*

Lily stared up at him, her whole body throbbing with desire, her lips bruised from his kisses. She had failed, she thought glumly. She had hoped to seduce him. Without a virgin, they couldn't banish the demon, but she didn't care. She couldn't bear to put Raedan's life at risk. She would rather have him as he was than not at all.

"I love you, Liliana," he said quietly. "I know you are afraid for me, but this is what I want. What I need. I cannot live with the demon inside me any longer. You cannot know how it torments me."

But she did know. She had felt his pain, at least a shadow of it, when the blood-demon had tortured him.

"Will you not help me, my sweet Liliana?"

Tears welled in her eyes when she heard the anguish, the soft pleading, in his voice. How could she refuse? Rising, she went into his arms and laid her cheek against his chest.

Whispering, "Thank you, love," he brushed a kiss across the top of her head before carrying her back to her own bed.

"Will you stay with me, Raedan?"

He nodded slowly. "Until you fall asleep." He waited until she slid under the covers, then he heeled off his boots and stretched out on the top of the covers beside her.

She wept quietly, her tears wetting his shirt, until sleep carried her away.

And still he stayed, content to hold her while she slept, until the sun peeked through her window. Knowing he might not survive the night, he continued to hold her, willing to endure the discomfort of sun's warmth to be near her a little longer.

When the pain grew unbearable, he kissed her cheek, then sought the lonely darkness of the attic.

CHAPTER THIRTY-FIVE

The pillow beside Lily's still bore the imprint of Raedan's head when she woke in the morning. She smiled inwardly, thinking he had stayed with her long after she had fallen asleep. And long after the rising of the sun. And then she sighed. He was determined to face the dragon alone. Ava and Mason had made no objection. Didn't they care that he might be killed? It was a disquieting thought. Even though Ava had stopped trying to dissuade her from seeing Raedan, Lily knew her great-grandmother didn't approve. Might never approve. She didn't think her parents ever would, either. Was it Raedan himself they objected to? Or the fact that he wasn't a Hungarian vampire? Or the fact that he was possessed by the blood-demon? Or all of the above?

Would they ever accept him? She knew her family loved her. Would always love her, no matter what. But it would be hard to visit them knowing they felt she had made a terrible mistake.

Sighing, she threw the covers aside and headed for the bathroom. She could be worrying for nothing, she thought, as she filled the tub, but she doubted it. He would be putting his life and their future together at risk when he went to the mountain to confront the dragon tonight. And as much as she longed to go with him, she knew he would never allow it, just as she feared that no spell she conjured would be strong enough to protect him. She could wear her invisibility cloak, but he would still know she was there because of the blood link they shared. Like it or not, there was nothing she could do to help.

She fretted all that day, her all-too-vivid imagination shifting into over-drive as it painted one horrible scenario after another. Ava and Mason tried to distract her by taking her to lunch at a popular restaurant in Transylvania. They toured the shops, had tea in a quaint little tea shop, watched a puppet show. And all the while, she imagined Raedan fighting the dragon, being torn to shreds by its razor-sharp talons, scorched by its fiery breath.

Knowing Raedan was safe until nightfall, Lily wished the day would never end. But, all too soon, the sun began its slow descent behind the hills. With the coming darkness, a horrible sense of doom descended on her.

Raedan was waiting for them when they returned to the house. Dressed in black from his shirt to his boots, he looked like the angel of death.

Lily ran to him and threw her arms around his neck. "Don't go!" she begged. "Please don't go."

Ava and Mason quietly left the room.

Raedan held her close, his hand stroking up and down her back while he murmured in her ear, whispering that he loved her, would always love her, promising that he would come back to her.

Leading her to the sofa, he sat and pulled her down beside him, his dark eyes searching hers.

She knew without asking what he wanted.

Pushing her hair away from her neck, she closed her eyes and pulled his head down, sighed as he bit her ever so gently. Pleasure surged through her and she knew that, strange as it seemed, in his own way, he was telling her that he loved her.

She would have been happy to let him take it all, but after only a moment, he lifted his head. "Thank you, my sweet Liliana."

"I love you," she whispered. "I'll never love anyone else."

"Ah, my darling girl, you must promise me that you will not spend your life alone if I do not return. I cannot bear the thought of you in another man's arms, but I would rather that than have you spend your life alone, with no one to love. And no one to love you."

His gaze moved over her face, as if to memorize every feature. "You have given me more happiness in these few months than I have known in nine hundred years."

Murmuring his name, she burst into tears.

He held her close until darkness covered the land.

When he stood, preternatural power radiated from him, raising the hairs along her arms, sending a chill down her spine. She stared up at him, thinking that, for the first time, she was seeing him for what he truly was. He was more than a man. More than a vampire. She felt the blood-demon raging inside him, an evil spirit trapped inside a supernatural being who intended to destroy him. His eyes were so dark, they were almost black.

For the first time since they had met, she was truly afraid of him.

She looked up as Ava and Mason came down the stairs. They came to an abrupt halt when they saw him.

"Lily," Ava said, very softly. "Come to me."

Moving slowly, Lily tiptoed toward her. She shrank back when Raedan turned to look at her.

"Do not mourn for me if I do not return," he said, and his voice was low and deep, like the rumble of distant thunder. "Only remember that wherever I am, I will always love you."

Blinking the tears from her eyes, Lily whispered, "Please come back to me."

But he was already gone.

Dark gray storm clouds hovered over the mountains, shutting out both moon and stars. Lightning flashed in the distance, promising rain before the night was over.

Raedan stood outside the house a moment before transporting himself to the place where they had encountered the dragon the night before.

He smelled the creature as soon as he arrived. A wicked slash of lightning split the skies and in the brief flash, he saw the dragon perched high atop one of the peaks, wings spread, tail whipping angrily back and forth.

Why are you here? The dragon's voice penetrated his mind like fire.

I need your blood.

Foolish man. It is I who will feast on your flesh and drink your blood before the night is through.

I did not come to destroy you.

The dragon's laughter sounded in his ears. *As if you could.*

I need only a cup. Surely you can spare that much.

The dragon hopped down from the peak. Standing so close, he towered over Raedan. Lowering his head, he sniffed Raedan's chest, and then reared back. *Demon, as I thought.*

One possesses me. I wish to rid myself its evil influence.

You think to give it to me?

No. I seek to destroy it. Raedan doubled over as the blood-demon unleashed its power. Excruciating pain, worse than anything he had known before, exploded through every fiber of his being, burning hotter than the sun. He dropped to his knees, his head bowed, as the pain went on and on, clawing at his vitals, turning his blood to fire, threatening to consume him from the inside out.

The dragon looked on impassively for several minutes. He had hated mankind for untold centuries, destroyed all those who had come hunting him and felt nothing at all. But this creature was not a mortal man.

Using one of his razor-sharp talons, the dragon made a tiny cut in the man's shoulder and lapped up the blood. And he felt the man's pain, his anguish, his love for the woman he had left behind. This man, too, had suffered for centuries. A kindred spirit, the dragon mused, as pain continued to rip through the helpless creature.

Raedan looked up when he felt the dragon's mind invade his. Their gazes met and he felt the dragon's pity. *We are alike, you and I. Both outcasts. Both hunted.*

The dragon nodded.

Raedan pulled a flask from his hip pocket and held it up. *Grant me that which I seek, or destroy me and put me out of my misery.*

The dragon regarded him for a long moment, then opened a shallow gash in his massive chest. Thick red blood, so dark it was almost black, oozed from the wound.

Teeth clenched against the agony that engulfed him, Raedan held the flask under the wound, capped the container when it was full. *May I?*

As much as you wish.

Lurching to his feet, Raedan licked the blood still dripping from the wound in the dragon's chest. It burned through him, momentarily distracting the demon and easing the agony that threatened to tear him to ribbons.

My thanks, Lord Dragon. If ever I can be of service, you have only to call my name and I will come.

The dragon dipped his head in acknowledgement, then took to the air as the heavens unleashed a torrent of rain.

Clutching the flask, Raedan transported himself to Ava's house in New Orleans. Feeling drained in mind and body, he burrowed into the soft earth behind the house. Wracked with pain beyond anything he had ever known as the blood-demon fought for control, he curled in on himself and closed his eyes.

Cradled in darkness, he wondered how much longer he could resist. Wondered if he would ever rise again. If it was not to be, if he was fated to rest here, in the bowels of mother earth for all eternity, at least he would be close to Liliana.

It was his last conscious thought before the dark sleep dragged him down into unfeeling oblivion.

CHAPTER THIRTY-SIX

Lily woke bleary-eyed and heart-sick. She had stayed up until dawn, waiting, praying, for Raedan to return, and feared the worst when he did not. *Raedan.* She called his name, searching for the link that bound them together and found only emptiness.

In the bathroom, she splashed cold water on her face, then stumbled into the kitchen.

Ava and Mason sat at the table, the remains of their breakfast still on the table.

Lily flinched at the look of pity in Ava's eyes. It was evident that her great-grandmother also thought Raedan had been destroyed by the dragon.

Rising, Mason nodded at Ava and excused himself from the room.

Lily sank into one of the chairs.

With a wave of her hand, Ava cleared the dishes from the table, then reached for Lily's hand. "There's still hope, child."

Lily shook her head. "He's not coming back."

"You can't be sure of that."

"I tried to contact him. Day or night, he's always answered me when he could." Twin tears trickled down Lily's cheeks. "How am I going to live without him?"

"Life goes on," Ava said quietly. "Even when we don't want it, too."

"I want to go home."

"To Savaria?"

"No, to your house. I don't want to see my parents right now."

It took only moments to gather their things. Ava cast a circle large enough to hold the three of them. When Mason returned, he quickly packed his belongings, then the three of them stood inside the circle while Ava sealed it with her blood. With their arms linked together, Ava chanted the words that carried them home to New Orleans.

When they arrived, Lily went straight to her room and closed the door. Throwing herself face down on the bed, she cried until she was sure she had no tears left, then pulled a blanket over her head and wept some more, until grief and exhaustion carried her away.

"She's young," Mason said, slipping his arm around Ava's shoulders. "She'll get over it, in time."

"I hope so, but they shared more than just a few kisses. He drank her blood. She was able to communicate with him telepathically, even though she never drank his blood in return. I don't know what kind of bond the blood-demon might have created between them, or if his death would sever it. She might grieve for him forever."

"Perhaps Quill can help."

"Or Andras. He's the oldest vampire in the family. If she's not feeling better in a few days, I'll call Callie and Quill. Until then, I think it's best to just leave her alone and let her grieve."

❧ ❧ ❧

Lily moved through the following days like a lost soul. She didn't eat, she rarely slept.

She spent her days curled up on the sofa and her nights outside in the dark because she felt closer to Raedan there. She knew Ava was worried about her, but she didn't care. Raedan had told her not to mourn for him if he didn't return, but how could she help it? In the short time she had known him, he had become her whole life.

She looked up at the sound of footsteps outside her bedroom door.

"Lily? May I come in?"

"Yes, Granny."

"I made your favorite chocolate mousse cake. I know you've forgotten it's my birthday, and I don't blame you. But won't you come down and share it with me?"

Lily nodded. How could she refuse? "I'm sorry," she said as she followed Ava down the stairs.

"It's all right, child. I know you're grieving. It's been over a week now. What do you say we go home to Savaria? Dominic and Maddy are going to stop there on their way home." She knew immediately it was the wrong thing to say.

Lily shook her head. The last thing she wanted was to see her brother and his family, to know they had found the kind of happiness she had only dreamed of.

"Never mind," Ava said. She cut three slices of cake and passed a plate to Mason and one to Lily.

"Happy birthday, Granny," Lily said. "I love you."

"I love you more."

To please her great-grandmother, Lily forced a smile as she ate the cake. She forced herself to participate in the conversation, to pretend she was having a good time, and all the while she was crying inside.

When Mason and Ava went up to bed, Lily went out in the back yard. A full moon hung low in the star-studded sky. Sinking down on one of the patio chairs, she gazed at the heavens. Raedan was gone. She had never spent much time wondering what happened after death, but she wondered now. Some people believed vampires had no soul. She hoped that wasn't true. How could it be? How could you walk and talk and think and feel without a soul? She had to believe that his spirit still lived, that somehow, some way, she would see him again, if not in this life, then the next.

She was about to go back into the house when a flicker of movement caught her eye. A startled cry erupted from her throat as a dark figure rose out of the earth. Too scared to move, she could only stand there as the specter shook off the dirt and debris that clung to its clothing.

"Liliana."

"Raedan!" He looked thin, pale, his hair unkempt for the first time since she had known him. Only his eyes were the same. Oddly, his clothes looked none the worse for wear. "Is it really you?"

Before he could answer, she ran toward him, tears of joy streaming down her cheeks. "I thought you were dead!"

He caught her in his arms and held her close, his nostrils filling with the scent of her hair, her skin, the warm red tide flowing through her veins. He swore softly as the demon stirred within him. "Liliana, I need to go."

"No!" Her arms tightened around him.

"Please, love, I need to feed the demon."

"You'll come back to me?"

"You know I will."

He kissed her quickly, then vanished into the darkness, leaving her to wonder if he had ever really been there at all, or if, in her grief, she had only imagined him.

Raedan prowled the night in search of prey. It was late, the streets were empty, but the nightclubs were still open. He entered the first one he saw, his gaze sweeping the occupants, his hunger growing with every passing moment, the demon growling inside him, demanding to be fed. Demanding Lily's blood.

Raedan summoned a woman sitting alone at the bar, compelled her to follow him outside.

As soon as he had her alone, he sank his fangs into her throat with no thought but to ease the awful pain knifing through him.

If you won't give me Liliana's blood, then give me this woman's, the demon demanded. Knowing he was taking too much, Raedan tried to stop, but the demon was unrelenting. Over a week without feeding had left Raedan too weak to resist and he buried his fangs in the woman's neck again. Warmth and power flowed through him and with it a sudden sense of guilt at what he was doing. What would Liliana think if she could see him now?

He jerked his head up. The woman was barely breathing, her heartbeat sluggish and unsteady, her face pale, her gaze unfocused.

Muttering an oath, he transported her to the nearest emergency room. Inside, he sat the woman in a chair and called for help and when a nurse appeared, he turned and left. Outside, he dissolved into mist before anyone could come after him.

❧ ❧ ❧

Lily paced the back yard. How long did it take to find prey? Was he really coming back?

Had he been buried here, in the ground, all this time?

She felt his presence moments before he materialized in front of her. Her gaze ran over him. He looked much better than he had before, more like his old self. It was the blood, she thought. It had restored him, strengthened him. She could feel the latent power within him, strong again. Invincible.

He watched her, his expression impassive. "Are you sure you want me to stay?"

She nodded. "Have you been buried here, in the backyard, the whole time?"

"Yes." It had taken the last of his waning strength to transport himself here. Seeing the question in her eyes, he said, "The earth, the darkness, are healing to my kind. It is late," he said, when she yawned behind her hand. "Let us talk of this tomorrow."

"Will you stay the night with me?"

"If you wish."

"I do." Taking his hand, she led him into the house and up the stairs.

He turned his back while she got ready for bed and then, as he had before, he removed his boots and stretched out on top of the covers beside her. "Go to sleep, my love," he murmured, his voice mesmerizing, hypnotic.

So many questions she wanted to ask, but her eyelids were so heavy. She felt his lips brush hers and then darkness enfolded her.

❧ ❧ ❧

Ava looked up as Lily skipped into the kitchen, a smile on her face.

"Good morning, Granny," she said cheerfully. "What's for breakfast?"

"Whatever you want, dear. You're quite chipper this morning."

"He's alive, Granny! Raedan is alive. I saw him last night."

"He's here?"

"Yes!" Grabbing Ava's hands, Lily twirled her around the room.

"Lily, you're making me dizzy."

"Sorry, I'm just so happy."

"Where has he been all this time?" Ava asked when the world righted itself again.

"He was … "

"Was what?"

"Buried in the ground in the back yard."

Ava nodded. "I've heard vampires do that when they're grievously wounded. Did he find the dragon?"

"I don't know. He didn't say."

"I guess we'll have to wait until tonight to find out," Ava said glumly.

"I hate waiting!" Lily exclaimed. It was hours until dark.

"Well, you might as well eat something. Fretting won't make the time go by any faster."

"You're right." A wave of her hand, a few words, and a waffle smothered in butter and blueberry jam appeared in front of her. "Do you want one?"

"Yes, thank you, dear."

Lily conjured a second waffle. "Where's Mason?"

"He went home."

"Home? Why?"

"Just to check on things," Ava said, adding butter and syrup to her breakfast. "He hasn't been there in quite a while, you know. He'll be back in a day or two."

"Where does he live, when he's not with you?"

"He has a house in Seattle."

"Have the two of you set a date yet?"

"No. We thought we'd wait a bit, until all this trouble is behind us."

She meant Raedan, Lily thought, annoyed that Ava thought of the man she loved as some kind of trouble to be dealt with, a problem to be solved. Well, maybe Ava had a right to feel that way, Lily mused. After all, Ava had pretty much put her life on hold to look after her these past months.

"Do we have a silver chalice?" Lily asked, frowning.

"I have an old one, but perhaps we should consider finding a new one."

"Good idea."

They went shopping after breakfast, wandering from one magic shop to another until Lily found a goblet she liked. The proprietor assured her it was a genuine antique found in an ancient tomb, but it was the dragon engraved around the base of the goblet that caught her eye. It was perfect.

Next on the list was nightshade, which they found in a little shop around the corner.

"It seems strange to add a poisonous plant to the blood," Lily mused aloud as they strolled down Bourbon Street. "Won't it kill Raedan?"

"No. Poison doesn't affect vampires."

"Are you sure?"

"Quite."

"What about demons?"

"Doubtful."

"Then what's it for?"

"I have no idea, child. Let's go home."

Lily thought the day would never end, but, finally the sun began it's slow descent. She had just stepped out of the shower, wrapped in a towel, when Raedan appeared in her bedroom.

"Oh!"

He grinned as she blushed from her hairline to the tips of her toes. "Guess I should have knocked."

"I guess so." She stared at him, eyes wide, as he padded toward her, a hungry look in his eyes. "Raedan..."

"Just a taste, love?"

"I don't think it's a good idea."

Wrapping her in his arms, he said, "I fed before I came."

"Are you sure?"

"Please, Liliana. I need it."

She closed her eyes as he lowered his head to her neck.

"Just a taste," he murmured.

She stilled when she felt his fangs at her throat, sighed when the familiar warmth of sensual pleasure spread through her. Was this what making love was like, this feeling of oneness, of surrender? She clung to him, her fears that he would never stop fading, forgotten.

Raedan jerked his head back with a horrified cry when he heard the demon's mocking laughter in the back of his mind. Damn! Had he taken too much? "Liliana? Liliana!"

He blew out a sigh when her eyelids fluttered open and she smiled at him, a slow, dreamy smile.

"You had better put some clothes on," he said, gruffly, "or we'll be looking for another virgin. I will wait for you downstairs." Taking a step back, he kissed her lightly on the tip of her nose and vanished from the room.

Still smiling, Lily pulled on a pair of jeans and a sweater and ran down the stairs. She found Ava and Raedan in the living room. Ava was sitting on the sofa, Raedan stood next to the fireplace, turning the silver goblet this way and that in his hands.

He looked up when she hurried into the room. "A dragon?"

"It seemed fitting," she said, with a shrug.

"I suppose."

"The moon will be full tomorrow night," Ava remarked. "Are you ready?"

"Damn right."

"How dangerous is this going to be for you?" Lily asked, going to stand beside him.

"I have no idea. But it matters not."

"It matters to me! I don't want to lose you."

Placing the goblet on the mantel, Raedan took her in his arms.

"If you love me, Raedan, please don't do this."

Raedan glanced at Ava. With a nod, she left the room.

"Please, Raedan. I'd rather have you and the demon than not have you at all."

Taking her hand, he moved to the sofa and drew her down on his lap. "Liliana, I know you cannot understand, but you do not know what it is like to feel him inside you," he said, his voice filled with anguish. "To be constantly struggling against his influence, to always be afraid that, in a moment of weakness, he will compel you to commit acts of violence and depravity that will haunt you the rest of your life."

"He's done that to you?"

Raedan nodded, his eyes dark and tormented. "More than once." Before he had gained the strength to resist the blood-demon's power, the creature had forced him to do terrible things, despicable things. Things that, centuries later, he still regretted. "The demon knew what I was after when I went to find the dragon. He tried to stop me…" He clenched his hands as the memory of the agony he had endured that night replayed in his mind.

Lily's eyes widened as her mind brushed his and she felt what he had felt—the excruciating pain, the anguish, the helplessness he had endured as the demon's power clawed at his vitals in a desperate effort to survive. It was like being burned alive from the inside out. How had he endured it? "Oh, Raedan," she murmured. "I didn't know."

"It was the blood-demon driving me to drink from you tonight, to take it all. I can feel his power growing. I didn't hear his voice urging me on. It was only when I stopped that I heard his mocking laughter."

He crushed her close. Ridding himself of the blood-demon was the only way he could ever trust himself to be with her. Risking his life was a small price to pay if it meant Liliana could be his.

CHAPTER THIRTY-SEVEN

They met in Ava's back yard twenty minutes before midnight. Ava had conjured a small stone altar covered with a black cloth. The silver chalice sat in the center. A small knife and a bottle of crushed nightshade stood to one side, the flask filled with the dragon's blood waited on the other.

Ava and Mason stood on one side of the altar. Raedan and Lily stood on the other side, hands tightly clasped. Lily glanced at the sky. The moon was full and bright above them.

Lily moved closer to Raedan. She was a young witch with much to learn, but she could feel magic gathering around them. It sizzled along her skin, made her stomach clench with anxiety. Squeezing Raedan's hand, she whispered, "Are you sure there's no other way?"

He smiled down at her. "I love you, Liliana, more than anything in this world. But in centuries, this is the only solution I have ever heard of. Even for you, I cannot wait any longer."

She flinched as his eyes took on a faint red glow.

"I am fighting him now," he said, his voice tight. "He is urging me to destroy the book, to devour you, to feast on Ava and Mason. I do not know how long I can resist." Releasing her hand, he took a step away from her. "The book, Ava. Now!"

Ava pulled the slim black volume from the pocket of her skirt and laid it on the table in front of the chalice. Picking up the knife, she said, "Liliana, give me your hand."

Taking a deep breath, Lily put her hand in Ava's, winced as her great-grandmother made a shallow cut in her palm.

After putting the knife aside, Ava held Lily's hand over the book. One, two, three drops, on the cover and the book opened by itself.

There was only one page of thick vellum inside.

"Three drops of virgin's blood," Ava murmured. "No more, no less."

A low growl rose in Raedan's throat as the scent of Lily's blood filled the air. There was a sharp, crackling sound as the crimson drops hit the page, followed by a flash of yellow lightning.

Ava handed the chalice to Raedan. "According to the book, you must add the ingredients."

He nodded, his jaw clenching as the silver burned his flesh. Picking up the flask that held the dragon's blood, he poured it into the goblet.

Ava took Lily's hand in hers again, made a small cut in the palm of her other hand, and held it over a small cup. "Seven drops," she murmured, and handed the cup to Raedan.

A plume of black smoke rose from the chalice as he added Lily's blood to that of the dragon.

Lastly, Ava handed him a vial. "Nightshade," she said.

Jaw clenched, Raedan added the last ingredient to the chalice.

And the smoke turned white.

Lily glanced at Raedan as Ava wrapped strips of cloth around her hands. He stood rigid beside her, his jaw tightly clenched. The hand that held the goblet trembled, the skin red and blistered from the silver. She could feel the pain rolling off him in waves as the blood-demon fought for its life.

Leaning forward, Lily read the words that would unleash the spell. "By dragon's blood and a virgin's pure, if thou art worthy, I hold the cure. Your lifeforce shall then ever be strong, the demon within forever be gone. If thou art false, thy heart and soul beyond saving, nightshade's poison will be your undoing."

Raedan took a deep breath, his gaze on Lily's face as he lifted the chalice to his lips and drank.

There was a sharp crack of thunder that shook the earth beneath their feet. Lightning crackled as it split the skies, unleashing a plume of fire that landed on the black book and turned it to ash.

Raedan dropped the chalice, then fell to his knees, arms wrapped around his middle as the demon fought to survive. Drops of dark red blood oozed from his pores. He writhed on the ground for several moments, his face a mask of agony.

He looked up when Lily knelt beside him. Crying, "No! Don't touch me!" he vanished from their sight.

Lily glanced at Ava. "What does it mean? Where has he gone?"

"I don't know, child," Ava said, taking Lily in her arms. "I don't know."

"Was he unworthy? Was my blood not pure?" Tears streamed down her cheeks. "I never should have let him drink that vile concoction!"

"It was his decision, Lily. Would you have rather let him live forever in pain?"

"No." Her tears came harder, faster.

"Lily…"

"I killed him!" She rocked back and forth, sobbing uncontrollably. "I killed him."

Ava sat on the chair at Lily's bedside, her thoughts turned inward. What had gone wrong? They had gathered the required ingredients, spoken the right words at midnight beneath a full moon. She wasn't sure what she had thought would happen when Raedan drank the potion, but certainly not the results she'd seen. Perhaps she had been naïve, but she had expected him to either be cured immediately, or drop dead at their feet. Instead, he had collapsed on the ground, his whole body wracked with pain unlike anything she had ever seen. How could anyone survive that kind of torture for more than a moment?

Lily had cried for an hour before exhaustion overcame her and she felt into a restless sleep. Mason had carried her up to bed. Ava had shooed him out of the room, undressed Lily and slipped a nightgown over her head. She had left Lily's side only once since then to call Quill and let him know what had happened. He would be here tomorrow to take Lily home.

That had been hours ago. It would be dawn soon. Guilt gnawed at her. She had failed to protect her great-granddaughter. Failed Raedan, who had done nothing more than love Lily. Failed Quill and Callie who had trusted her to keep their daughter safe and out of danger.

With a sigh, she closed her eyes and wept quietly.

A moment later, she felt Mason's hand on her shoulder.

"It's not your fault," he said. "Nothing you could have said or done would have kept Lily and Raedan apart. Lily could not change Raedan's mind. He knew the risk and was willing to take it. If you must blame yourself, you must also blame Lily's parents, and Lily, too."

"I don't know how she'll ever get over this."

"She comes from good stock. Her heart will mend, in time."

"I hope so," Ava murmured as she stroked Lily's brow. "Heaven help me, I hope so."

Feeling weak and in pain, Raedan headed for Bourbon Street. He didn't know if it was the concoction burning through him causing him such agony or if it was the demon's last, frantic efforts to survive. All he knew was that he needed blood, he needed it desperately, and he needed it now.

It was an hour until dawn when he staggered into the bar favored by the Master of the City. He found her in her favorite booth, drinking from a slender young man. Tonight, she wore a gown of deep purple taffeta that revealed a generous amount of tawny cleavage.

Claret looked up, blood dripping from her fangs, when he practically fell onto the seat opposite hers. "What happened to you?" she exclaimed.

"No time to explain. I need blood."

"This one has some left. Help yourself."

Raedan shook his head. "Your blood." Vampires rarely shared blood with one another, but tonight something told him nothing else would do.

"Mine?" She stared at him as if he had lost his mind. "I don't share my blood with anyone."

"I need the blood of a vampire, and you are the only one I know."

Leaning forward, she inhaled sharply. "What is that smell?"

"Dragon's blood. Liliana's blood. Nightshade."

"It reeks." She drew another breath, a frown creasing her brow as her gaze met his. "There is something different about you. What is it?"

"I tried to destroy the blood-demon tonight. I am not sure I succeeded."

"And you need my blood why?"

"To strengthen my own."

"What will you give me in return?"

Raedan groaned low in his throat. "Dammit, woman, I do not have the time or the strength to play games. Are you going to help me or not?"

"I will expect some Hungarian blood in return. Dominic's will do. Quill's would be better."

"Fine."

With an aggrieved sigh, she thrust her arm across the table toward him, then quickly withdrew it. "Wait! How do I know this isn't just some sneaky way to transfer the demon to me?"

"I can no longer feel it. I can only assume we succeeded in destroying it."

She regarded him through narrowed eyes a moment, then offered him her arm again.

Raedan grasped her wrist in both hands and sank his fangs into her flesh. She was an old vampire, though not nearly as old as he. Still, her blood was powerful. He felt it move through his veins like heat lightning, healing the wounds left behind by the demon, strengthening his own power. He didn't know what had driven him to search for vampire blood, all he knew was that no mortal could have given him as much as he needed and still survived. He closed his eyes as he felt Claret's blood mingle with that of the dragon, Liliana's, and his own, sighed as the combination seemed to eradicate the last vestiges of the demon's hellish power.

"Enough."

One last taste and Raedan lifted his head. "I owe you a life debt."

"Indeed. I've told you what I expect in payment. I will accept nothing less."

"I will see that you get it," he vowed. "Again, my thanks."

With a queenly wave of dismissal, she tuned back to her prey and buried her fangs in his throat once more.

The sun was rising when Raedan stepped out of the night club. His skin tingled as he transported himself to his lair. Falling back on the bed, he closed his eyes and summoned Liliana's image.

He whispered her name as blessed darkness engulfed him, carrying him down, down, down, into blessed oblivion.

CHAPTER THIRTY-EIGHT

Quill glanced at the clock over the fireplace as he paced the floor of Ava's parlor. "Maybe we should wake her up."

"She had a bad night," Ava said. "Let her rest."

"I agree with Ava," Callie said. "The sleep will do her more good than anything else."

"What do you think happened to Raedan?" Quill asked.

Ava blew out a sigh. "I have no idea. We did everything right. At least I think we did. How can we know for sure? I doubt if that incantation has ever been used before."

"Well, I can't help being relieved he's gone," Quill admitted.

"Quill! That's a terrible thing to say!" Callie exclaimed.

"Tell me you're sorry he's out of the picture."

"Of course I am. But Lily loves...loved him. She's not going to get over it any time soon. Perhaps never."

Quill snorted. "It's not like they were married. Hell, they've only known each other a short time."

"Sometimes you know right away," Callie reminded him.

"She'll feel better when she gets home," he muttered.

"Lily!" Ava exclaimed.

Lily glanced around the room, surprised to see her father pacing the floor, her mother sitting on one of the easy chairs, Ava and Mason sharing the sofa. "What's going on?"

"We've come to take you home," Quill said, putting his arm around her shoulders.

"Oh."

"Ava told us about Raedan," Callie said. "We're so sorry."

Lily blinked back the quick sting of tears in her eyes.

"We thought we'd leave as soon as you're packed," Quill said. "Is that all right with you?"

"Whatever you want," she said listlessly.

Quill and Callie exchanged looks, disheartened by the lack of interest in her voice, the dispirited slump of her shoulders.

"Would you like me to help you pack?" Callie asked.

"No. I can do it." Turning, Lily headed back to her room, her steps slow and heavy.

"It's worse than I thought," Callie said. "She's lost the will to live."

In her room, Lily sat on the edge of her bed. Her parents had come to take her home, as if that would make everything better. But wherever she went, her heart would always be with Raedan.

Rising, she pulled her suitcase from the closet and tossed it on the bed. Opening her dresser drawers, she tossed her things into the suitcase. *Raedan, Raedan, where are you?*

"Standing right behind you, love."

She whirled around, a wordless cry of joy rising in her throat as she threw her arms around his neck "Oh, Raedan, I thought I'd lost you forever!"

"You very nearly did." He held her close, reveling in the warmth of her body against his, the scent of her hair, her skin, the sweetness of her lips as he covered her mouth with his own. It was heaven to hold her in his embrace without the blood-demon screaming in his mind, demanding that he sink his fangs into her throat and drain her dry.

Lily hugged him tightly, tears of joy trickling down her cheeks. He was here. He was alive, and nothing else mattered.

Finally, unable to wait any longer, she asked the question uppermost in her mind. "Is he gone?"

"Yes, love." He smiled down at her, feeling at peace for the first time in centuries.

"What happened? Where did you go?"

"The demon didn't die easily. He struggled to break his ties with me, to transfer to another host. To you."

"Me?" She stared at him. "That's why you told me not to touch you? Why you disappeared?"

He nodded. "I could not let his evil infect you."

"I thought the demon only inhabited vampires."

"Usually, yes. But even though you are not a vampire, you carry your father's blood. The demon could have survived inside you until he found another vampire host. Your father, or perhaps your brother."

She shivered, remembering the pain the blood-demon had inflicted on him. "But you're okay now?"

"Yes, thanks to Claret."

"Claret! What does she have to do with anything?"

"The demon fought me for hours. I was about to give up the fight when I realized the only thing that might help me was vampire blood. "

"Odd, there was nothing in either book about vampire blood being necessary," Lily mused.

"I have a feeling it was there, but the demon prevented me from seeing it."

"Why?"

"Perhaps he was tired of fighting with me and wanted a new host. At any rate, I found Claret at her club and she agreed to help me. For a price."

"What did she want, I'm afraid to ask."

"Blood. Hungarian blood."

"My father's," Lily murmured.

"Or your brother's."

Lily frowned. "You kept the demon from transferring to me, but why didn't it infect Claret?"

"By the time I found her, I could no longer feel the demon inside me." Which had led him to believe it was dead, inert, or no longer a threat. "She almost refused to help me, but apparently she decided the risk was worth the promise of your father's blood." His gaze searched hers. "So much has happened in such a short time, my sweet Liliana. Have your feelings for me changed?"

"No. Never. I will always love you." She bit down on her lower lip. "Have your feelings for me changed?"

"That will never happen. You are my love, my life." He caressed her cheek with the backs of his knuckles. "Will you marry me now, Liliana?"

"Yes. Oh, yes!"

"Are you sure? Think it over, love. Your parents will not approve. I doubt they will ever accept me."

"I don't care."

"I cannot give you children." His jaw clenched as he watched the play of emotions cross her face. His mind brushed hers. She was thinking of her brother's baby, her heart filling with sadness at the thought of never having a son or daughter of her own.

"Raedan…"

He pressed his fingers to her lip. "I understand."

Lily tilted her head to the side. "What is it you think you understand?"

"You have changed your mind."

"Oh?"

"I have no right to ask you to give up a normal life to be with me." He shook his head, his expression bleak. "You deserve so much more—a man who can share your whole life, give you children, grow old by your side. Share a meal with you."

Lily took a step back, hands fisted on her hips, eyes narrowed and flashing fire. "You asked me to marry you not two minutes ago. Are you already trying to back out of your proposal, mister?"

"No." He stared at her, confused by her anger. "No, but I thought…"

"Stop thinking. You asked me to marry you and I said yes. So now you're stuck with me. Is that understood? As for sharing my whole life, I think we've done just fine so far. So, we can't have children of our own. We can always adopt a couple. There are kids all over the world who need parents, and furthermore…"

Feeling his heart swell with love, Raedan swept Liliana into his arms and kissed her, a long, searing kiss that branded her his for all time.

Going up on her tiptoes, Lily twined her arms around his neck, holding on for dear life as he kissed her again and yet again, his hand sliding seductively up and down her thigh while the other delved into the hair at her nape.

A cough from the doorway brought a rush of heat to Lily's cheeks. "Mom," she squeaked. "Dad. Guess what? We're getting married!"

Raedan sat beside Liliana on the sofa in Ava's parlor, his face impassive as he listened to the women talk about the wedding—where should they hold it, here or in Savaria? Who would they invite? Should it be a small gathering or a large one? Liliana texted her brother to tell them the good news. Dominic said they would be home as soon as they packed. When the initial fuss quieted down, Ava remarked they'd be having two weddings, and the next thing Raedan knew, the women were planning a double ceremony.

Raedan glanced at his future father-in-law. Quill stood by the fireplace, arms folded across his chest, his blatant disapproval evident in every line of his body.

Finally, when Raedan had decided the women were going to talk all night, Ava yawned. Ten minutes later, Raedan and Liliana were finally alone.

"You didn't say much," Lily remarked.

"Your father hates me."

Lily stared at him, then burst out laughing.

"You think it is funny?"

"Yes, in a way." Laying her hand on his arm, she said, "He would have hated anyone I chose. Don't you know that?"

Raedan grunted. He thought of his own daughter, gone these many centuries. Had his life not changed so drastically, had his children grown to adulthood, he likely would not have been happy with any man who stole his daughter's heart and took her away.

"He'll get over it," Lily assured him, "when he sees how happy I am."

"So, what did you all decide about the wedding?"

"We're going to have a small, double ceremony here, in the church down the street. Just the immediate family. You and I will have to go to Savaria within the year for a formal announcement, but we don't have to worry about that now." She cupped his face in her hands and kissed him lightly. "How do you feel?"

"What do you mean?"

"I don't know. I thought you'd be different somehow when the blood-demon was gone."

"Demon or not, I am still a vampire, love. But there is a difference. I am no longer constantly fighting him for control." He smiled into her eyes. "I can be close to you, hold you, without wanting to sink my fangs into your throat and devour you."

"That *is* good news," she said, laughing. "I love you, Raedan. I'll try to make you happy."

"You already make me happy, witch woman. It is late," he said, rising and pulling her to her feet. "You should get some rest."

"I wish you could stay the night with me." Trailing her fingertips over his chest, she murmured, "I wish we could make love."

"No more than I do," he said, his voice rough with desire. "But I am afraid your father would destroy me while I rested if I made you mine before the wedding."

Chapter Thirty-Nine

Quill sat on the edge of the bed, watching Callie brush her hair. "Are we really going to let our only daughter marry this Transylvanian vampire?"

"I don't see any way to stop it," Callie replied calmly. "Do you?"

"A stake in his heart would quickly solve the problem."

"Quill! What a thing to say!" she exclaimed. But one look at his face and she knew that he meant every word.

"What kind of life can she have with him? He'll never be accepted by our people. She'll never have children or any kind of normal life. Gradually, she'll adjust her hours to his and the daylight will be lost to her. In time..."

Moving toward the bed, Callie placed her hand over his mouth. "Hush. You don't want Lily to hear you, do you? Or worse, Raedan."

Quill muttered an oath. Slipping his arm around her waist, he fell back on the bed, drawing her down on top of him, all thought of Lily and Raedan momentarily forgotten as Callie magicked their clothes away and turned out the lights.

"I'm happy for her," Ava said as she snuggled against Mason. "Raedan seems different now that the demon is gone. He's no longer at war with himself, no longer constantly on edge. And he loves her. A blind man could see that."

"He's not like the vampires in her family," Mason remarked. "He doesn't eat. He can't give her a child. He's rarely awake during the day. Transylvanian vampires are nothing like the ones she's used to. Save for their need for blood, Hungarian vampires are more like mortals."

"She'll adjust," Ava said confidently.

"And what if he turns her?" Mason asked quietly. "What then?"

Ava stared at him. It was, after all, a very real possibility, whether he did it on purpose or by accident. Stars above, she hated to think what Quill would do if Raedan turned Lily.

✿ ✿ ✿

Dominic paced the floor of the hotel. How could Maddy sit there and calmly pack their suitcases when his little sister was about to marry the enemy? Dammit, it wasn't right. He didn't know a blessed thing about the man Liliana intended to marry, nor could he believe their father hadn't put a stop to it.

"Dom, calm down. I'm sure Lily knows what she's doing."

"No way! She's never even dated anybody else and now she's getting married. To a Transylvanian vampire!"

"Ava says they're in love."

Dominic snorted. "I'm sure *he's* in love, all right. With her blood. Nothing like having a ready-made snack for a wife."

Maddy looked at him, her brow furrowed, her arms folded tightly over her chest. "Is that all I am to you, Dominic Falconer? Just a ready-made snack?"

"What? No! Of course not."

"If the vampire's as despicable as you seem to think, Ava would have turned him into a toad by now. Or Quill would have lopped off his head."

Dominic glared at her.

Maddy grinned inwardly. There was no talking to him when he was in a mood like this. But she knew how to get his mind off Lily and Raedan.

Closing the suitcase, she changed into her sexiest black lace nightgown and turned off the lights. She summoned a candle and lit it with a word. Soon, the seductive scent of musk filled the air. Hips swaying, she brushed by Dominic and climbed into bed.

A moment later, he slid under the covers, all thoughts of his sister forgotten as he gathered the love of his life into his arms.

CHAPTER FORTY

Lily stared at her reflection in the mirror. She had never looked so good. There was a glow in her eyes that had never been there before. Was it the dress that made her feel so beautiful, or Raedan's love? She twirled slowly in front of the floor-length mirror. The dress was white, studded with brilliants across the bodice. The neckline was round, the sleeves long and ended in points at her wrists. The skirt swirled around her ankles as she turned. She felt like a storybook princess about to marry the handsome prince.

"Here, Lily, let's try this one," Callie said, veil in hand.

Lily turned to face her mother as Callie set the delicate, shoulder-length veil in place.

"Perfect!" Ava exclaimed.

"You're the most beautiful bride I've ever seen," Callie said, blinking back her tears. "I can't believe my little girl is getting married."

"Did you find a gown you like, Granny?" Lily asked.

"Yes. It's hanging in the dressing room."

"Well, let's see it," Callie said.

Ava stepped into the dressing room.

Lily smiled at her reflection. In a few days, she would be Raedan's wife. The very thought unleashed butterflies of happiness in the pit of her stomach. Wife. Was there ever a more beautiful word?

She glanced over her shoulder as Ava came to stand beside her.

"Granny, I love it," Lily exclaimed. The gown was pale pink silk, simple and elegant. Instead of a veil, she wore a circlet of pink roses in her hair.

"Callie, what do you think?"

"I'm with Lily. I love it. Now, what am *I* going to wear?"

Lily smiled at Raedan as they walked through the park that night. "I found a dress today. I can't wait for you to see it."

"I am sure you look beautiful in it." Pausing, he drew her into his arms, unable to believe she was his, that soon he would be able to hold her, kiss her, make love to her all night long.

"Where are we going for our honeymoon?" Lily asked.

"Anywhere you want."

"I don't know. I've never been anywhere, but you, you've been everywhere."

"But never with you."

She smiled, pleased. "Where would you suggest?"

"Anywhere with a bed," he muttered.

Lily stared at him, then burst out laughing.

"You think it is funny?"

"No. I'm sorry I laughed."

Taking her hand, he started walking again, hoping the exercise would cool his desire. She would never know how hard it was for him to be near her. Even without the demon, his desire for her blood, his yearning to possess her, was a constant temptation. He had never loved anyone the way he loved her. Her laughter, her generosity of spirit, her faith and trust in him, her willingness to ease his pain … in nine hundred years, he had never known a woman like her.

He sighed when they returned to Ava's house. His future in-laws were inside with Ava and Mason. Dominic and Maddy would be here tomorrow night.

They were about to go inside when Claret appeared on the porch beside them.

Lily let out a gasp of surprise when she saw the vampire.

Raedan grimaced.

"I see my blood did the trick," Claret remarked with a smirk. "I've come for what is owed me."

The hunger in the vampire's eyes sent an icy chill down Lily's spine. Claret had given Raedan her blood when he desperately needed it and he had promised her Hungarian blood in return. And now she was here to collect.

"Liliana," Raedan said. "Go inside."

"No."

His gaze caressed her. "Please, do as I say."

"Oh, all right."

"Ask your father to come out."

With a nod, she opened the door, stepped into the house, and closed the door behind her.

"I think you should make yourself scarce while I talk to Quill," Raedan suggested.

"As you wish." A wave of her hand, and she was gone.

Raedan paced the porch as he waited for Liliana's father. Five minutes passed. Ten, before he came outside.

"What do you want?"

"Let us take a walk."

Quill raised one brow, but followed him down the steps to the sidewalk. "What's this all about?"

"When I fought to destroy the demon, it weakened me badly. I needed blood … "

"You didn't!" Quill hissed.

"No. I knew Liliana could not give me what I needed. I needed the blood of a vampire so I sought out the only one I knew."

"Claret."

Raedan smiled faintly, not at all surprised that Quill could sense he carried the blood of the other vampire. "She agreed to help me, for a price."

"And did it help?"

"I am standing here, am I not?"

"So the price was *my* blood," Quill said flatly.

Raedan nodded. "She has come to collect."

"And if I refuse?"

Before Raedan could reply, Claret materialized beside them, radiant in a gown of ice-blue silk. "You would not refuse an old friend, would you, Quill?"

A slow smile spread over Quill's face. He had no love for her. She could be ruthless, cruel, totally without a sense of right and wrong. And yet he harbored a mild affection for her that he could neither understand nor explain.

"It seems our paths keep crossing," Quill remarked.

She smiled at him as she raked her nails lightly down his cheek. "May it ever be so."

Raedan glanced from one to the other, bemused by the obvious love-hate relationship between them. He wondered what had happened in the past to bring them together.

In a move too quick to follow, Quill pulled Claret into his arms. "Let's get this over with before Callie comes looking for me."

Raedan watched as Quill canted his head to the side. Claret's eyes went red as her fangs extended. She stroked Quill's neck with her tongue before she bit him. A minute passed. Two. Three, before Quill said, "Enough!" and put her away from him.

Raedan felt an odd sensation as the two vampires parted.

Claret let out a sigh of pleasure as she licked Quill's blood from her lips. "A pleasure, as always," she murmured. "Give my love to Callie."

"I think not," Quill said dryly.

Claret's laughter hung in the air as she vanished from their sight.

Raedan shook his head. "Well, that was the damnedest thing I have ever seen. A Hungarian vampire willingly giving his blood to one of my kind. Will wonders never cease?"

Quill glared at him.

"I have heard that your blood is like catnip to my kind."

"Have you?"

"Indeed. Is it as addictive as they say?"

"I wouldn't know."

"It certainly seems that way. Perhaps one day you will give me a taste?"

Quill bared his fangs. "I wouldn't count on it, if I were you."

Raedan threw back his head and laughed as Lily's father turned and headed back to the house, hands tightly clenched at his sides, his back rigid.

It was her wedding day. Or night, Lily amended, as she bounded out of bed. In a few hours, Raedan would be hers and she would be his. Things would have been perfect if not for her brother and father both taking her aside late last night for private chats where each of them, in his own way, tried to convince her she was making a huge mistake. She couldn't blame them. They loved her, they worried about her marrying a man they considered an enemy, but nothing they said had changed her mind. No marriage was perfect. If she yearned for a child in a year or two, they could always adopt a baby. Raedan preferred to rest during the day, but he could be awake if he desired. She could stay up later at night, sleep longer in the morning, thereby giving them more time together. He didn't eat, but that was no big deal. She was a witch. She could conjure a meal wherever and whenever she wished. It would all work out.

The family gathered around the table for breakfast. The men didn't say much. Her mother, Ava, and Maddy gave Lily marital advice—be sure to turn on the light in the bathroom at night—men tended to leave the toilet seat up. Men hated to ask for directions. They left their socks wherever they took them off. They rarely made a bed or washed a dish.

Lily laughed good-naturedly, knowing it was all in fun. And that, in her father's case, it was all true.

After breakfast, Lily spent some time getting acquainted with her nephew. He was a darling child, the spitting image of his father. She knew a moment of regret that she would never bear Raedan's child, and quickly thrust the thought away.

As the sun began to set, Lily went up to her room to get ready. Raedan would meet them at the church.

"Lily?"

"Come in, Mom."

Callie stepped into the room and closed the door behind her.

"How do I look?" Lily asked, doing a pirouette.

"Just as beautiful as I knew you would. The dress is almost perfect."

"Almost?"

"It just needs one more thing," Callie said as she fastened a gold chain around Lily's neck from which hung a small gold heart. "So you'll never forget how much we love you."

"Thanks, Mom. I love it. Please be happy for me."

"I am. Give me a hug now. It's time to go. Your Dad is waiting for you downstairs. He wanted a few minutes alone with you. I'm riding to the church with Dominic and Maddy."

Lily held her mother tight. "I love you."

Callie cupped Lily's cheek in her hand. "I'll see you there."

Lily sent a last look in the mirror, took a deep breath, and hurried out of the room.

Her father was waiting for her at the foot of the stairs. He looked quite handsome in his tux and it occurred to her that he looked exactly the same now as he had when she was a little girl, and that he would always look that way. Funny, she had never thought of that before, and it occurred to her that Raedan, too, would always look the way he did now.

"You look wonderful," Quill said.

"Thank you, Papa."

"Are you sure this is what you want?"

"Yes, very sure."

"No sense in putting if off then. Let's go, Princess."

The church was small and old. Made of white stone, it shone like a diamond in the moonlight.

Lily took a deep breath as she peeked into the chapel. Her mother, Ava and Mason, sat in the first pew on the left, Dominic and Maddy sat in the one on the right. J.D. sat on

Maddy's lap, his eyes round and wide as he looked at the flickering candles and the statues of the saints. Her great-grandfather had called that morning. He had apologized for their absence, but promised to be there as soon as his business in Africa was complete.

She was shocked to see Claret sitting primly in the last row, her hands folded in her lap. For once, the vampire was modestly attired in a simple navy blue sheath that still managed to show off every curve.

And then she saw Raedan standing in front of the altar and everything and everyone else faded into the background. He looked more handsome than ever. The black tux, the crisp white shirt, perfectly complimented his dark good looks, the width of his shoulders. When his gaze met hers, a wave of desire swept through her. A faint smile twitched his lips and she knew he was perfectly aware of what she was thinking, feeling.

At a nod from the minister, the organist began to play *The Wedding March.*

"Ready, Princess?" her father asked.

Lily nodded.

"Here we go."

Lily's heart was pounding with joyful anticipation as they glided slowly down the aisle. It was really happening.

"Who giveth this woman to this man?" the minister asked.

Placing Lily's hand in Raedan's, Quill said, "Her mother and I do."

Her father gave her a kiss on the cheek, then stepped back to take his place beside Callie.

Lily was scarcely aware of the rest of the ceremony. She couldn't stop gazing into Raedan's eyes, which seemed darker, more mesmerizing than ever. She winced as his hand tightened on hers, let out a gasp when his eyes took on a faint red glow.

As the minister pronounced them man and wife, Raedan pushed Lily away, let out a harsh cry of denial as he clutched his stomach and fell to his knees.

The minister took one look at him, murmured, "Heaven help us, he is possessed!" and fled the chapel, the organist close on his heels.

Lily looked at her father in horror. "It can't be … "

When Dominic and Mason moved toward Raedan, he growled, "Get the hell away from me!"

"But we destroyed the demon," Lily said, glancing helplessly at Ava and Mason.

"Apparently not," Dominic remarked.

"But we did everything right!" she insisted.

Quill watched impassively as Raedan writhed on the floor, being destroyed from the inside out. Ava had told him of the ritual they had performed. Watching Raedan, it was obvious that something had gone terribly wrong. Whatever they had done hadn't destroyed the demon, only drained its strength for a time.

Tugging on Dominic's arm, Maddy whispered, "I'm taking J.D. home," and quickly left the chapel.

Quill looked up as Claret came forward. "My blood helped him last time. Perhaps it can again."

"For the same price?" Quill asked dryly.

"Who cares what it costs if it helps!" Lily cried. "Can't you see he's dying!"

She fell to her knees beside him, wanting to help but not knowing what to do. He was being ripped apart. She could feel the blood-demon clawing at Raedan's vitals, the demon weakening Raedan as it grew stronger. "Claret! Do something!"

The vampire looked at Quill. "Do we have a deal?"

"No."

"No?" Lily stared at her father in disbelief. "I know you hate him but if you love me, you won't let him die."

"Lily, get away from him now!"

Startled by the harsh tone of her father's voice, she scrambled to her feet and backed away.

Kneeling beside Raedan, Quill rolled up his shirt sleeve. "He's not going to die. Dominic, Mason, hold him down."

When they had Raedan subdued, Quill bit into his wrist, forced Raedan's mouth open and let his blood drip onto his tongue.

Raedan growled low in his throat as he wrenched one arm free and took hold of Quill's arm. Eyes as red as flame, he drank. And drank.

Silence fell over the chapel as the scent of hot, fresh blood filled the air.

Lily held her breath, a silent prayer rising in her heart, as Raedan continued to drink. She glanced at her father. How much blood could he spare? What if the demon transferred to her father?

A violent shudder wracked Raedan's body. Throwing back his head, he let out a howl that sent an icy shiver slithering down Lily's spine.

Mason and Dominic stood and backed away from him.

Raedan convulsed again and then lay still, his eyes closed, his body slack.

Lily looked at her father, tears welling in her eyes. "Is...is he dead?"

"No," he said, rising.

Lily glanced at Raedan again. He lay as before, not moving, not seeming to breathe. "Are you sure?"

Quill nodded. "He knew instinctively that he needed vampire blood to complete the ritual and destroy the demon. That's why he went to Claret for help." He glanced around for the vampire, but she was nowhere to be found. "The only thing is, he went to the wrong breed of vampire."

Suddenly hopeful, Lily knelt beside Raedan and kissed his cheek.

"You can do better than that, can you not, wife?" he asked.

"Raedan!" When he sat up, she threw her arms around his neck. "I was so afraid." Her worried gaze searched his. "Is the demon really gone this time?"

"Yes. Your father's blood did the trick. I felt him die this time." Taking Liliana's hand in his, Raedan stood and lifted her to het feet.

"I think a thank you is in order, don't you?" Quill remarked.

"I guess you and I are blood brothers now," Raedan said with a grin. "And you know what? Hungarian blood really is as good as they say."

Quill snorted.

"Seriously, my thanks," Raedan said. "I know what that cost you."

"See that I don't regret it," Quill said gruffly. "Let's go home."

CHAPTER FORTY-ONE

Since they hadn't yet decided where to go on their honeymoon, Raedan and Lily bid good night to the family and checked into the bridal suite at the best hotel in town.

When they reached their room, Raedan swung her into his arms and carried her across the threshold. "Here we are, bride of my heart."

"Here we are," she murmured, and wondered why she was suddenly so nervous. She had been waiting for this moment practically from the night they met.

Now it was here. What if she disappointed him? He had been married before. No doubt, in nine hundred years he had made love to many women. How many, she wondered. And how would she compare?

"Happy?" he asked.

"Of course."

"What is wrong, Liliana?"

"Wrong? Nothing. Why do you ask?"

"You cannot lie to me," he said. "What is it that troubles you?"

"I'm afraid."

He set her lightly on her feet and took a step back. "Of me?"

"No! I...you...I've never..." She looked down at the floor as a rush of heat flooded her cheeks.

"Liliana, look at me."

When she refused, he placed his finger under her chin and lifted her head. "We can wait until you are ready."

She stared at him, wide-eyed with surprise. "But I thought..."

"What? That I would throw you on the bed, rip off your gown, and ravish you?"

She laughed, her blush deepening. This was Raedan. There was nothing to be afraid of.

She bit down on her lower lip when he drew her gently into his arms.

"I want you," he said, his voice husky with desire.

"And I want you, but..."

"But what? Tell me what is bothering you."

"I'm afraid I'll disappoint you. You've been with so many women, and I know nothing of pleasing a man."

"Everything about you pleases me. Your lips, your eyes, your sweet smile." He kissed her tenderly. "Your laugh." He kissed her again, his hand sliding up and down her back as he drew her closer. "The way you sigh when you are in my arms." Taking her hand in his, he pressed it to his chest. "Why do you not get ready for bed while I take a shower?"

She nodded, grateful for his understanding, confused by her feelings. She had waited for this moment, dreamed of it. Why was she so hesitant?

Brow furrowed, she padded into the bedroom and closed the door. She stepped out of her shoes, removed her veil, her wedding dress and her underwear. A murmured word clothed her in a long white nightgown. Chiding herself for her foolish fears, she opened the connecting door to the bathroom and peeked inside.

Raedan stood inside the stall, his back toward her, a study in sheer masculine perfection. Her gaze caressed his broad shoulders, his trim waist, his long, muscular legs. A gasp escaped her lips when he turned around and found her standing there, staring at him.

The nightgown she wore left nothing to the imagination and his body reacted instantly. Her cheeks turned bright pink when she saw the blatant evidence of his desire.

Raedan turned off the water, opened the door, grabbed a towel and wrapped it around his hips.

And still she stood there, watching him avidly, her lips slightly parted. He heard the rapid beating of her heart as the scent of her desire filled the air. She didn't back away when he moved slowly toward her. Instead, she ran her hands over his chest, let her fingertips follow the line of dark hair that disappeared beneath the towel.

"Careful, little girl," he warned. "You are playing with fire."

Feeling suddenly bold, she wrapped her arms around his neck, went up on her tiptoes, and kissed him.

He crushed her close a moment before sweeping her into his arms and carrying her to bed. She didn't remember removing her nightgown, but it was suddenly gone and they were lying side by side.

"What should I do?" she asked.

"Anything you want," he replied, and groaned softly as her curious hands moved over him. It was pleasure and torment combined as she acquainted herself with his body. And when he could stand it no longer, he turned the tables on her and began an exploration of his own, worshipping her with his hands and his lips, whispering love words to her in his native tongue as he aroused her.

Lily moaned softly as his body merged with hers, filling her with pleasure even as she reached for something just beyond her grasp. And just when she thought she would never find it, pleasure exploded deep within her. A moment later, Raedan thrust into her one last time, then fell still, his head pillowed on her shoulder.

Feeling more relaxed and content than she ever had in her whole life, Lily closed her eyes, thinking she would be happy to lie there in his arms forever. She smiled, thinking that if she was a cat, she would be purring now. She laughed inwardly, thinking how surprised he would be if she suddenly morphed into a feline, something Ava had done long ago.

Raedan rolled onto his side, carrying her with him so they lay face to face.

Feeling his gaze, Lily opened her eyes to find him watching her intently.

"Did I hurt you?" he asked, brushing a lock of hair behind her ear.

"Terribly." She laughed softly at the look of horror on his face. "It was wonderful," she murmured. "Maybe we could do it again some time. If you want to."

Now it was his turn to laugh. "Count on it, love." He ran his knuckles along her cheek. She would never know how much she meant to him, how he cherished her love, her trust. He had lived in darkness with no end in sight and then she had come along, her smile as bright as the sun's light, chasing away the eternal darkness of his existence, warming the cold that had been a part of him for so long.

He held her close, murmuring that he loved her, would always love her. And she gave it back to him with both hands, making him feel whole again. Making him feel like a man again instead of a monster. And that was the greatest gift of all.

CHAPTER FORTY-TWO

L ily looked at the calendar. And frowned. She was two
months late. Had she not been married to a Transylvanian
vampire, she would have thought herself pregnant. But that
was impossible. Maybe it was just the excitement of coming home from their honeymoon in Europe. Maybe she was
coming down with the flu. Maybe it was the stress of waiting
to see if the offer they'd made on a house in New Orleans
would be accepted.

Ava and Mason had decided to stay in Ava's home in
Portland until Lily and Raedan found a place to live, insist-
ing that all the newlyweds needed some privacy.

A glance out the window told her Raedan would be
rising soon. With that in mind, she fixed a bowl of soup
and a sandwich for dinner and carried it into the living
room to watch TV while she ate. She loved being married,
loved every minute she and Raedan spent together. With
the demon gone, he was more relaxed. His insatiable hunger had disappeared and though he still required blood
to survive, his thirst was easily controlled. Best of all, the
tense relationship between her father and Raedan seemed
to have resolved itself the night the demon had finally
been destroyed. Raedan had joked that he and her father
were blood brothers, and while Quill scoffed at the notion,
there was obviously some truth to it. They had even gone

hunting together one night before her parents returned to Savaria.

She smiled when she heard the shower come on upstairs. Her husband was awake. A wave of her hand sent the dishes into the kitchen and she ran up the stairs, thinking she would join him in the shower.

She barely made it into the bathroom before her stomach began to heave. Dropping to her knees, she vomited into the toilet.

Raedan was immediately at her side. Dripping wet, he knelt beside her. "Are you sick?"

He had no idea how to handle the illnesses of the day. It had been centuries since he had been ill. Sometimes he forgot how fragile mortals were, how easily they could be hurt. How quickly they could succumb to any number of diseases. "Liliana, are you ill?"

"I don't think so."

"Then why are you throwing up?"

"I don't know. I just felt queasy all of a sudden."

He grabbed a wash cloth, wet it, and handed it to her, his eyes narrowed with concern as she wiped her mouth. Helping her to her feet, he placed his hand on her brow. It was cool to his touch.

"It's probably nothing," Lily said. "Something I ate must have disagreed with me."

He nodded slowly. His biggest fear was that he would lose her. Time and again he had considered asking her permission to bring her across, but he had never found the nerve to broach the subject. He knew her parents would object. Even though they seemed to have accepted him into the family, he wasn't one of them and he never would be. He was certain that turning Liliana into a vampire would break the tenuous peace between himself and her family.

Seeing the worry in his eyes, Lily grinned at him. "I'm fine," she assured him. "Why don't you finish your shower and I'll wash your back?"

Lily didn't mention her upset stomach to anyone else, but she began to worry when it happened several mornings in a row. She didn't mention the incidents to Raedan for fear of worrying him. She was scared enough for both of them. Scared enough that she'd made an appointment with a doctor for the following morning. She hadn't mentioned that to Raedan, either.

"Are you feeling all right?" he asked when he rose that night.

"I'm fine," she said brightly. "Stop worrying about me."

"Would you like to go out?" he asked. "You haven't been out of the house for days."

"Sure, if you want to."

Taking her in his arms, he gazed into her eyes. Something was troubling her. It would have been so easy to read her mind, but he had promised not to do it once they were married. She deserved her privacy. But if this went on much longer, he was going to break that promise.

Resting his chin lightly on the top of her head, he closed his eyes. And frowned. Liliana's heart beat slow and steady but he detected another heartbeat, one that beat faster.

Lifting his head, he opened his preternatural senses. What he was sensing was beyond impossible, yet there was no denying it.

Liliana was pregnant.

And there was no way he could be the father.

Cursing under his breath, he put her away from him, his eyes blazing red. "What have you done?"

Liliana stared at him, every instinct for self-preservation on high alert. His rage was a palpable thing. "I...I don't know what you mean."

"No?"

"Raedan, you're scaring me. What's wrong?"

"Who is the father?"

Lily blinked at him. Had he lost his mind? "What on earth are you talking about?"

"You are pregnant," he hissed. "And we both know it cannot be mine!"

Pregnant! "But...But that's impossible!"

"Tell me his name."

Tears burned her eyes. "I can't believe you think I've been unfaithful to you!"

"Stop lying to me, Liliana. I can hear the baby's heartbeat. I can sense his presence in your womb."

Pregnant? She wrapped her arms around her waist in an age-old gesture of protection. Pregnant? That explained everything—why her breasts were so tender, why she had been nauseous every morning, why she was tired all the time. Pregnant.

"I have a doctor's appointment in the morning," she said. "Blood tests will prove who the father is."

Lily went to bed early, mainly to avoid Raedan. How could he believe she had been unfaithful to him? And yet, she couldn't really blame him for what he was thinking. Transylvanian vampires couldn't sire children. Everyone knew that. And then she frowned. But Raedan carried her father's blood—a lot of it.

She smiled into the darkness. That had to be the answer.

Raedan entered Liliana's bedroom. She lay on her side, her cheek resting on her hand, her hair, black as the night, spread across the pillow. Sitting on the edge of the mattress, he placed his hand over her belly and opened his preternatural senses once more. And then he bit her, ever so gently. Her blood was warm and sweet and familiar.

And he knew without a doubt that the child was his.

"Liliana?" He whispered her name. "Liliana?"

Her eyelids fluttered open. He flinched when he saw the fear reflected there. "What's wrong?"

"I am sorry I thought you had betrayed me," he said, his fingers stroking her cheek. "But what else could I think?"

"You could have trusted me."

He nodded as guilt pierced his heart. "I should have known you would never betray me. But how could I believe otherwise? It is impossible for me to father a child."

"You drank from my father," she said, sitting up. "I think his blood made a change in your DNA or whatever vampires have. His blood is very powerful, you know."

He thought that over a moment. He carried Quill's blood, as did Liliana. Somehow, it had allowed them to conceive. "Can you forgive me?" he asked, taking her hand in his.

"I love you, Raedan. There's nothing to forgive," she said. And then she laughed. "I can't wait to see the look on everyone's face when we tell them."

His arms went around her, hugging her tightly. "I do not know what I ever did to deserve your love and your trust," he murmured. "But you mean the world to me."

"Show me." Falling back on the mattress, she held out her arms. "Show me how much."

"Always my pleasure," he said, his voice husky with desire.

Lifting her hips to receive him, she murmured, "May it ever be so," and gasped with pleasure as he possessed her, body and soul.

EPILOGUE

Three days after the baby was born, Lily's family gathered at the Raedan home. They were all there—her parents, grandparents, great-grandparents, her brother and his wife and J.D. They had all been at the hospital when her son was born, of course. But now they could stay as long as they wished, hold the baby for more than a few moments. He was a strong, healthy boy, with thick black hair and dark blue eyes. They named him Ryder Andras Falconer.

"It's a miracle," Callie murmured.

"Yes, indeed," Ava agreed.

"I still can't believe it's true," Quill said, as he gazed at the tiny infant cradled in his arms.

Sitting up in bed, Lily said, "We owe it all to you, Papa."

"Hey," Raedan protested. "I would like to think I had *something* to do with it."

"Of course you did," she said with a smile. "Just remember, *I* did all the hard work!"

He couldn't argue with that. He thought he would rather endure the blood-demon's torture than endure the pains of childbirth. It had been sheer hell, watching Liliana suffer as she brought their child into the world. He knew it could have been worse. Ava and Callie had worked their magic to lessen the pain when the contractions came hard and fast. He had watched in awe as his son slipped into the doctor's hands and took his first breath. There were no words to describe how he felt. He had never expected to father another child. Somehow, it helped to ease the pain he still carried over the children he had lost so long ago.

He waited patiently for Liliana's family to go home so he could be alone with his wife and son. Quill was the last to leave. He kissed the baby on the forehead before placing the infant in Liliana's arms.

Lily watched her father and Raedan shake hands. They would never be close friends, she thought as her father left the house, but at least they were no longer enemies.

"Happy?" she asked, looking up at Raedan.

"Beyond happy." Taking her hand in his, he kissed it. "You have given me everything I ever wanted and more."

Lily smiled up at him, eyes glinting with merriment. "Maybe next time, we'll be blessed with a girl."

Raedan stared at her, amazed that she would want to go through childbirth again. And then he grinned at her. "Maybe if we try hard enough, we will have twins!"

~finis~

About the Author

Amanda Ashley started writing for the fun of it. Her first book, a historical romance written as Madeline Baker, was published in 1985. Since then, she has published numerous historical and paranormal romances and novellas, many of which have appeared on various bestseller lists, including the *New York Times* Bestseller List and *USA Today*.

Amanda makes her home in Southern California, where she and her husband share their house with a Pomeranian named Lady, a cat named Kitty, and a tortoise named Buddy.

For more information on her books, please visit her websites at:

www.amandaashley.net

and

www.madelinebaker.net

Email: darkwritr@aol.com

ABOUT THE PUBLISHER

This book is published on behalf of the author by the Ethan Ellenberg Literary Agency.
https://ethancllenberg.com
Email: agent@ethanellenberg.com
Facebook: https://www.facebook.com/EthanEllenberg LiteraryAgency/